STORM OF PASSION

a Men of Danger novel

REBECCA A. CORIO

Relax. Read. Repeat.

STORM OF PASSION
(a Men of Danger novel, Book 1)
By Rebecca A. Corio
Published by TouchPoint Press
Brookland, AR 72417
www.touchpointpress.com

ISBN-13: 978-1-956851-01-4

Editor: Scott Bury
Cover Design: ColbieMyles.com
Cover images: Night shot with palm trees and milky way in background by Taiga
(Adobe Stock); Dark sea stormy background by Konstiantyn (Adobe Stock)

Connect with the author:
www.rebeccaacorio.com

 @rebeccacorio @rebeccaacorio

First Edition

Printed in the United States of America.

To my family who put up with me and never gave up on my ability to write The End. To my agent Julie who always picks up my call and patiently answers my questions. To my editor Scott, you deserve to be knighted. This book would not be here without you. To everyone at TouchPoint, thank you for taking a chance on me.

CHAPTER ONE

"Did you hear? The mayor called a press conference," the head of HR called from where she leaned in the doorway of the Safety Manager's office.

"A what?" Savanah Jordan looked up at the sound of her friend Leayne's voice, in surprise.

"You know . . . that thing where somebody important stands in front of people and says something everyone already knows."

"I know what a press conference is. I just don't believe it."

"About the press conference or the fact everyone knows what's going to be said?" Leayne shot back.

Savanah gave Leayne a friendly roll of the eyes. "The press conference. Maybe the mayor meant to call it something different. This is Hawaii. Do we even have enough people who call themselves 'press' to call it a press conference? Or are we counting mynahs?"

Savanah and Leayne both laughed. Mynah birds were everywhere in the islands, and mainly a nuisance. If you couldn't find anyone else to talk to, there was always one of the brown-and-black noise makers around. The talkative birds were always willing to squawk back.

"We are pretty third-world," Leayne admitted.

"We are not third-world. This is my home you're talking about."

"Yeah. It's my home too. You were the one who wondered whether the mayor knew what a press conference was. And you know it's true. How many times have you been asked if you need a green card or a passport to go to *the States?*"

Savanah wanted to argue but couldn't. If she had tried, Leayne would have called bullshit on her in a heartbeat. Hawaii was like no other state in the United States.

Savanah had been born in Hawaii, just like her parents and the generations before them. So, it was different for her.

She and Leayne were unlikely friends. A local girl and a *haole. Haole* meant a non-native Hawaiian, a foreigner, often thought to simply mean any white person. But locals had very specific ideas of who was haole white and who wasn't. If you were from Europe, that somehow excluded you from the derogatory grouping. No, haole in its most insulting form had come to be directed almost exclusively at Caucasians from the contiguous forty-eight.

Savanah didn't like how prejudiced that sounded. Her parents had taught her that all people had their place on the planet and all life should be respected. Deep down, though, she knew that being born and raised beneath the blue Hawaiian skies meant there was a magical quality to life. A mental and spiritual balance that distanced those born of Hawaii and everyone else on the planet. The land, the ocean, every breath taken when standing on their homeland, were necessary for native Hawaiians to thrive and be at peace.

"We are part of the United States. Not because we belong to them, but because we are one of them. We are a state," Savanah said with a frown. "I would never ask that of someone. If they needed a green card to go somewhere. It just sounds stupid. And it's rude."

"Just because you're nice doesn't mean everyone is, Savanah. I'm not," Leayne replied.

"Yes, you are. You just don't let it interfere with your job. I know how much it affects you when you have to let someone go. Besides, you know I'm not as nice as most people think I am."

"I know sometimes you're too nice for your own good. You care too much about people. When you're being mean, you're doing what you think is right. You've just made the decision that you are willing to take the consequences if it isn't the most popular course."

"You care about people, Leayne."

"But you worry what people think of you. I don't. And you have a much sweeter smile than mine." Leayne added her smile for evidence.

It had taken some time for them to realize that they really did think a lot alike. Savanah loved Leayne's sarcasm. She was a reality check for anyone who'd forgotten to put on their big girl panties that morning. But Savanah hadn't ever seen Leayne say something that wasn't true. "People mistake the truth for unkindness, because the whole world is turning into marshmallow," Leayne had said once. The memory of that made Savanah laugh out loud again.

"What?" Leayne asked at Savanah's laughter.

"Nothing. Just had the random thought that people are turning into marshmallows, and no one knows how to handle a good disagreement anymore." Savanah explained.

"Most people are wusses . . . and I love to toast marshmallows. Come on. We'll watch in my office." Leayne suggested. "That way we can laugh together."

Savanah locked her computer screen before pushing her wheelchair away from her desk. "We could watch it here, you know."

"We could. But then we'd have to head to my office anyway to start the paperwork. I'm being practical."

3

Savanah made sure no one was around before she replied. "They've never announced who's been selected for the Civil Defense Director position with a press conference before. Why would they do it now?"

Leayne was the only person at work who knew Savanah had applied for the position. That had been more than a year ago, and the County hadn't issued a word about why the process had taken longer than usual. Savanah hoped the extra time had worked in her favor.

She'd almost forgotten about it. More pressing things had taken precedence for Savanah. While surfing one morning two weeks after she'd turned in her application, Savanah had wiped out badly enough to need rescuing. Once she woke up on the hospital, the only thing on her mind was recovering from her injuries and learning how to walk again. A job application had receded to the back of her mind as insignificant in comparison.

Things were different now. There was an end in sight. Her rehab was almost done, and her doctor was talking about giving her a full release. Savanah could go back to thinking about the future and moving her life forward, now that getting out of her wheelchair was more than a dream.

That didn't mean she was going to kid herself. Especially about this job. This application. Going from a resort Safety Director to Civil Defense director for the entire island was a big step forward. Onimura Resort was the biggest on the island. She and her people were responsible for over 4,000 guests and staff. That was a far cry from the full 200,000-strong population of the island of Hawaii.

Savanah knew she could do the job. But there were things working against her. The biggest was that she was trying to break into the "good 'ole boys club" of the Big Island's County network. Specifically, the County Civil Defense office, which was as steeped in nepotism as you could get. There were the obligatory female secretaries. But women in positions of authority? No way.

"They're just starting." Leayne turned her screen so Savanah could see it as they waited to hear the mayor and the news that he'd deemed press conference worthy.

Within minutes they were both staring at the monitor in shocked silence. Neither of them saying a word until the conference concluded. Leayne hit the mute button once it was over. She looked to where Savanah sat. The utter stillness with which her friend sat in her wheelchair was as telling as any words Savanah might have said.

CHAPTER TWO

Savanah was stunned. From the moment the mayor started speaking, she knew she wasn't getting the job. That didn't mean she wasn't shocked by his announcement of whom had been chosen. She'd thought she knew all the other applicants. They'd all been invited to the Civil Defense bunker for a meet-and-greet several months before. This was uncharacteristic of the County's hiring process, but understandable since no matter who was awarded the position, everyone would need to continue working together for the common good of the island. Which made it even more surprising that the man the mayor had just announced as the new director hadn't been among the men Savanah had met that day.

Savanah couldn't hold it in any longer. "He's not even from one of the other islands. He isn't from Hawaii at all. He moved here a few years ago. How the hell does that make him the best candidate? He's an outsider . . ."

"The mayor said he meets the qualifications." Leayne seemed at a loss to offer any real words of comfort following the surprising news.

"*I* meet all the qualifications. On paper, plus ones they can't measure."

As the daughter of a native Hawaiian father, and a Japanese-Hawaiian mother, Savanah had a unique knowledge base that came from generations, not just her short lifetime. Knowledge that wasn't simply something learned from some book. Knowledge she was sure would help her do the job of protecting the Big Island and its people.

Savanah's shock boiled over into anger. "Whoever this jackass Race Weston is, he didn't even bother to show up so he could be introduced at the press conference."

Leayne shut the door then settled her hand on her friend's shoulder. "I know how much you wanted the position. Protecting the land and the people of Hawaii matters to you in ways, and for reasons, most of us can't claim." Leayne moved back behind her desk. "I know it's been a difficult year, Savanah. Getting the job would have been a signal your life was finally moving forward."

"I want to know what made him the best candidate," Savanah responded.

"Things happen for a reason. You know that," Leayne offered.

"We both know the reasons I didn't get the job. I'm betting it's the same reasons Clark's suddenly being such a jerk." Savanah's teeth snapped together as she closed her eyes, fighting to get a hold of her emotions. Making unfounded remarks out of anger wasn't going to help the situation. It only resulted in making people look ignorant. She knew better.

"I'm still trying to figure that one out, Savanah. I don't know what his problem is lately. He's acting strange with everyone. Not just with you." Leayne suggested, leaning back in her chair as a frown knitted her brows.

Savanah remembered when Clark Dieter had come on board. She had been pleasantly surprised at the new CEO's outward show of community spirit. Lately, though, things had felt different. Savanah was starting to think the man had his own agenda. Up until recently, he'd seemed happy with the way she was running the Safety Office for the resort. But something had changed. Now it seemed she couldn't make any decision Clark agreed with.

7

"Clark is making it real clear what the problem is as far as I'm concerned." Savanah clipped her words so short she almost bit her tongue.

"Has he said something to you?" The springs on Leayne's chair protested the sudden shift forward.

Savanah knew that as the head of Human Resources for the resort, Leayne wouldn't tolerate harassment or discrimination. Even if it was from someone in management. Correction. Especially if it came from management.

"Not anything I can turn him in for. But his tone is definitely different." Savanah took a deep breath and held it, counting to herself for several seconds as she willed her body to let her anger, and the ugliness it brought, go.

"Why don't you take the rest of the day off." Leayne's voice was quiet even though it was just the two of them in the office.

"No."

"You know no one will question it. Your crew can handle."

"If I were a wuss, I'd take you up on that." Savanah turned her wheelchair and started toward the door. Looking back at her friend, she said, "That sounds like something Clark would have expected of me. You didn't really think I would take off just because I didn't get the job, did you?"

Leayne flicked an imaginary bug from the organized surface of her desk. "Nope."

Savanah chuckled, giving a shake of her head at the reverse psychology Leayne had employed. It was enough misdirection to give Savanah the time to pull in a breath and concentrate on nothing but the feeling of the air making its way into her lungs. She held it momentarily before exhaling it along with her anger. "I'm sorry for blowing up in your office."

"Blow up any time. That's what I'm here for. As for Civil Defense, they couldn't have handled you, anyway. Everyone knows that office is nothing but pussies."

Savanah choked at her friend's bald comment as laughter threatened to break through the slackening muscles of her jaw. Sometimes Leayne wasn't anything like what you expected the head of HR should be. She was far too human, which was what made her so good at her job. And was just one more thing Savanah loved about her.

It was a moment before Savanah could speak without laughing. "We'll have to wait and see if Race Weston has a pair or follows suit with the rest of them. Will it be about the money tourism brings or what's best for the island?" Savanah's lips pursed to one side as she raised a brow. Then her face sobered. Her voice dropping lower. "Thanks."

"Don't mention it. Not going to lie, part of me is glad I don't have to do your exit paperwork."

Savanah felt her anger evaporate, thanks to Leayne. All things did happen for a reason. She would just have to be patient to understand what it was.

CHAPTER THREE

Savanah tilted her glass so the contents could make its way down her throat. Thank God for bananas and lilikoi, commonly known outside the islands as passionfruit. Otherwise, she wasn't sure she'd have been able to stomach her morning meal for the last eight months. She'd still have swallowed the mixture of vitamins, protein, and herbs. Her body needed all the help it could get in its fight to rebuild and recover. But it would have seriously sucked.

Letting it get warm wouldn't help, either. She took another long drink to finish the concoction, gratefully replacing the container into the cup holder as the soft vibration against her wrist told her it was time to go.

The alarm wasn't necessary. The light spilling over the mountains and across the island was already enough to let her know it was time to head to the office. Still, Savanah took those last few seconds to take in everything around her. Her gaze traced the streaks of gold making their way from behind her and through the mass of greenery that lay all around. The glowing light proof the sun was gaining strength as it cleared the mountain top. The palm fronds overhead barely moved in the early morning calm, the wind a gentle caress that turned from *mauka* to *makai*, from the mountain to the ocean. Even the ocean itself had chosen a quiet start to its day. A soft whooshing provided the only evidence of the crystal waters caressing the sand beneath the deck she stood on. Savanah smiled as the sound made her think of the steady, reassuring voices of her parents. But unlike her parents' calm, the ocean caressing the sand with its greeting was deceptive, the gentle sound a façade for the destructive power that lay beneath. A power Savanah knew all too well.

The loud calls of a flock of parrots overhead prompted Savanah to turn the wheelchair and begin making her way gingerly back to her apartment. Had there been enough wave action for surfing, it would have been harder to leave. Even calm, the ocean's lure was as strong as it had always been. The water was a part of her soul. She got that from her father. It was a necessity, for at least a moment of every day, to make her way to the lifeblood of Hawaii. Those quiet moments floating, held by the water's hand, allowed her to make peace with herself and for the universe to reset.

Savanah took it all in as if it were the first time she'd seen it, rather than having been born to it. She never grew tired of the sights and sounds of her home. Each day more beautiful than the last. Gawking like some visiting tourist standing in awe at their first sunrise in Hawaii. Of course, if she had really been a tourist, she'd most likely still be in bed, recovering from too many mai tais upon finally reaching the Aloha State. And missing out on some of the most beautiful moments Paradise offered.

With a last look over her shoulder, she acknowledged the beginning of another glorious day. There wasn't a single sign that anything was amiss as she looked out across the water. No way to know that in a week's time, she'd once again be fighting to survive. Only this time, she wouldn't be alone.

"Good morning, Duke. Thank you for picking me up."

Savanah greeted her youngest staff member warmly as he helped her into the cart. She could have gotten in by herself, but she didn't protest. Her parents had brought her up to believe that if someone was attempting to be helpful, let them. And make sure you expressed your thanks for it. As for Duke, his upbringing wouldn't allow him to not assist her. Plus, Savanah knew her staff meant well when they tried to help. They had become very protective after her accident.

Had the tables been turned, she would have done the same.

"Any waves this morning?" Duke asked.

"Who says I checked?"

"Your DNA. Same as mine does," Duke scoffed. "Just because you can't get on your board right now, doesn't make a damn bit of difference. Unless that maybe you look at it more now."

"You're right," Savanah laughed. "Smooth as glass . . . It would have made for great waterskiing."

"Good for trolling, you mean," Duke's laughter joined his boss's as he released the brake and put the cart in motion.

"You'd be surprised what people think is a good idea." Savanah had found herself having to explain to more than one visitor that waterskiing and Hawaii, did not go together.

Waterskiing was a sport meant for mainland people and the little bodies of water they were so fond of. In Hawaii, if you were foolish enough to hang yourself at the end of a tow rope and bounce around in the churning water behind a boat, you had better be worried about some *grander* coming up for you.

"Tourists just don't think things through." Duke agreed.

Visitors assumed it was the sharks you had to worry about. They were wrong. In the deep blue waters off the Kona Coast, people needed to worry about blue marlin. As far as a thousand-pound grander was concerned, a skier was nothing more than bait ringing the dinner bell. An experience Savanah listed in the top five things she didn't want to take part in.

Which hadn't made a difference to the number one thing on her list. Drowning. The water gods had deemed fit for her to be bent like a pretzel while her lungs filled with water. Yet they hadn't chosen for her to stay dead. Savanah had to be okay with what had happened, given how it was working out.

"Did I ever tell you I know how to ski?" Duke steered carefully, avoiding sharp turns and bumps as he ferried his boss to her office.

"You didn't." Savanah was surprised. She knew he'd been an avid snowboarder while at school on the mainland. She'd never heard him talk about waterskiing.

"One of my friends in college had family nearby. I spent a summer there instead of coming home. We went to a lake called Fern Ridge almost every weekend. They meant well, but a lake is no substitute for the ocean. It was a cool summer, though."

"She wasn't cool enough to make you stay in Oregon permanently." Savanah couldn't help the knowing smile she gave Duke. His answering blush all the confirmation necessary that his friend had indeed been female.

"No way. I'm a Hawaii boy. I need my fish and poi, and my surfboard."

Savanah had no trouble imagining how attracted women would have been to Duke during his college days on the mainland. He was a good-looking man: tall, dark, and handsome enough that he could appear on any month of a *Men of Hawaii* calendar.

13

Looking again at him, she was struck by their similarities. Easy, open smiles. Their matching sun-kissed skin. Defined shoulders. There was no mistaking that she, like Duke, had been born a water baby. Her body, and her personality, sculpted by countless hours in the pull of the ocean, just as his was.

For all their similarities, there was one difference that couldn't be overlooked: their eyes. While Duke's were the warm brown so common among Hawaiian people, Savanah's were a glacial blue. A recessive gene caused an eye color so striking as to decorate entire family lines. The starburst affect that had her eyes bleeding from blue to white was something that Savanah had never seen outside someone of Hawaiian descent.

Savanah was struck by the fact, despite these similarities, she had no such claim to the easy-going charm as she knew the men of Hawaii had. Age-old beliefs that the men were the important ones and the women only there to serve were imprinted upon her. So, while the men were relaxed and confident, the women found themselves always fighting some unknown adversary as they struggled to find their place in the world.

"Those mainland girls sure do love us local boys. I swear sometimes they'd look at me like they'd never seen a man before." Duke didn't bother trying to hide his smile.

"That must have been really hard for you," Savanah teased him good naturedly. "I'm sure you did us proud, though."

"I did my best." His smile echoed that unique innocent charm of a local boy.

Duke parked the cart and jumped out, quickly going around to the other side so he could assist his boss. "But there was never any question I was coming home to marry a local girl. The whole time I was gone, I never felt like anyone on the mainland really understood me."

Savanah knew what he meant. There was just something different about the way you thought when you were from the islands. Sometimes it was hard to put a finger on. Other times, it was as easy as saying life was simpler in Hawaii. You could laugh, love, care, and not have to hide it. Growing up in Hawaii meant everything in your heart came first in your life, without ever having to explain or make an excuse as to why.

She envied Duke. He'd moved home after college and found the woman who completed him. One look at Duke and his wife, Merry, and there was no question they were meant for each other. The woman was her husband's twin, but in feminine form. She was graceful and calm, with an inner strength that matched Duke's brawn. Savanah knew if he were ever threatened, Merry would move heaven and earth to protect him. As he would for her.

Meanwhile, Savanah was still waiting for the tall Hawaiian that would sweep her off her feet, as her father had done with her mother.

Savanah took the hand Duke offered. "Bet you'll be happy when you don't have to babysit the boss and help put me in my stroller anymore."

They'd done this often enough over the last months that the transition went smoothly. Duke positioned her wheelchair so she could slide from one seat to the other with almost no effort. There were no words for Savanah to express how grateful she was for her staff and everyone who'd been there to help her. She was well enough to have walked the few steps from the cart to the sidewalk. She knew she could have even walked from her car in the parking lot. Her therapy regime was far more rigorous than a few steps. But no one was taking any chances. Until the doctor said okay, she stayed in the wheelchair.

Duke shook his head. "Bet you'll be glad to be rid of this thing for good. I don't mind. None of us do. Your doctor making you use these wheels so you could heal was smart. He didn't rush you or give up on you. That's why you're recovering." Duke hesitated. "When we first heard, we didn't think walking again was going to be an option."

"Shows what you know," Savanah laughed. "Not walking was never an option."

"If it would have been me . . . if I thought I might not ever walk again, never have the privilege of my freedom in the ocean . . ." For a moment, Duke's body slumped. His eyes took on a look akin to terror. But then he met Savanah's gaze and the look turned to pride. "You just keep recovering. Merry says she wants to be there, the first time you're back on your board. Even if all you two do is sit."

Savanah laid a hand on Duke's shoulder but didn't say anything. She was afraid to. If she'd ever considered she might not walk again, Savanah knew, she would have hated the wheelchair.

CHAPTER FOUR

Race Weston was always early to work. Not the few minutes, just enough time to get a cup of coffee from the breakroom, kind of early. He liked to walk into the office an hour before the shift change that brought in the morning crew. As the new Civil Defense Director, or CDD for the island of Hawaii, missing something and endangering lives because he wanted to hit the snooze wasn't happening. He had never understood people who had to drag themselves to work. Race felt most comfortable, and most *alive*, when he was in the middle of a seven-day work week, with days that went round the clock.

Race didn't pretend to be anything but who he was. No nonsense. From his haircut to his shoes, he was about efficiency. Waterproof hiking boots were his everyday wear. He wasn't going to make someone wait to view a disaster area while he changed out of shoes that couldn't take a little mud. Same went for his clothes. Growing up in Australia meant he wore pants and shirts that were useful. Pockets were a must. He didn't go anywhere without a utility knife, rope and matches, a practice he saw no reason to change just because of his new position.

His haircut was military short on the sides and only slightly longer on top. There was no sign of facial hair. He was old-school: clean-shaven meant people could trust you. Trust and respect were integral to him doing his job, as was staying in shape.

Race ran every day to keep his blood pressure down and worked out to make sure the emergency responders doing the dirty work didn't discount him simply because he looked like a desk jockey. As far as he was concerned, being physically able to keep up with the unpredictable demands of any emergency was part of the job—even when that meant shoveling sand or hauling a fire hose.

Picking up the reports from the previous evening, he made his way around the room, ensuring he spoke with everyone. He wanted to hear from the outgoing shift personally rather than just looking at words on a sheet of paper. Most of the crew had been at their position for years. Race considered that experience invaluable. He knew there was often more information in how something was said or the look in someone's eyes, than the words they'd written in a report.

Talking one-on-one also gave him a chance to gauge work ethic. When he'd joined the Hawaii Civil Defense, the air of complacency he'd felt surprised him. As if the group planned to sit back and drink their coffee while assessing the new guy. Worse yet, it seemed they also planned on the new guy failing. They apparently didn't realize something very important: if he failed, they all did. It would be the people of the Big Island who suffered from it.

Race had wasted no time in setting the record straight: "Put out or get out."

It had earned him his first reprimand from the County Human Resources department. Obviously, the people in his new office were more sensitive than he'd realized and hadn't appreciated him being a man of few words. He'd have to keep that in mind.

Or not.

Race had made it clear he valued each of them and the experience they brought to their job. And then he'd made his expectations equally clear: their collective duty was to keep the public safe, no matter how many hours, how many sleepless nights, how many missed meals that took. And he expected people to own up to their mistakes. There would be no hiding or sweeping things under the rug on his watch. He'd taken the time to meet the eyes of each of his staff in turn. "It won't take the legislature ordering an investigation to tell us we've made a ballistic missile mistake."

When he referenced the most embarrassing moment in the state's emergency warning system history, everyone in the Big Island's Civil Defense operations gasped at once. Race was well aware of the colossal screw-up by the State Emergency Management Office on Oahu. A mistake had turned a routine procedure into a horrifying emergency message going out to the whole state: "BALLISTIC MISSILE THREAT INBOUND TO HAWAII. SEEK IMMEDIATE SHELTER. THIS IS NOT A DRILL."

It had taken the state thirty-eight minutes to send out a retraction. Worse, it had taken days to learn how such a mistake had happened. The incident shattered the credibility of every emergency management office in the state.

Race had given everyone in the Civil Defense Office who disagreed with his work ethic the option to ask HR for reassignment. It hadn't bothered him at all that his reputation as an egotistical hard-ass began on day one.

"I am going to assume you know the job to which you are assigned. As long as you do your job, we'll get along just fine. If you can't, I will find someone who can. It would be a mistake on your part to assume otherwise." That had earned him reprimand number two.

It was the beginning of hurricane season in the Pacific. Meteorologists predicted a quiet year. Which didn't mean a thing to Race. It only took one storm, not even of hurricane strength, to devastate a community and the lives of everyone in it. Every blip on the radar, every quake beneath their feet, was a threat. It was his job, their job, to watch and prepare for everything, until all possibility of harm passed.

His rounds done, Race approached the man who'd had the misfortune of being assigned as his assistant. From what Race had learned, Steve Chan had a wife and a new baby at home. Yet the man was at his desk at half-past the crack of dawn. He had adjusted his schedule to coincide with Race's without having been asked, or told, to do so. That spoke volumes about Steve's work ethic. Race's respect for his right-hand man had grown from that day.

Race didn't bother with pleasantries. As far as he was concerned, his words constituted a greeting. "I don't like the way Garth is moving," he said as he approached Steve's desk. They'd been tracking the tropical storm for several days now.

"Officially Hurricane Garth at the 06:00 update. And no sir, NHC doesn't like it, either." Steve handed the newest printout to Race without flinching from his boss's darkening focus.

The Civil Defense office received reports from around the world, about everything from volcanoes to earthquakes to hurricanes. Right now, the National Hurricane Center was taking center stage. Race didn't check to see whether Steve was following. The man had learned quickly: his new boss didn't like to say things twice.

Chapter Five

Savanah pushed the wheels of her ultralight chair toward the door. A modified athletic wheelchair, it weighed barely ten pounds and was far more maneuverable than a traditional wheelchair. It had been specially designed with electrodes that delivered pulses to the injured area at her lower back, to interrupt the spasms that still occurred. The design was experimental, and Savanah was one of only a handful of patients to use it.

So far, it had worked. The seizures in her back were less frequent. Still, the intensity of the spasms that still came had not diminished as much as the doctor had hoped. While no longer rendering her unconscious if Savanah was seated in her chair, they were still powerful enough to leave her immobile for long minutes afterwards.

Even though it was an ultralight model, the difficulty to move it had shocked Savanah, as had how quickly she tired. She had thought her upper-body strength was pretty good. She'd been wrong.

The doctors had explained that much of her weakness was due to the complexity of her injuries and how much energy the healing process required. They explained that the years of paddling, surfing, and training for competition in an outrigger canoe, had made a major difference. Without that experience, her injuries could have been even more severe. And regaining the muscle tone required to get herself around would have taken much longer.

In the early days after her injury, she had hated needing the help of others to push the chair for her. It had been the first thing she had set her mind to overcoming.

Savanah and her parents had believed in Dr. Antone and followed his orders faithfully. He took a cutting-edge approach to spinal injuries and medicine. In addition, rather than discounting her parents' beliefs and suggestions, Dr. Antone had worked with them. It was one of the things that made him unique. He had welcomed the Native Hawaiian aspects of medicine and healing and integrated them with modern medicine. He even modified Savanah's physical therapy, all with the single goal of returning Savanah to complete health.

He had begun Savanah's therapy in the controlled conditions of an indoor pool, only allowing Savanah to return to the ocean when she was strong enough. Savanah's father had been there for all of it. She would never forget how in the beginning, when she'd been too weak, her father had lifted her from the bed to act as her legs, taking her wherever she needed to go.

As soon as the doctor allowed it, Savanah returned to the ocean's healing waters. Kyle Jordan would carry his daughter into the water, his wife Wainani, Savanah's mother, beside him. Her parents worked as one, moving Savanah's legs when she couldn't. Their first goal had been to keep her muscles from further atrophy. Then, later, to help her regain strength.

Savanah had always known her father was strong, but it was only when he started aiding with her recovery that she'd seen how powerful he truly was—strong in ways that had nothing to do with muscle mass. His strength had been the rock that she and her mother relied on. Kyle Jordan had never let his daughter quit. He never let her consider she wouldn't recover fully. He was a constant by her side and still met her at the ocean as she continued to grow stronger.

The weakness in her legs wasn't the worst of her problems. The wave that took her down had damaged her nerves, leaving her with debilitating pain. Spasms racked her body, radiating from her spine and seizing up every muscle and ligament until her mind chose the oblivion of unconsciousness to escape it.

She'd wake to find her mother or father, or both, massaging the knotted muscles of her back, their tears matching hers as they shared her pain. Her parents had never expressed any shame over the tears, or the pain-filled sobs Savanah couldn't hold back. Wainani Jordan had assured her daughter that every teardrop was a sign of strength.

Kyle and Wainani had refused to give up on their daughter's recovery. Savanah was barely conscious during the days they disappeared into the forested depths of Mauna Loa, returning with sacred herbs that they made into a salve to work into her skin daily. Apologizing for the pain even the gentlest touch caused, her mother and father worked tirelessly until Savanah's body responded. Savanah remembered the smell, so disgusting that thinking about it even now made her grimace. But it had always helped to ease the pain and relax the muscles.

The salve had worked so well that Dr. Antone had asked for the ingredients, so he could make it available for his other patients. Savanah didn't know whether it would work the same way on others. Much of the effectiveness was born of the gathering process and her parents' prayers. She didn't think that was something that could be applied to mass production.

Savanah knew the journey her mother and father had to make to harvest the ingredients was as important as the items themselves. The difficulty, their dedication to doing anything needed to help their child, and the time it took, were all necessary. They had been able to pray. And pray Kyle and Wainani did, with every step and every labored breath, that the gods new and old would see their love for their daughter and bless their efforts.

Savanah had never questioned her parents' actions. The beliefs of her culture weren't folklore, nor tales created by travelers to explain forbidden escapades after becoming drunk on Hawaii's exotic beauty. Savanah knew every step her parents had taken, every word, every flower plucked and root dug, had been based on centuries of knowledge from their Hawaiian and Japanese ancestries.

Savanah prayed her thanks daily for having such supportive parents, doctor, and staff.

At the Safety Office, Savanah greeted the morning crew. Now that Duke had delivered her to the office, his day was complete. He'd worked the graveyard shift and was on his way home. *Babysitters indeed*, she thought with chagrin.

The man who had relieved Duke looked up, smiling, as Savanah entered. "Anything exciting I should know about, Manny?" Savanah asked.

"Not really. A couple late-night pool and Jacuzzi users. Duke escorted them to their tower and rechecked the area to keep them from sneaking back down." Manny wriggled his eyebrows as he chuckled.

Savanah thought his smile almost looked like admiration. "Sounds like something you'd do."

"You know it. If the guard wasn't on it, I'd be back in the Jacuzzi with my girl in a heartbeat."

Manny had been kicked out of places just like theirs for similar stunts in his younger years. Savanah always laughed when he told her that former rebellious nature was what helped him stay a step ahead of their guests.

He was still smiling as he finished the update: "Garth has been upgraded. H-1 so far. That's really the only thing new, boss."

Savanah wheeled to Manny's screen. He opened the notice from Civil Defense that showed what had been Tropical Storm Garth, was now a Category 1 hurricane. It was official. Garth had graduated to the big leagues.

Her office didn't just handle overzealous resort guests. She was responsible for having a plan for every conceivable emergency. She and her staff responded to everything from bandages to belligerence. Smoke, fire, missing keys, natural disasters, and weather issues. They were all trained in first aid at an expert level. That wasn't the resort's requirement; it was hers. Doing so meant her people were as prepared as she could make them. She also required they get self-defense training. You never knew when a guest who'd had one too many piña coladas would turn on you at being told no peeing in the pool.

The hurricane was still too far away to be able to predict its effect on Hawaii. As the resort's Safety Manager, Savanah was responsible for planning their response to Garth. *Prepare for the worst. Hope for the best,* was the safety creed. The rest of the resort would rely on her office to keep them updated and instruct them on what to do if the storm worsened.

Savanah rubbed her arms where they prickled with her familiar sixth sense. "I'll be in my office for a while. Let me know if you need me."

"Figured that. Poured your coffee when Duke pulled up with you." Manny turned to watch his boss as she wheeled expertly across the floor. "Your mom still making those shakes for you every morning?"

"Yep. Every morning."

"The taste get any better?"

Savanah shook her head, a hand covering her mouth. "Not even a little."

Sliding the ultralight wheelchair to her desk, Savanah opened the National Oceanic and Atmospheric Administration website and reviewed Garth's behavior as a tropical storm. She studied the different tracks and projections now that it was Hurricane Garth. Taking into consideration the estimated timelines, she made notes for herself. She would send her first email to the resort's CEO and managers with a heads-up regarding the storm's upgrade to hurricane status, and potential threats.

Savanah dialed Leayne as she continued to review the information on the NOAA website.

"How's the back this morning?"

Savanah couldn't help but smile as her friends' voice came through the phone. As usual, Leayne was direct and to the point.

"Good. I haven't had an episode in a while now. I'm hoping that's a sign of things to come."

Leayne knew everything about Savanah's injuries. Not just because they were friends, but as head of Human Resources for the resort, Leayne needed to know what Savanah was capable of when she had asked to return to work.

"Is Dr. Antone still saying he might release you from the wheelchair completely by the end of the month?" Leayne's question was as much business as personal concern for Savanah.

"He is. And I'm doing everything I'm supposed to do to make that happen."

Savanah knew why Leayne was asking. It was a conversation they'd had frequently in the last month or so, at work and over glasses of wine after, when they could talk freely.

"It's going to be a fight with Dieter. From everything he's said to me, he isn't going to just accept that, Savanah."

"Why wouldn't he want me to be cleared and out of this stroller?" Savanah chewed the inside of her cheek in frustration. Her eyes narrowed as her forehead wrinkled, working to think of any reason why the CEO would want her to remain disabled. There'd been whisperings of aggressive outbursts. But that was a long way from explaining why he seemed so suddenly at odds with Savanah's recovery.

"I'm beginning to get an idea, but don't have anything concrete. I'll let you know when I do," Leayne assured her. "Did you need something this morning? I've got a new hire coming in."

"I was just wondering if you saw the track on Garth. Officially Hurricane Garth now."

"You thinking it looks like Iniki?" Leayne asked.

Thirty years earlier, Hurricane Iniki had caught the Hawaiian Islands by surprise. It wasn't because they hadn't known it was out there. They had. But when it passed south of the Big Island, every meteorologist on the planet had thought the danger was past and gave Hawaii the all-clear. Residents and visitors had gone back to their lives and enjoying fun in the sun. Hours later, Iniki had intensified to a Category 4 and made an unprecedented turn north. Instead of days, people had only hours to prepare. When it struck, Iniki broke all records for hurricanes that made landfall on Hawaii, beating the hell out of the islands. The devastation to the island of Kauai had been catastrophic.

Savanah tapped her pen against her desk as she studied the screen before her. "It's still too far out to know what's going to happen. But yeah, for some reason I can't shake thinking of Iniki when I look at Garth."

"But there isn't anything to back that thought up with yet. Evidence, I mean."

Leayne's question didn't offend Savanah. She huffed in frustration because her friend was right. "There isn't. Just how I feel. That's why I was wondering what you thought of it. Checking if I'm crazy."

Leayne's laughter broke the tension. "Of course, you're crazy." Leayne laughed again. "But you do your job. You aren't up in Clark's office whining about needing more staff or more money. You haven't once used your injuries or your wheelchair as an excuse when there was a problem, or your office fucked up. You take care of the shit that's your responsibility. Like a manager is supposed to."

Savanah didn't see whatever point Leayne was trying to make. "That's what I get paid for."

Leayne snorted. "Exactly. So, if you tell me batten down the hatches, I'm doing it. It's why you'd have made a damn good CDD. You've got instincts about this stuff. And nobody works harder than you. You aren't a wuss."

"Thanks, Leayne. Good luck with the new hire." Savanah hung up the phone. The continued tapping of her pen was the only sound in her office, as if the rhythm could reveal the future.

Not likely. They were all going to need some luck. Leayne because good employees were hard to find, and she wasted hours every month on people who didn't last the first week. And the rest of them if Garth decided to get up close and personal.

Staring at a computer monitor wouldn't get her work done. Clipping her pen to the neck of her shirt and tucking her phone and iPad into her bag, Savanah pushed away from her desk. It was almost check-out time. The lobby would start to fill up with guests on their way home or their next destination. Between the press of people and the increasing humid heat of the day, things could get rowdy. She would do a pass through just to make sure everyone was okay. Then she'd make a round of the entire property. It would give her a chance to soak in some sunshine and salt air. If not for what it might tell her, then just for the pleasure of it.

CHAPTER SIX

Outside his office, Race looked at the sky as if it would give him the answers he needed. Sometimes it did. Cloud formations, sky color, the wind on his face, all said something about the weather. Every region was different. You just needed to know what language the weather spoke where you were standing.

And that was the problem: where he stood, the language was foreign. As if it was purposely trying to deceive him. In Hawaii, every day was beautiful— until it wasn't.

"You're worried it isn't going to blow out or turn?" Steve asked.

Race nodded. Hurricane Garth had continued toward them for the last several days since reaching official hurricane strength, holding at a solid Category 2. The National Weather Service reported it would upgrade Garth to a Category 3 by day's end.

There was no science yet to back up his concerns. And he'd pored over the reports. Just like everyone else had. But Race couldn't shake the feeling there was something wrong about the almost casual manner this storm exhibited as it meandered across the Pacific. As if it were out for nothing more than a Sunday stroll.

"When it upgrades, send out a message that it's time to take steps to get visitors out or plan to house them. For our residents, I want them checking and then double-checking their disaster preparedness list." Race didn't take his eyes off the horizon, even though Garth was still some eight hundred miles away. Squinting uselessly behind his sunglasses as if that would help him see the storm.

There was still a chance the low-pressure system that was coming in from the north would help the storm blow itself out. Race's chest was telling him that wasn't going to happen. As if he had an internal barometer where his lungs should be, he could feel the tightness that said Garth was sucking up the air as far as it could reach. All with the intent of becoming a monster.

Race knew the island didn't need to be hit directly to be devastated. Even a glancing blow by a tropical storm would do millions of dollars in damage and threaten countless lives.

"Whoa. Hold on a minute, Race," Steve said. "The hotels and resorts are not going to like that. Hell, none of the businesses are going to like that. You'll probably get a call from the tourism office as soon as we put that out." Steve's next words came out slowly. "They're going to think you're being premature and scaring everyone for no reason."

The way Steve chose his words carefully, looking around before speaking, made Race wonder if the man was trying to sugar-coat things for his new boss. While many thought that emotions had no place in emergency preparedness, Race didn't subscribe to that belief. Emotions made people human. Being able to *control* one's emotions when it was necessary was the important thing.

Race wasn't always good at that. He was still learning.

Steve's face wasn't as blank as Race bet the man was aiming for. "Race, you do know tourism is *the* business for the State of Hawaii. All of the islands, not just Oahu where Five-O is filmed. For us here on the Big Island, too."

Race gave Steve his full attention. He pushed his sunglasses on top of his head so he could give the eye contact the discussion warranted. "I'm sure I read that somewhere, mate."

"You do realize that thanks to those eruptions last year wiping out a whole subdivision and reshaping the southern coastline, we've moved up a few notches on the list of places to visit." Steve didn't look away.

Race didn't back down. "I happen to be aware of that, too." He had done his homework before applying for the job. Race knew all about the eruptions from the Kilauea volcano. The sudden volcanic activity had brought people from all over the globe to see it. Kilauea had opened twenty-two new fissures at a pace that was seen as a come one, come all, invitation for scientists and tourists alike. The eruptions had gone on for nearly four months, and the lava had claimed more than seven hundred homes. The geothermal plant that provided nearly a quarter of the island's power had been forced to shut down and seal all twelve of their deep-water vents.

Plant management had waited until the last possible moment, hoping the volcano would stop before they had to end a generous revenue stream. That calculated delay had turned in to a nightmare when two of the deep ocean vents, and the flowing lava, hadn't cooperated with the engineers' estimates. Water started boiling up through the pipes, fueled by a heat so intense it melted everything being used to plug them.

The engineers realized their mistake too late. They hadn't considered what was moving underground. Their calculations were based on what they could see flowing. In the end, they'd gotten lucky: the plugs had held long enough for the lava itself to seal the vents permanently.

This, the longest emergency the island had ever endured, had been an eight hundred million-dollar lesson with nearly thirty casualties. After reading all the reports, Race felt it was due more to luck than anything else that the results had not been far worse.

Steve was still waiting for him to say something. Race clapped the man on the shoulder, giving it a shake. "Remember when people had enough sense to run away from two-thousand-degree stuff that would kill them instantly? Those were the days. Now we have to worry about protecting people from themselves."

The two men stood a few moments longer. The calm waters of Hilo Bay gave no indication of anything amiss.

"Send it out. And forward the calls to my office." Race gave a last glance at the horizon before meeting Steve's guarded gaze. "I'll throw the party if I'm wrong."

"Manny, I'm shutting the door."

Savanah expected her phone to ring any minute. Based on the latest update from Civil Defense, she had sent an email to the resort staff, suggesting they begin preliminary procedures for shutting down the resort. It had been a long, uneventful week watching the hurricane amble across open water, its trajectory uncertain. But she agreed with Race Weston and his notification that time had come to begin preparations for an impact. Even though the hurricane hadn't shown any sign of turning, the increase in strength warranted it. Savanah didn't believe they could count on the current harmless track of the hurricane continuing. They needed to put the next several days to good use.

"Good luck. He's not going to be happy, boss," Manny called as he shut her door.

Manny's comment confirmed what Savanah already knew. She didn't have to look at her phone to know who was on the other end as it began ringing before her door settled in the frame.

"Good afternoon, Clark," Savanah answered calmly.

"Who the hell do you think you are, issuing a directive to start shutdown procedures? You don't have that kind of authority, Jordan," Clark Dieter yelled.

Savanah kept her voice level, hoping to counteract the hostile pitch of her boss. "Civil Defense has issued a directive to begin evacuations and I see no reason we should dispute it. We are at full occupancy and aren't the only ones. The airports will be jammed the closer Garth gets to landfall. If people can evacuate now, that's better for everyone."

Lesson one in the "dealing with people" manual: don't match intensity. It's hard to maintain the energy necessary to yell at someone who isn't yelling back. But Savanah doubted the strategy would work with the CEO.

"It's not better for us. You have no idea what that will cost or how much money we'll lose. You aren't qualified to make a decision like that. It's business as usual until I say different," Clark reprimanded sharply.

"Actually Clark, I believe these are exactly the decisions I'm here for. The decisions you are paying me to make." Savanah didn't think standing her ground was being disrespectful.

"No. They're not. You're still around because it looks good on paper. Not because we need you. You're here to do exactly as I tell you. If I want you to make a decision, I'll tell you what it is and when to make it. Understand?"

Okay, so that was clear. Even alone in the office, Savanah felt her cheeks coloring. She was a good employee. She'd never given Clark a reason to speak to her in such a manner. His insults seemed purposely cruel, as if he were hoping to push her to react in kind. Her boss had to know she would never engage in an argument with him. And certainly not in the manner he was speaking to her.

Savanah's grip tightened around the handset as she reminded herself of rule number one: They who keep their cool, wins. Clark Dieter might be her boss and the CEO of the resort. But right now, he was losing.

Savanah stared at the phone, telling herself to just breathe as she wondered what the hell was going on with her boss. She'd expected him to be angry. But she could hear him spitting through the phone. Savanah wondered if his face was as red as she imagined it must be.

His remarks were so inflammatory, his rage so palpable, Savanah couldn't justify them with the current situation or what she'd done. She wondered if his anger weren't stemming from some other frustration. But there was his comment she was only still around because it looked good on paper. She knew it wasn't the time to ask him to explain what he meant by his remark. But neither would she forget it.

Savanah waited until Clark had to take a breath and interjected calmly. "We're required to report back to Civil Defense with our plan and the timetable, including numbers on occupancy. They aren't going to like us not complying." Maybe knowing they had to respond to Civil Defense would help the CEO calm down.

"I don't give a damn what Civil Defense does or doesn't like. Those morons don't have any idea what it takes to run a business. If they can't figure out when we do or don't have a ballistic missile crisis, I'm for damn sure not going along with them when they hit the panic button about a storm that isn't anywhere near us. Ignore them and their instructions." Clark cleared his throat. The vehemence of his words choked him. "I say what goes here. And from now on, Jordan, when you feel like sending out an email, you send it to me first. Is that clear?"

Clark's voice had gone down a notch in volume, but he was still hissing as he spoke. Savanah saw no evidence of the reasonable man he'd once been.

"Crystal." Savanah didn't waste any other words.

"Good. Now I've got to go calm everyone down and fix what you've started. Like I don't have enough to do already without your incompetence adding to things."

Savanah wasn't surprised to hear the click of the line closing. The man had been angrier than she'd ever seen or heard before. He'd always taken the time to hear her out and let her explain the reasoning behind her actions. But this conversation hadn't even come close to being two-way. In no uncertain terms, he'd just handed her own ass to her.

And for the life of her, she didn't understand why.

Denied the relief of pacing, Savanah pushed back from the desk and went to the window. Staring through the flower-laden plumeria tree, Savanah saw the brilliant blue sky beyond. She closed her eyes, wishing for the warm breeze, heavy with the sweet scent of the soft yellow and white flowers.

Savanah's hands resting on the wheels of her chair had her rocking unconsciously. Nothing more than a reflex to expend energy as she replayed the conversation in her mind. Clark, like so many others, hadn't forgotten the mistake by the Civil Defense Office on Oahu. She didn't argue the severity of incorrectly saying ballistic missiles were inbound to Hawaii. But in all fairness, the message hadn't come from the Big Island office. Theirs was but one of the four offices that covered the Hawaiian Islands. The message, and the mistake, had come from the State office. Still, it was a mistake every emergency management office continued feeling the effects of. Clark's comment confirmed that.

Taking a deep breath to push back some of the anger Clark had showered on her, Savanah typed out a response to the Civil Defense Director. She carefully explained that Onimura Hotel and Resort wouldn't be following his directive at this time. It felt for all the world like she'd just written "Dear John" to the new CD Director. Savanah didn't have much hope that her response would be received with a smile.

Race had to reread the email he'd just received. Who the hell was Savanah Jordan and what did she think she was doing? Safety Manager Jordan had stated the numbers of visitors currently registered at the Onimura property. She had then, matter-of-factly, informed his office they would not be taking any steps to prepare for impending inclement weather, as in the resort's opinion, such steps weren't warranted at this time.

Grabbing his jacket, he pulled the door with enough force it slammed behind him. "I'm headed to the other side of the island," he told the staff. "I'll be back in the morning. Call me for anything that you feel warrants it."

Race wasn't about to waste time with an electronic pissing contest to determine whose authority trumped whose. The email had come from the Onimura Resort's Safety Office. It would take him a few hours to drive across the island, at which time he'd find the office and straighten this out face to face. Because obviously Savanah Jordan had no idea what her job was or how to do it.

CHAPTER SEVEN

By the time Race had driven from one shore of the Big Island to the other, he had his emotions under control. He had to admit that his initial reaction had been somewhat ego-based. The audacity of questioning his authority at his first directive had surprised him. He had expected to have to prove himself to the people of Hawaii. He just hadn't expected skepticism to be so blatant.

Making his way through the maze of streets of the hotel district along the Kona Coast, Race cringed. Like so much of the populated areas on the Big Island, the upscale hotels and condominiums were at sea level. It would take very little change in water level to flood things. It was a disaster waiting to happen.

All the Hawaiian Islands had that geographical nightmare in common. The population lay clustered along the beautiful coastlines, where it was exposed, rather than inhabiting the interior of the land masses where the elevation would afford some protection. This was due to the largely uninhabitable, mountainous terrain at the center of the islands. Terrain that had been shaped by active volcanoes long ago.

Oahu had the most development of its interior, but even then, hundreds of thousands of acres remained untouched, far too remote and forbidding to be viable for development. This left villages, towns, and cities unprotected against anything that swept off the ocean.

Hawaii, the Big Island, had one major difference from the others. Its size came from the merger of five mountains. Two peaks, Mauna Loa and Mauna Kea, towered so tall and wide, they deflected the fiercest storms. Giant protectors, shrouded in cloud, myth, and legend. Instead of generating fear for their volcanic potential to blow the island apart, they inspired faith in their ability to protect against weather that would have otherwise devastated the island.

Meteorologists from all over the world argued the validity of Hawaiians' claims that the mountains protected them. To those who lived on the island, it wasn't speculation or boastfulness. It was geographical, indisputable, generationally proven fact.

Race had studied countless reports. He had watched the radar recordings and reached the same conclusion. Storms that threatened the Big Island suddenly came to a halt. The land masses forced weather systems to seek new paths with less resistance. As inconceivable as it sounded, the meteorologists who continued to discredit the role Hawaii's mountains played were wrong.

"Excuse me. Can I help you with something?"

Race blinked, bringing himself back to what he was doing. He'd followed the signs that read Onimura Resort. Most resorts were laid out similarly, and he was looking for a maintenance yard or administrative building. Something that didn't have the typical "little grass shack" feel as the guests' housing. He'd parked, intending to go inside and ask directions for the Safety Office and Savanah Jordan. He'd gotten side-tracked as he sat lost in thought in his SUV staring at Mauna Kea. Looking around, he didn't see the voice that had interrupted his thoughts.

"Down here."

Race looked out his window and was surprised to see there was a woman he'd not even noticed approach him. Maybe that was because she was unbelievably short. Her head was below his window.

When he opened the door, he realized she wasn't actually that short. She was sitting in a wheelchair, which he hadn't been able to see from the driver's seat as she was so close to the Suburban. He tried to guess her age, which was difficult to tell. Island women's caramel-colored skin and exotic eyes masked it well.

The woman waiting patiently before him was a perfect example. She had the coloring of someone born in Hawaii. Women all over the world tried everything from sprays to days of sun exposure to emulate what came naturally to the woman sitting before him. The easy air of grace and beauty that surrounded her made him want to smile.

Her eyes were the most exotic he'd ever seen. Blazing azure beams of light surrounded by luxurious black lashes. Her hair was bound up on her head and he felt cheated to not have the pleasure of confirming what he was sure it would look like. A genuine smile extended from her lips to her eyes. That was when he realized he was still frowning. He changed his expression. It was easy to return her open smile as he stepped closer. He didn't bother to look again at the wheelchair, which she seemed more than comfortable in. There were many other things he found more interesting about her.

When Savanah saw the SUV with county plates in the parking lot, she rolled close to the vehicle and saw a man sitting inside. At first, she thought he was listening to earbuds that she could not see, but when she looked closer, he didn't appear to be talking on his phone. Instead, the man's eyes were fixed on the mountains in the distance. He was so focused, he hadn't noticed her rolling up to him.

The door emblem indicated the vehicle belonged to Civil Defense. She couldn't help but wonder if CD had decided to send someone over to discuss the email she'd sent that morning. If that was the case, she had her proof of how poorly it had been received. She shared that opinion, even though she wouldn't be able to admit it. She didn't agree with Clark Dieter about anything. But he was the boss.

As the man climbed from the vehicle, she watched with unashamed interest. There was something about him that she found instantly attractive.

Savanah could see by the tension in his face the man was unhappy about something. She wondered if he always showed his feelings so plainly. Even someone less attuned to reading people would have been able to feel the anger in the air around him. She tried to figure out what she found attractive. Was it something so simple as his build? Or maybe the confidence of his movements. She admitted his rough edges had a gritty appeal. That surprised her. She wasn't normally attracted to men who didn't control their emotions.

Savanah was vehemently opposed to men who exhibited their manhood by beating women up, physically or verbally. Clark's conversation with her earlier that morning was an excellent example. The CEO had tried to intimidate her because, being bigger and stronger, he considered himself dominant and to have that right. Even if the belief was in his subconscious, it acted as the guide for his actions.

Savanah didn't mind that the man who stepped out of the Suburban was looking her over. She'd done the same to him. Which was why she was smiling. The tingle of mutual attraction was something she hadn't felt for a long time. "Can I help you with something?" She asked again when his eyes came back to hers.

"I'm looking for the Safety Office."

Her gaze swept over the man again at the surprising sound of his accent. The elongated vowels of his accent, almost lazy with self-confidence, identified him as Australian rather than British. Something his open demeanor and easy warmth confirmed. Savanah felt an immediate urge to keep him talking for the simple pleasure of hearing the exotic cadence. A desire cut short as she remembered his request.

Of course, he was looking for her office. She didn't know whether to swear or congratulate herself at having been right. It would depend on how the conversation went. "It can be a little tricky to find. Come on. I'll show you where it is."

"Do you need a hand? The parking lot is pretty rough," he offered smoothly.

"Thanks for asking. But I've got it. I'm used to it." Savanah replied just as smoothly.

She liked that his gaze hadn't dwelled on her chair. Again, she wished she weren't in it. She would have preferred him assessing her without it.

"I can see that."

"Is that so? What do you think you see?" Savanah glanced upwards.

He had all but stopped to look her over a second time. Savanah found that very interesting. Most men were so intimidated by the frame she sat in, they didn't notice anything else.

She didn't know what to think when he reached down to the scrollwork of the silver bracelet on her wrist. Her skin responded to the brush of his thumb across the engraving as if the metal weren't the object of the caress.

"Steel plumerias?"

Points for him. Most people didn't read the etching on her bracelet, let alone ask about it. Hawaiian bracelets were the most recognizable adornment next to having a flower tucked in one's hair. Both instantly said where you came from. Most women had several bracelets and wore them all at the same time. Savanah had only two, one silver and one gold. Both so special they didn't come off her wrist. Ever.

Her parents had given her the gold one on her sixteenth birthday. The silver one she had received when she lay in the hospital after her accident. On the inside were the names of eight other women, friends who had remained constantly at her side, with her family. The bracelet was their way of letting her know she wasn't alone, and their strength was hers for as long as she needed it. Savanah wasn't the first of the group to have received one. The tradition had started several years earlier, when Leayne had lost her father suddenly.

"It's a movie reference. Chick flick. An old chick flick. You've probably never heard of it," Savanah offered.

"Have you ever seen a magnolia flower? They're huge. But the colors aren't so different from plumerias," the man replied.

That stopped Savanah, causing her to turn to look up at the man whose cologne invited her closer. Neither men nor women in the islands bothered with cologne or perfume. When the air surrounded you with fragrance, there just didn't seem a need for it. You only had to walk out your door and pluck a blossom from the nearest bush or tree to wear the natural fragrance all day long. For most people, spraying on something extra was only for church on Sunday or weddings. That said, Savanah's father wore cologne, so she noticed it when other men did.

"Okay. I'm impressed." Savanah was also sorry when he withdrew his hand. She could still feel the whisper of sensation where his fingers had touched her skin as he'd inspected her bracelets.

He made no move to open the door. "If that impresses you, we should have dinner some time."

A thrill went through her at the subtle trap he had her in as he kept the door from opening. "Dinner? That sounds like quite a leap of faith." Savanah thought it would be interesting to sit across from the intensity she saw in the eyes staring back at her. Blue but so different from her own. There was something in them she couldn't identify.

"The way you handled that parking lot, dancing doesn't seem out of the question."

Savanah couldn't help but laugh. His sense of humor was a surprise given the seriousness of his expression when they'd first begun talking. "Dinner and dancing? I don't even know your name."

He offered his hand, smiling. Savanah didn't hesitate to lay hers into his upturned palm. Her lips parted with a silent intake at how good the instant warmth of their skin-to-skin contact was. His fingers flexed tighter around hers. She stared at their hands wondering if he, too, had felt something.

"My name's Race. And it is a pleasure to meet you."

Savanah almost groaned aloud. It had been too much to hope her day might end on a good note. How many men were named Race? Men driving a Civil Defense vehicle and looking for the resort Safety Office? She would bet her paycheck that the man holding the door for her was none other than the new CDD. Her assumption that her email would not be well-received now seemed a colossal underestimate. Not that she was surprised. If it had been her on the other end, she probably would have interpreted it exactly as she was guessing he had.

Hey, new guy: piss off.

RACE WATCHED THE MUSCLES OF THE WOMAN'S upper body working smoothly as she moved herself along effortlessly. She didn't look as physically challenged as being in a wheelchair suggested. The thought sparked an unexpected feeling of relief. She seemed full of life in a manner that defied whatever her disability might be.

Race wanted to place his hand beneath her chin and hold her face still for the simple reason he wasn't ready for the sight of her gazing at him through the plush dark lashes to end. The starburst of her eyes twinkled with mischievous curiosity. He'd never seen irises of white and blue before. Arresting in a way that stopped time when he gazed into them.

It was rude to stare, so Race settled for keeping the warmth of her hand in his.

He hoped he hadn't offended her. So far, she hadn't given any indication she was. Not even when his fingers had teased along the bands adorning her arm. There had been an instant spark of electricity from her skin to his. Like there was now as he held her hand.

The door opened from within and Race was forced to move. He reluctantly let the woman's hand go. After the way was clear, he held the door so she could go through.

"The Safety Office is at the end of the hall. Are you here to see anyone particular?" she asked him.

"I'm here to speak with the Manager . . ." Race hesitated, his frown and his anger threatening to return. It had receded while he'd been flirting with the beautiful woman who'd offered help. He was selfishly trying to hold onto the smile she'd given him a while longer. Race gave himself a shake. He was supposed to be there for business.

"Savanah Jordan," she said, her forehead wrinkling slightly.

Race felt the tic of a muscle at the side of his neck. Something about the look on her face made him think his conversation with the Safety Manager wasn't going to be pleasant. That thought made him appreciate the few moments of easygoing flirting he'd enjoyed with the woman in front of him as they'd crossed the parking lot together.

"Yes. That's the one. Savanah Jordan," Race confirmed as he followed through an open door which read Safety Office on the glass.

The man behind the desk raised his head above the monitors he was watching, a quizzical expression on his face.

"Manny, this is Race Weston. He's come all the way over from the other side of the island to see Savanah." The woman who was now his escort waited as Race stuck out his hand at her introduction.

"Welcome to Onimura Resort," Manny coughed.

"Right this way, Mr. Weston." Race nodded at Manny before turning to the office the woman pointed to. If she hadn't been following so closely behind, he would have turned back at the muttered "Oh shit" he barely heard.

"Would you mind getting the door, Manny."

CHAPTER EIGHT

"As Manny said, welcome to Onimura." She waved at the chairs in front of the desk. "Please, have a seat. How can I help you, Race?"

"Excuse me?" Race looked around the neatly organized office. The remnants of the half-grin he'd been wearing since they started talking, gave way to confusion.

"I'm sorry. We didn't get to finish our introduction earlier. I'm Savanah Jordan." She held her hand out again. "It's a pleasure to meet you as well, Race. I believe you said you've come to see me. How is it that I can help you?"

Under normal circumstances, Race felt sure he would have controlled the emotions crossing his face. But now, caught off guard as he was, he knew his confusion was evident. His eyes narrowed as he looked at the woman he'd been so enamored with only moments before. What the hell was going on here?

"You're Savanah? Savanah Jordan? The Safety Manager?" He hastily scanned the interior of the office, taking in the signs she was telling him the truth. There was no chair behind the desk, and the office was noticeably devoid of clutter, making it accessible for someone in a wheelchair.

Even to Race's ears, her reply sounded calm. "I can see you were expecting someone else. I'm sorry to disappoint you."

"Perhaps I've misunderstood . . ." He stopped abruptly. His mind working furiously.

Race didn't want her to be who he'd come to see. He'd meant what he said when he'd suggested dinner. He had found himself instantly attracted to the bright flame behind her eyes. Now, he regretted flirting with her in the parking lot. She was the person whom he'd come to set straight about the email dismissing his precaution instructions.

He pushed his thoughts aside and refocused on his purpose. "Is there someone else I can speak with? Your boss, perhaps."

He was here because of his office's responsibility to the people of Hawaii. People like Savanah Jordan. Someone like her would be in particular danger if a hurricane struck the island. Who would help her? His mind filled with reasons why the woman in front of him had no business being a safety manager. How could she respond to emergencies effectively?

"Again, sorry to disappoint you. Yes, I really am the manager and no, there isn't someone else you should be talking to," Savanah answered. The frown knitting her brow matched his. "Why don't you go ahead and explain why you've come all this way without so much as a phone call ahead to ensure I was able to meet with you? To what do I owe the pleasure of a visit, Director?"

Her reprimand made him bristle. "You know who I am." He wondered if she'd known who he was before he introduced himself. He'd only given his name, not his title.

"It comes with the territory. Knowing who people are. Chief of Police. Fire Marshall. Civil Defense Director. So yes, Mr. Weston. I am aware you are the new Civil Defense Director. Now back to the question of why you're here . . ."

"Very well. If that's how you want to handle things. You are aware there is a hurricane coming?" If the situation hadn't become such a frustrating cluster of confusion, Race would have admired the way she hadn't backed down.

"I am," Savanah replied.

"Yet your email stated you are refusing to begin evacuation preparations, as advised."

"It did."

Race found himself quickly becoming annoyed by her short responses. "You do understand the purpose of the Civil Defense Office is to make recommendations, and then people are supposed to follow them."

"I do."

"That's so people without the proper training or information aren't left to make these decisions themselves. Decisions they shouldn't be expected to make."

Her eyes narrowed. "Perhaps you meant that as noble. From where I'm sitting, your statement feels rather insulting, Director. It sounds like you're saying the poor, uneducated people of Hawaii need saving."

"Noble . . . that's not what I said."

"How generous, magnanimous of you, to come here and save us . . ." she countered.

"Magnanimous . . ." Race didn't have a clue where the fight had come from, but his shoulders were twitching as if his body were deflecting blows.

"I'm afraid I don't understand your confusion, Director Weston. Do you not like my choice of words, or the implication? Are you surprised I have them in my vocabulary? How *very good* of you, then. Is that more what you expect of someone like me?"

"Someone like you . . ." Race's bewilderment gave way to his instinctual authority. "What I expect is for people to follow protocol."

"Thank you for clearing that up. You aren't just insulting me. You are insulting my people, the people of Hawaii, as well." Her eyes flashed.

"It doesn't matter who you are. The point is I have given a directive."
The woman was maddening, and Race didn't feel like he was gaining ground.

"You expect people to do what you tell them."

"If what I'm telling them is the right thing to do."

"And you're always right."

"Yes," Race replied without hesitation.

She sat back in her chair, a satisfied look on her face.

Damn it. Once he'd said it, Race couldn't think of a graceful way to take it back without looking like even more of an ass. That would cause him to lose even more ground to the tenacious woman across from him. He *was* right most of the time. But blatantly saying he was always right was an open invitation for karma to kick him to the curb. The smug air that Savanah Jordan had assumed didn't help.

"The recommendations of the Civil Defense office are to begin hurricane protocols and preliminary evacuations," Race reiterated.

"I am aware of that."

"You are refusing to follow my recommendations."

"As my email stated, Onimura Resort feels the recommendations currently posted by the Hawaii County Civil Defense Office are not warranted at this time. As such, the Resort will not be following them."

Race found her response both formal and illogical. She had decided to disregard his recommendations.

"If that's your decision, then you obviously don't know what you're doing. It makes me doubt your qualifications to make the decision in the first place. Perhaps gaining additional experience outside of the islands might help you in the future. But this is about the here and now."

There was a sudden quiet to the room. Race felt a dangerous riptide swirling in the air around Savanah Jordan. He flexed his shoulders to rid himself of the inexplicable threat.

"That seems to be the popular opinion of the day. Sadly, you'll have to take a number, Mr. Weston."

"Take a number? What the hell? This is serious. You're gambling with people's lives. If you'd take the time to listen to me, you'd understand that I'm right." Race was beyond frustrated with Savanah's cool composure. It was like trying to crack open a nut that continually rolls away, unharmed, from beneath a hammer. Nothing he said seemed to make an impression on her.

Race Weston was proving to be arrogant and assuming. It was ironic, almost humorous, that the man was having a meltdown over a recommendation which she agreed with. Maybe someday she could explain why the situation was funny, even though it shouldn't have been.

She hadn't made the decision on her own. In truth she hadn't made that decision at all. That had been all Clark. But the email had come from the Safety Office of Onimura Resort—her office. Under the circumstances, Savanah felt saying "*we*" was appropriate. And she was certain the man across from her hadn't heard the difference.

As it was, she chose her words carefully—another thing Savanah was sure was lost on the irate Civil Defense Director. It would have been inappropriate to tell the man across from her how at odds she and her boss were over the decision. Savanah wouldn't even consider such a breach of confidence. But neither was she happy about the position she found herself in with Race, nor the opinions he'd formed of her.

It was an impossible situation.

The buzz of her phone saved her from having to reply further to Race. "Please excuse me. I need to take this."

She knew Manny wouldn't interrupt without a good reason. He knew who Race Weston was, and even if he couldn't hear the words through the door, Savanah was sure he could hear Race's increasingly irate tone.

"Sorry Savanah. The *Big Man* just called wanting to know if you were in the office. I told him you were, and he said he'll be right down to see you."

"He's coming now?" Savanah shouldn't have been surprised at the timing. She wished, briefly, she could wind time back to meeting Race in the parking lot so she could find a way to change how the day was going. Looking at Race fuming, she said, "Great. That sounds perfect."

Savanah's lips twitched. The situation was becoming laughable. She could sell tickets to watch the irritated Civil Defense Director try to convince the irrational CEO. Though she doubted Clark would find a verbal sparring match with Race Weston as much fun as she had. Then again, she doubted very much the CDD would be as charming with Clark as he'd been with her before discovering who she was.

"Send him in when he arrives, Manny."

When Savanah hung up the phone, Race began, "We seem to have gotten off on the wrong foot."

"Are you referring to the part where you suggested we have dinner, or the part where you told me I wasn't fit for my job?"

Savanah should have let it go and accepted Race's attempt to reclaim some sort of professionalism. His change of tone was a textbook dial-down for the spiraling situation. She could almost hear Leayne praising him for it, while telling her to quit pushing the man's buttons. Unfortunately, his sentiments so closely echoed Clark's words that morning, they were too much to ignore. She was owed an apology. By both men.

"Our conversation in the parking lot was unfortunate. Asking you to dinner . . ." Race fell silent.

"You no longer think I would make an acceptable dinner companion." Savanah wasn't about to let him off the hook.

"Why, of course not. I mean, of course you would be. Not, of course you wouldn't be . . ." Race hesitated. "You seem to be a charming, beautiful woman. But we're talking business now. I should never . . . Dammit. Why you?" Race's voice trailed off, his face flushing.

"Indeed. Why me?" Savanah was not about to back down, even a little bit. Instead, she martialed her feelings and channeled them to show him she wouldn't forget a moment or a single word, while watching his emotions leak out like water through a sieve.

"Ms. Jordan," Race began again. "I'm sure there's good reason why your company employs you. But I think we are both adult enough and intelligent enough to admit this is not the job for you. There is no possible way you can respond effectively to emergency situations. I suppose if it's a Band-Aid in the parking lot, you can assist. But your ability to do anything else . . . safety related . . ."

Race exhaled loudly. "You seem determined to make this as difficult as possible."

Her eyes widened at his words. She blinked several times before speaking. "I do apologize for making *this* difficult. Please do go ahead expressing your thoughts, Mr. Weston. I assure you, I am very interested in hearing what else you might have to say."

"If there is an emergency which requires you to run . . ."

"In other words, a situation that requires anything other than sitting prettily in this chair."

The words burned as they crossed her tongue. She made sure to speak slowly and clearly, enunciating each one in case the man across from her didn't get the message. He had immediately blamed her wheelchair for what he thought was wrong with the situation. The fact she was female and from Hawaii were icing to his apparent assessment of her. She couldn't help thinking Race Weston epitomized haoles' reputation as rude, discriminating, assholes.

"That's not what I said. You simply do not have the mobility a position such as this requires. Even if there weren't a hurricane coming. The fact there is, and you have chosen to disregard my recommendations . . ."

The door opened, but Race kept talking. "Your refusal to do what's prudent given the impending weather seems an indicator of thoughtlessness about the safety and wellbeing of others, as well as yourself, that shouldn't be ignored."

Savanah didn't let the sound of the door distract her. She kept her attention on Race. His hesitation could only mean one thing: the kicker was coming. The statement which would wrap everything up with a bow. She raised an eyebrow in silent permission for him to finish.

Not that he was waiting for permission. Race Weston was on a roll and seemed intent on voicing his opinion no matter whom he hurt. Savanah kept her hands clasped in her lap. Enduring was something she was good at.

"If I may speak frankly," Race concluded, "you'll be one of the people who will need saving when the time comes."

The air went out of the room.

"I couldn't agree with you more . . ."

CHAPTER NINE

"You agree with what?" Savanah visibly blanched as she retreated a fraction of an inch into her chair.

Race followed Savanah's gaze to the man who'd walked in unannounced and thrown his hat in the ring, seemingly on his side. He took stock of the new player in the room. The polo shirt the man wore had the resort logo and was tucked neatly into a pair of slacks over matching oxfords. The air of smugness made Race think here was someone who resided higher up the food chain. There was also the fact he'd walked in without hesitation.

The interruption would have been enough, but something about the man's tone rubbed Race the wrong way. Race felt torn between asking what the man agreed with and ignoring him altogether. The argument was between him and Savanah Jordan.

The man stuck out his hand, offering a smile and a practiced air of *aloha*. "Clark Dieter. CEO. Aloha and welcome to the island."

"Race Weston. Hawaii Island Civil Defense Director."

Race ended the handshake as soon as acceptable. The other man's demeanor felt too manufactured for Race's liking. A stark contrast to the warmth he'd felt upon meeting Savanah.

"Good to meet you, Weston. How can we be of help to the new CDD?" Clark asked, showing his teeth as he smiled. "Nothing like a big 'ole hurricane to see what you're made of right off the bat. This will be your first disaster, if I'm not mistaken."

"You're mistaken," Race corrected firmly, bristling. "This isn't my first disaster."

Race cast his eyes between Clark Dieter, standing with his fake smile, to Savanah sitting silent behind her desk. She was doing a masterful job of masking her thoughts. Her face was blank. He stared harder. That was when he noticed the tension in her neck. Something that, despite their heated conversation, he hadn't seen before the CEO's entrance.

Race saw her eyes move carefully from him to her boss. She seemed suddenly wary. There was something going on that he'd fallen into the middle of.

"Your first emergency situation here with us, then. You know what I mean. As you were saying, something about Savanah will need saving . . . continue." Clark prompted.

Race tasted a bitterness at the words he'd been speaking moments earlier. He decided on a new course now that he was speaking with the CEO of the resort. "I was curious why Ms. Jordan decided it wasn't necessary to follow the suggested protocols Civil Defense issued this morning."

"You mean the protocols you issued," Clark amended.

Race wondered whether the other man believed what he did with his lips could be mistaken for a smile.

"They are one and the same," Race replied calmly.

"Perhaps I was misinformed how your position works. I understood the hierarchy of things was the Director made the decisions. A dictatorship rather than a democracy." Clark shrugged in dismissal.

Race chose to ignore the man's musings. If he didn't know better, Clark Dieter was being deliberately insulting. He understood Savanah's wariness. He redirected the conversation back to the reason he was here. "While I appreciate Ms. Jordan's immediate response, and supplying the requested information on occupancy and other matters, none of that negates refusing to prepare for evacuation." Whatever was going on between Savanah and her boss wasn't his concern.

Race refused to mitigate what Savanah had done. The presence of the other man helped him rein in his rampant emotions. Race pushed away the nagging voice that said he owed the woman across from him an apology. Now that he'd been joined by the resort's CEO, he could concentrate on resolving the situation. That was what he'd come for and what was important. Surely the Safety Manager couldn't, wouldn't, disagree with them both.

"I believe there was also something about dear Savanah not being a good fit for the job." Clark held his hand up as if to stop Savanah from speaking. "You perhaps once were, my dear. But we need to face facts. As you're so fond of saying, it is always the best course of action to deal with the reality of things."

Savanah had her mouth clamped shut so tightly, Race could see her lips paling. He didn't blame her. Her boss seemed to be purposely baiting her. Race felt embarrassed for her. He didn't need to add to her discomfort for being privy to an issue that should be between her and her boss.

"I'm only here to discuss the recommendations of my office. And this company's lack of compliance." Race regretted his harsh words earlier. He hadn't given Savanah much of a chance to explain her actions. He'd been too busy jamming his title and the respect he expected down her throat.

"Excellent. Perhaps now that we're both here, Savanah will listen to reason. Something I thought I had taken care of this morning. Obviously based on your statements, I was wrong." Clark nodded as if the two men had clapped one another on the back in agreement.

If it was possible, Savanah eyes widened further at Clark's remarks.

"I'm afraid I'm not following you," Race said.

Clark sent a smug glance to Savanah. "Why, as soon as I saw your email, Weston, I called right down to Savanah about activating our procedures based on your preliminary evacuation suggestions. Savanah was quite vocal about disagreeing with what I was saying and the advisories from your office."

Clark rubbed his chin for a moment. "I thought I made myself clear and that she would follow my instructions. Which of course were to follow yours. Your presence here clearly says she did not."

Savanah stared at Clark, who returned her gaze with an unblinking one of his own. The man appeared comfortable with being the source of her humiliation. The CEO was clearly enjoying himself.

"Perhaps she will better understand the necessity of these actions now that we have both explained things to her," Clark finished, offering another manufactured look of concern towards Race.

"Are you saying you aren't aware of the email Ms. Jordan sent my office, informing me this resort would not comply?" It was too incredible for Race to comprehend.

He couldn't help looking at Savanah in disbelief. Perhaps she really wasn't any more than a pretty face with a sunny personality. The thought turned his stomach.

"Now you're getting the picture. Give me the gist of her reply to you, if you don't mind."

"The gist of it . . ." Race looked at the CEO in shock. "Your resort will not be enacting any emergency preparedness procedures at this time. Procedures you feel aren't warranted." Race thought he'd made that clear several times already.

He turned again to Savanah as he continued to address the CEO. If it was possible, she'd become quieter. Had he known her better, her silence might speak volumes. But what was there for her to say? The CEO had explained clearly what she'd done.

Clark rose to his feet, a look of disappointment on his face. "I'm sorry for the trouble, Weston. I gave specific instructions to follow the recommendations sent out by your office this morning. Thank you for bringing this to my attention. We will of course be complying immediately. As for my employee, rest assured I will be supervising her more carefully and the dereliction of duty will be appropriately addressed, given this obvious proof that her capabilities are compromised."

Race didn't know what to say. The woman who fifteen minutes ago had attracted him now seemed like a different person. If she were his employee, he'd have fired her on the spot. The fact that Savanah's boss seemed willing to work with her despite such gross misconduct was a credit to the man that Race hadn't anticipated.

Clark held the door open. "The staff will escort you back to the parking lot. Thanks again for bringing this to my attention. Good luck with the hurricane and the job and all. I'll just have a word with Savanah."

Clark Dieter propelled Race forward until he was outside Savanah's office. He turned to speak, only to find the door shut in his face, severing the connection. What the hell had just happened? Clark Dieter had just dismissed him like he was another employee. Who the hell did he think he was? Race felt a new anger beginning to burn.

CHAPTER TEN

Clark turned back to Savanah, his face hard, his lips in a thin line. Savanah almost choked at how easily he transitioned from the feigned innocence and outright lies. She felt the walls of her office closing in. She'd walked into a trap, one that she should have seen.

There was no way for the Civil Defense Director to know the resort CEO was lying. And no reason for Race to believe her. Especially given he was so quick to think sitting in a wheelchair meant she wasn't capable of anything. The meeting and Clark's behavior were ludicrous. But Savanah couldn't bring herself to laugh about it. She felt like throwing up.

She spoke slowly. "Do I understand you correctly that we will now be complying with the Civil Defense directive?" She reminded herself that the safety of the staff and guests was what mattered, repeating "sticks and stones" in her mind. Both men had thrown words at her. She just needed to continue letting them bounce off without breaking her.

"Don't be stupid. We aren't doing anything of the sort. We just needed that Civil Defense moron off the property and out of our hair. This storm will bounce off like all the rest. He should get back to the other side of the island and worry about things there and leave us alone," Clark snapped.

Savanah blinked in a shock. "You just told Race . . ."

Clark leaned across the desk. "And if you wanted to make a scene and disagree with anything I said, you missed your chance."

Savanah was so stunned she almost didn't know what to say. "I'm not going to have an argument with my boss in front of someone. Challenging what you said would have been unprofessional."

Clark barked, "I know what I said. And I know what I'm telling you now." He glared at her. "And now Civil Defense knows anything that goes wrong here will be the result of your incompetence. I expect you to do exactly as you're told from here on out. Otherwise, I'll make sure the whole island hears of your poor decision-making. You won't be able to find work at a mini-mart."

Clark turned and left the office without another word, leaving Savanah to stare at the door behind him. She couldn't breathe, the air in her office poisoned by the dark personality of the CEO.

Her head went back, and her eyes closed. Savanah's upbringing prevented her from correcting Clark or speaking out against him while Race had been there. She'd been raised to respect authority and would never embarrass herself or her family by speaking to anyone in the workplace, let alone her boss, as Clark had addressed her. Her place was to be the rock that others could rely on to do her job without complaining. That's what she'd been trying to do.

But maybe, this time, I was wrong.

With a long sigh, she dialed Leayne, hoping her friend would still be at her desk. Like Savanah, Leayne tended to put in extra time, rarely leaving at the end of the scheduled workday. Savanah sighed with relief as she heard her friend's voice on the other end. "Leayne, I need to talk to you."

"Are you okay? You don't sound good. Did you have a seizure?" Leayne asked quickly.

"No, I'm fine. Unless you want to count my heart about to explode out of my chest." Savanah had to tell someone about what had happened. Leayne was the logical choice, just in case Clark decided to make good on his threats and fire her for something she didn't do. "I'd like to come and see you officially before I leave the property."

"Of course. I'll be here," Leayne responded.

Savanah wasn't surprised that Leayne didn't interrupt as she described the debacle that had taken place in her office but scribbled extensive notes.

According to Leayne, there was plenty for Savanah to file a complaint. Something Savanah declined doing. That wasn't going to help with whatever Clark's problem was with her. Savanah would just need to keep her eyes open and make sure she did her job.

Savanah took comfort that Leayne had agreed with her. That confirmed she was not overreacting. Still, the more she thought about the situation, the more incredible it seemed. Savanah didn't like the "wait and see if it goes away" method. Staying away from Clark as Leayne suggested sounded too much like hiding.

Her hands tightened on the wheels of her chair, bringing it to a stop in the middle of the sidewalk. She hadn't done anything wrong. Savanah wasn't willing to argue in front of an outsider or another employee. But confronting Clark and asking him for an explanation seemed fair.

Instead of heading to her office, Savanah whipped her chair in an expert U-turn on the sidewalk, toward Clark's. Determination had her pushing the wheels expertly down the empty path. There was always the chance he would be gone for the day. That thought kept her from calling to ask Leayne to accompany her. She thought that if she spoke with Clark, and it resulted in a repeat of the meeting with Race Weston, then Savanah would make sure the head of HR was there for any subsequent attempts at conversation.

"Sorry Lea'." Savanah sent the apology into the air. She knew Leayne would be pissed about her confronting Clark. Leayne had made her recommendation clear. Every interaction between the two of them from then on had to be documented, whether Savanah thought it important or not.

Savanah saw Clark's BMW was still in his reserved spot. The remainder of the employee parking lot was almost empty, as the day shift gave way to the evening staff. With the administration offices closed, only service personnel who interacted directly with the guests remained. Other than that, it was only Savanah's staff and someone from maintenance on property around the clock.

As she wheeled past the few vehicles left, she was struck by the view. License plates and taillights. No wonder so many children and older people were struck by vehicles. From where she sat in her wheelchair, no driver would have seen her, either. She had never realized that before.

That was probably why Clark didn't see her even as Savanah heard him talking. At first, she thought for a moment he was talking to her. His tone conveyed the same anger he'd used that morning. She applied pressure to the wheels, stopping behind a truck as she realized he had to be speaking to someone else.

"I told you. I'll take care of it," Clark said angrily. "None of your damned business how."

So Savanah wasn't the only one Clark talked to like that. Knowing that should have eased something inside her, but it didn't. She couldn't help but wonder who the poor soul might be on the other end. She hugged tighter to the bumper of the truck she hid behind. It was wrong for her to be listening to his conversation, but Savanah couldn't help herself.

There was a long pause before Clark added in a more solicitous tone, "I'll get the money. Your hounding me isn't helping. I have everything under control."

The silence that followed indicated the caller on the other end was talking again.

"No. I don't need you to come here." Now there was a tremor underlying the CEO's words that Savanah would never have believed if she hadn't heard it herself.

She strained forward to hear, but Clark's voice dropped to a murmur for the rest of the conversation. There was nothing more than guttural sounds of agreement. Savanah had an image of a dog ducking its head, tail between its legs as it whined apologetically in the hopes of escaping being struck.

Footfalls froze her in place. She prayed that the owner of the truck wouldn't appear. Savanah needed to shelter behind it for just a few minutes longer. She hadn't intended to eavesdrop, but she could not pretend she wasn't. If Clark found her, Savanah could imagine how furious he would be.

She still didn't know what was going on. But at least now, she felt relieved that her guess had been right. The anger her boss had unleashed on her stemmed from something else. Her email had just been the spark to light whatever her boss had buried himself in.

Savanah peered cautiously around the tailgate toward Clark's parking spot as she heard the bang of his door. He gunned the engine and sped out of the driveway. She quickly moved to the other side of the truck in case he looked in his rearview mirror. As he crossed lanes erratically and pulled onto the road, she hoped that he wasn't paying attention to anything but what was in front of him.

Chapter Eleven

Race talked to himself as he drove. He couldn't remember the last time he'd left a meeting feeling so frustrated. Despite the CEO having agreed with him and assuring him the resort would begin evacuation preparations, Race found himself doubting the man's sincerity. He kept picturing the stoic look on Savanah Jordan's face as her boss gave her up as the problem. He believed nothing Clark Dieter had said. Yet Savanah hadn't disputed the statement, which unequivocally pointed to the woman in the wheelchair as the one who'd defied his instructions.

He almost stomped on the brake at a thought: was he disinclined to believe that Savanah Jordan was at fault because of an unconscious consideration for whatever her condition might be? He had found her captivating and had already been thinking of reasons to speak with her again. If he didn't want to believe she had such poor judgement, was it also possible his interest in her was out of some sympathetic reaction to a beautiful woman being confined to a wheelchair?

He swore at his confusion. "Jesus. Get it together. You don't have time for this shit."

Forcing his mind back on track, Race had to command Siri twice before she recognized his voice and played back his new voicemail. Steve confirmed that Hurricane Garth had been upgraded to a Category 3. The good news was the 200-mile-wide storm had slowed and seemed to be drifting south, taking it away from the Big Island.

Race didn't find the news comforting. The storm wasn't far enough away to be dismissed yet. Or maybe he was still too angry to accept the news.

Race continued along the coastal highway, turning down small roads to the water's edge when he found them, making mental notes for the next update his office would issue. Each district of the Big Island would have its own challenges, on top of those common to the entire island: mass flooding and virtually no protection from the destructive winds.

As dusk fell, he circled back the way he'd come. He might as well grab dinner before driving home to the other side of the island. It wasn't long before he was sitting above the pier at the center of Kona. The vantage point overlooking the road and the seawall afforded him a perfect view of the beach and the swimmers who seemed determined to make the most of the last of the daylight, refusing to get out of the pristine waters of the Kona coast until the very end.

That was when he noticed the wheelchair at the edge of the sidewalk, beside the stone steps that lead to the sand and water below. Race sat up straighter, scanning the water. Was it possible the woman he'd only just met and who had consumed his thoughts was somewhere down there? The wheelchair certainly looked like hers.

Then he saw her, swimming with a man at her side. From what he could see, Savanah was a better swimmer than Race was, her confidence evident in the easy swing of her arms. Before he could tell how much of a role her legs played, the seawall hid her from view.

Race leaned forward over the rail, impatient to see Savanah Jordan reappear. Her companion came into view first, as he stood head and shoulders above the woman he held. His arms were securely around Savanah's body. From where Race sat, he couldn't determine how much of her weight the man supported. He certainly looked capable of carrying her. Before they took the steps up to the pier, another man appeared, his outstretched arms offering assistance. This man was younger, closer to Savanah's age from what Race could see. By the way they interacted, they all knew one another as they walked with Savanah toward the wheelchair.

Race found the scene baffling. Savanah could walk. Had he not met her personally and seen her in the wheelchair, there was nothing about her physical appearance that gave any indication she needed it. But it was clear by the undivided attention of the two men with her, something wasn't right.

It irritated him that he still found her damned attractive. A continued echo of his original train of thought when he'd met her in the parking lot. Now, as she exited the water, there was more to see. All that tanned skin revealed by the brilliant yellow bikini was tantalizing. Race couldn't help but appreciate her perfectly proportioned curves. *What exactly was the wheelchair for?*

As if cued by his thoughts, Race saw Savanah stumble despite the hands that held her. Her body grew taut, stiffening without warning. Only their arms going around her kept her from falling to the ground.

Race leaned over the rail, unable to look away. He gripped the metal, his knuckles whitening as the beautiful Savanah Jordan contorted to the point that he feared she would break. The big man who'd watched her so carefully in the water held on securely as Savanah's body bent backwards in what looked, to Race, like a seizure.

Whatever was happening, it was clear, her body wasn't under her control any longer.

The younger man stood, anxiously watching, as did passers-by who stopped when they realized something was wrong. Many hands reached out, ready to help. Race felt an urge to run down to the beach and do the same.

But he realized there were already enough people around to help. He would be just another onlooker, or worse, get in the way. From his vantage point on the restaurant deck, he could continue to watch without adding to the spectacle the growing crowd created.

Race couldn't take his eyes from what was happening, his dinner forgotten as he watched how gently the two men handled Savanah. They seemed prepared when, as suddenly as the seizure started, her body gave a last shudder and fell limp in their arms. Watching her now confirmed that she did not have the full use of her legs.

The crowd remained silent as the older man wrapped Savanah with a towel while the younger one held her securely. Race watched as they finally lowered her into the wheelchair. He could almost feel the collective release of air from the bystanders that the emergency was over. He peered harder, attempting to hold back dusk by his will alone and allow him to watch how things with Savanah would end. But the shadows of night fell and hid her from his view.

Tiki torches flickered as the evening breeze came down from the mountain. Race pulled his eyes from the scene on the pier to the darkness offshore. He didn't know what had happened down there. But he hadn't been wrong. Savanah Jordan wouldn't be saving anyone if the hurricane hit. She'd be one of those in need of help. Just like moments ago.

Race pulled out his phone. The man he guessed was Savanah Jordan's father flashed in and out of view beneath the streetlights, as he pushed the wheelchair and its exotic occupant from view. He couldn't help feeling a little deprived now that there was nothing more to see on the darkening shore.

"Steve. I know it's late. I want a fully functioning office set up and running in the next twenty-four hours over on the west side of the Island . . . Yes, I know that's never been done before. We're doing it now."

Race had read the reports of past disasters on the Big Island. The CDD always stayed put, buried safely in his bunker, giving orders to those trying to survive outside. But Race didn't operate like that. He wasn't one to wait until the emergency was over, when a new day would allow him to emerge and assess things safely. He preferred to be in the thick of things.

Hurricane Garth was moving south of the island. For once, the windward or eastern side didn't appear to be first in line for damage. Until Garth was no longer a threat, Race resolved to run things from what was usually the leeward side. It was long past time his office recognized the population there.

Race pushed his now cold dinner around the plate. He had a reputation as a man of action. There were several reasons to support situating himself on the west side of the island for this event. He dismissed the concern that his decision had anything to do with the dark-haired woman who had managed to monopolize his thoughts.

Savanah looked at her father. "One more, Dad. There's time to do one more."

"Your body is tired, Savanah. Pushing it too far will do more harm than good."

"I'm still really angry, Dad."

Kyle did not respond. He knew his daughter was upset and gave her the space to work things out for herself.

"Angry or not, the shark will enjoy you for dinner just the same. It is time we get out of the water."

He watched her laughter overcome a retort. "Okay Dad, you win."

"No. They win. It is their ocean, and we are but borrowing space in it for such time as they allow."

Savanah took a deep breath and held it for several seconds as she lay on her back. She closed her eyes and floated in the water. Letting her breath out slowly, she met her father's gaze.

"I love you, Dad."

Kyle smiled knowingly at his daughter. He would never forget what standing in the hospital next to her had felt like before they knew whether she would live. Even now, fourteen months later, the awful memories would come back to him in the middle of the night. He could hear her crying as she gripped their hands, apologizing for her tears. Apologizing for her weakness as the pain robbed her of control. He and her mother had assured her countless times that her tears were a sign of strength, not the lack of it.

Father and daughter made their way to the beach. Kyle Jordan moved closer, making sure he was on his feet before she was. He would never forgive himself if he let her progress be interrupted because he allowed something so simple as a slip on the sand.

"Dad, I can do it," Savanah said as he reached for her. He stood almost waist-deep in the water, while her feet were barely able to touch bottom, as she took his hand.

"I know you can," he agreed without letting go of her hand.

Savanah put her feet down, making sure they were secure as her Dad began to walk slowly backward. The transition from water to land, where Savanah's body and spine would engage to take her weight, was a perilous one. The smallest misstep on her part, taking a wave while not being secure on her feet, could bring her to her knees.

As she emerged from the water, her legs quivered and she slowed her steps. "You're right. My legs are a little tired," she admitted with a guilty smile.

There was no need to reply to what he had observed. Instead, he carefully lifted his daughter from the pull of the wet sand, making sure to place her feet securely on the concrete edge. It wasn't wide enough for both of them, so he walked in the water beside her, ignoring the waves that licked at his ankles. The height of the concrete walk brought his daughter's eyes to his level. He watched carefully for any sign of her instability.

"I am also right the shark would happily eat us for his evening meal if we were so foolish to be in the water at twilight."

Kyle had taught his daughter from birth about the danger of being in the water during the transition times of the day. Ocean creatures loved to rise to the surface at sunrise and sunset. It was an opportune mealtime when the mix of shadows hid the ocean predators easily. It was why fisherman started their work before dawn, bait already in the water as the sky began to lighten. As someone who'd been surfing his entire life, Kyle knew the predators' feeding schedule. Just as the men who waited to feed their family by their catch knew it. Neither father nor daughter had any desire to be on the menu.

"I've got her, Uncle."

Savanah and her father looked up. They hadn't noticed Duke on the steps, waiting to take Savanah's hands. "Merry is drying off Leila over on the other side," Duke explained as Savanah's father handed her over.

Neither of them thought anything of Duke referring to Savanah's father as *Uncle*. It was a sign of respect in Hawaii. It had nothing to do with whether you were a blood relative to someone. It was just part of what *ohana* meant. What it was to be born and raised in Hawaii. Sometimes people understood it. Kyle felt sorry for those who didn't.

"Thanks Duke," Savanah said as she reached for her towel on the seat of her chair.

Maybe she made too much of a stretch. Or the angle was more acute than she realized. Maybe her father was right, and she'd pushed herself too hard. Whatever the reason, Savanah gasped in pain. "Daa-aaaad!"

Kyle spun at the unmistakable sound of pain in his daughter's voice. The sight of her body growing rigid told him all he needed to know. Her knees buckled as he caught her stiff body. He held her securely as she grasped him blindly.

"Here's her chair." Duke was already moving the wheelchair into place behind Savanah.

"No. Don't . . . I'm too wet . . . I can't . . ." Savanah gasped as another spike of pain ripped through her.

"Just breathe. Keep breathing. It will pass," Kyle Jordan told his daughter over and over, his voice even and calm. He held her steady in his arms as she struggled to stay conscious. "Look at me. Focus on me, Savanah."

Savanah fought to keep the blackness from overtaking her. She prayed the ringing in her ears wasn't the sound of her screaming, but she couldn't tell as her body refused all her attempts at control.

Savanah could hear her father talking to her, soothing words over and over. What was he saying? Savanah couldn't make it out, but she didn't need to. For now, it was enough to follow the calm cadence, a lifeline as she fought her way from beneath the waves of pain.

"I'm sorry," she managed to whisper between gasps of air.

Her vision cleared enough for her to see her father above her. Relief filled his gaze as her eyes focused on him in recognition. "You have nothing to be sorry for, Savanah."

"I made a scene. You were right. I pushed too hard." Savanah was still panting, her heart racing, her hands locked on her father's forearms.

"You didn't do anything wrong," her father reassured her. "Duke, give me her towel."

Kyle nodded a silent thanks to the passers-by who had stopped and were still watching the intense scene. There were those who knew them and were aware of Savanah's condition and others who'd just wanted to help, sensing someone in need. That's how it was. He waved to indicate things would be fine.

"Did I . . ." Savanah didn't want to ask if she'd made any noise. In the beginning she'd been unable to keep from it.

"No. You didn't make a sound," Kyle comforted his daughter.

Even now it was still one of the things that bothered her the most. Savanah hated when she couldn't bear the pain in silence. It added to the weakness she felt at not being able to control the seizing of her back.

"I'm going to let Duke take you for a moment, while I dry you off. Don't worry. We've got you."

Savanah's attempt at a nod was nothing more than a spastic jerk of her neck. It was always like that afterwards—as if every muscle and nerve had to reestablish its own connection with her brain. Random twitches of an engine sparking in vain as it attempts to turn over. She felt Duke take her weight from her father's arms but even if she wanted to protest, she could do nothing but allow it.

CHAPTER TWELVE

Savanah sat at her desk, comparing the latest predictions for Garth. Since the disastrous meeting in her office two days earlier, she'd not heard another word from her boss, nor Race Weston. Other than the island-wide updates that his office published, the Civil Defense Director seemed to have forgotten all about her. Something Savanah was sure she should be grateful for.

Then why wasn't she? It wasn't like her to not be able to put it out of her mind. But there was something about those first few minutes that she couldn't forget. Every time she thought about them, a smile came to her lips.

She pushed her keyboard away in frustration as she thought about why she felt so cheated. There'd been something captivating in the depth of Race's eyes. Despite how hard she was fighting it, Savanah admitted, she was disappointed at how things had turned out. She rolled her eyes as she voiced her irritation. She laced her fingers behind her head and drew her torso up straight. Slowly, she began to lean to one side, over the arm of her wheelchair. Savanah moved carefully as she elongated the opposite half of her body. She straightened with the same amount of caution before leaning in the other direction. The stretches that were part of her ongoing therapy had become a daily routine and helped her release more tension than just that of her injured back.

"Okay. Fine. I admit it. I wish things hadn't turned out the way they did. And yes, it would have been interesting to find out what kind of dinner companion Race Weston might have made," she said aloud as she moved.

Only when she'd done twice the number of sets required, did she slow down. "Happy now? Then get back to work, why don't you, Savanah."

Garth was still several hundred miles away, seeming to trace the island's outline. Rainfall was sporadic, but high waves and powerful winds were already slamming into the southern portion of the island. Conditions characteristic of South Point. If it continued along this track, the edge of the storm would pass them less than one hundred miles away. That was still close enough to deliver torrential rains and damaging winds over at least the southern end of the island.

Savanah pulled up the records from Hurricane Iniki, which had hit the islands thirty years earlier. Too young to remember it herself, she had heard the stories of it from her relatives. Iniki had originally caused barely a hiccup in the weather as it made its way westward, passing well south of the Hawaiian Islands. Its initial track predicted almost a straight line across the Pacific. And then, after everyone had written the storm off, it had made an unexpected ninety-degree change of course. Though the hastily issued hurricane watch was upgraded to a warning within hours, it was too late. The sudden storm had barreled straight northward, sweeping directly over the small island of Kauai, leveling everything in its path that wasn't made of millennia-old lava. Residents and guests alike had been left with no time and no choice to do anything but shelter in place. And pray.

Luck and the grace of God had kept the loss of life low. But the devastating damage to the island taught residents a painful lesson. They didn't wait to be told to prepare. They didn't breathe relief when storms weakened. Only after the wind shear from the mountains decapitated storms and broke the rotation into harmless pockets of clouds, would life go back to normal.

Savanah reached for her phone as it rang, not taking her eyes from the screen in front of her. She compared the projected paths of Garth against that of Iniki, as she knew the meteorologists were doing. They all had the same goal: to predict how effective Mauna Loa and Mauna Kea would be in pushing Garth away if it changed course.

"Aloha," Savanah answered automatically, still wondering what it was about Garth that had her so nervous.

"Ms. Jordan."

Savanah sat back in her chair at the sound of Race Weston's voice. The thrill at hearing him quickly faded to wondering why he was calling her. Hadn't things been bad enough the first time around? "Director Weston."

"I was wondering if you might have time to meet this afternoon. I had some questions I was hoping you might answer. The insights you have as someone born and raised on the west side of the island could prove valuable."

"I'm sure there are others much better suited to supply you with whatever information you're looking for." The memory of the way he had treated her once he'd learned she was the Safety Manager, and the humiliation of what had happened in the office flooded back. She wasn't about to give him another chance to tell her how inept he thought she was.

Savanah heard the frustrated intake of breath as he replied. "You aren't going to make this easy, are you? I owe you an apology and was hoping to make it in person."

"I'm sorry to have been a problem for you." Savanah replied immediately. "Please let me make things easy now. There's no need to apologize and I unfortunately don't have time to meet with you. This afternoon, or if I have a preference, ever. I understand how full your schedule must be with your continuing hurricane preparedness recommendations." She hesitated, concern finally winning against the memory of what had happened. "We aren't in the clear yet and it would be foolish for you to believe we are. Aloha, Director Weston."

Savanah hung up the phone without waiting for a response. It didn't matter what he would have said, her answer was no. For all she knew, Race and Clark were now best friends and communicating directly with one another. Clark still lying his face off, and Race continuing to believe she was incompetent.

Savanah stared at the picture sitting on the corner of her desk. It was her college graduation. There was such pride on her parents' faces. She picked the photo up, her fingers tracing over the image.

"I swear I haven't forgotten what you've taught me." Savanah's mind was made up. She was going to do what was right. Even if that meant disregarding a direct order from her CEO.

The picture went back to its place, and Savanah turned back to the list she'd been working on before answering Race's call. Race and Clark deserved one another and could both go jump in a lava flow for all she cared. She was busy trying to do her best for the people that counted on her. People that didn't disregard her because she was a woman, a local, or because she pushed herself along in a wheelchair.

"Come on now. Give a bloke a fair go of it . . ."

The words slipped out. He'd lived in the States long enough to control his Australian accent and diction. Usually. That the words had escaped now showed how unhappy Race was over what had happened with Savanah.

Several seconds passed before he realized Savanah had hung up. Race wasn't sure whether he should be thankful or insulted. Part of him knew he deserved the rebuke. He was a better man than their first meeting had shown him to be. He wasn't just some bludger, mucking about. But how could he talk sense into her if she wouldn't even hear his apology? And then there was the fact he was halfway to her office. He had been sure he could convince Savanah to meet with him.

He thought about her parting words. What had she meant about not being in the clear yet? If she thought that, why had she resisted following his directive?

It was enough to make him dial another number. Race stared at the bright blue sky as he waited for Steve to pick up his call.

"Steve, has there been a change in Garth's projected path?"

"No, sir. Still on its way passing South Point. It does appear to be slowing down again, but no shift in direction at this time."

"We aren't letting go of this until we are positive it isn't coming back at us," Race stated.

"Roger that, Race. I'll make sure everyone keeps on top of things. I'll contact you the moment there are any changes. If there are any."

"Good man. I'm out of the office but can be back in less than thirty." It was essential that Steve be aware of where his boss was at all times. Knowing how long it would take any member of the team to return to their post was an essential part of the job.

An idea came to him as he checked his watch. If Savanah Jordan wouldn't agree to a meeting, perhaps he could manage to run into her some other way. There was more than enough time before she should be leaving her office for him to buy the necessary items.

If she kept normal hours.

Race knew he would have to hope for luck. So far, he'd come up short on that.

CHAPTER THIRTEEN

Her mind still distracted by Race Weston wanting to see her again, Savanah was surprised by the knock at her door. Looking up, she waved Duke in. He was working on his day off, picking up additional hours in preparation for the birth of his second child.

It was nice to have him around in the daytime. His usual third-watch schedule meant she missed out on how great he was to work with. The young man lived and breathed the aloha spirit. A personality like his was a waste on the graveyard shift, but it was the shift that worked for him.

"Thanks for your help the other day." It was the first time since the episode at the pier that she had the chance to talk with him. "Sorry you got stuck—"

"You don't have to thank me. Glad I was there to give Uncle a hand." Duke shrugged as he settled into the chair on the other side of the desk. "No worries. It wasn't a big deal. That one didn't look as bad. Are the seizures getting better?"

"I'm sure there's at least one social media post of it out there from the tourists passing by. Who knows, I could be famous," Savanah joked. "Yes. They are getting better . . . too slowly to suit me, but better."

"You didn't pass out this time."

"You're right. Which is what we've been aiming for. Once I can control that, then the doc will let me out of this chair. Until then, it's my safety net." Savanah made a face. "As you saw, though, I'm still fairly useless until it's over and I've had time to recover."

"You shouldn't let that bother you so much, Savanah. Given what your body goes through, it's understandable."

"You're not the one feeling like you've just taken a taser strike meant for an elephant to your spine." She knew Duke meant well, and that she wasn't taking his concern as gracefully as she should have. Savanah appreciated how much everyone had drawn together to help her. But learning to let the guilt and embarrassment go was easier said than done. Which was why she made a point of saying something about what had happened. "Did you need something?" she asked.

"There wasn't anything in the briefing this morning about the new emergency procedures the front desk is going through today. I only found out about them when I was making my rounds just now. The girls over at check-in seem pretty uncomfortable about it. I was just wondering what's up with that."

Savanah leaned back in her chair, frowning at Duke. "I don't know anything about it. What procedures are you talking about?"

"Pinky said they've been told to encourage all guests to put their valuables in the resort safe rather than the ones in the rooms. Bagging and tagging every guest's belonging is causing a lot of extra work for her and her crew. I got the impression they're used to singular deposits. Not the whole resort," Duke explained.

"Did Pinky say where the order came from?"

"The big man himself."

Savanah couldn't believe what she was hearing. "Clark told the front desk to start telling the guests not to use the room safes? When?"

"I think just this morning. It's been nonstop at the front desk ever since." Duke quit talking when Savanah picked up her phone.

"Clark. It's Savanah. I just heard you've given instructions for the front desk to tell guests not to store their valuable in the rooms. Is that true?"

Savanah found it disturbing that the man whose job put him at the top of the food chain didn't think he should inform any of his managers about what he was doing or why. With a hurricane on the horizon, he seemed to be communicating even less than usual. Not a single meeting had been scheduled in the last few months—not even to address the threat of Hurricane Garth. It was no way to run a business. Certainly not one as big as their resort.

"I did," Clark snapped.

Savanah's mouth fell open. "Why?"

"Are you questioning my authority, Jordan? Because if you are, I have a solution for that."

Savanah knew her job was on the line. But she was determined to fulfil her responsibility. "No. I'm just trying to understand what's going on. Maybe knowing why will help me understand." She didn't want this to be a repeat of their last conversation. Especially not with Duke sitting there.

"You really aren't very smart, are you? I would think even someone like you could reason this out. It's a matter of preparedness. As you pointed out, we have a hurricane off our coastline. While the resort is built to withstand such things, I don't want our guests to worry. I also don't want to take any unnecessary chances that would have our insurance companies paying any more than they have to, in the event the worst does happen. Our guests' valuables will be at much less of a risk in the resort safe."

The argument stunned Savanah. "You're worried about jewelry but aren't worried about evacuating the guests who own it? Or our staff?"

"Which shows your utter lack of comprehension about the dollar amounts involved with such decisions. Again Jordan, do as I tell you. When I tell you. And not a word otherwise."

The receiver she still held to her ear buzzed with the sound of the dead connection.

"Tell him to fuck off, Savanah," Duke said, righteous anger blazing. "If you won't, I will." The CEO's tone had had come through loud and clear, even if the words hadn't. "You're one of his managers. And that's no way to talk to you."

Savanah understood why Duke was so bothered. He had been raised with a sense of respect for his elders, for authority, and yes, even for the fact she was a woman. Maybe that was old-fashioned to the rest of the world. But this wasn't the rest of the world. This was Hawaii.

Everything about the CEO's attitude grated against Duke's upbringing.

"He can't talk to you like that. I heard him threaten you," Duke continued.

"It's fine. Duke, I need you to calm down. You need to let it go." The conversation bothered her, too. She didn't want to show how much. That would only make the embarrassment of Duke witnessing the exchange worse.

Clark's words confirmed to Savanah, more than ever, there was something else going on with the CEO. Something he was trying keep secret. But for now, she had bigger things to deal with. "I know it's not right, Duke. And I expect you not to repeat any of what you just heard." Calming Duke helped her maintain her own composure. *Fake it 'til you make it, sister.* Savanah forced herself to continue with the business at hand.

"I need you to forget about what just happened and concentrate on something else. I need your help. I want you to look at something."

She turned her computer screen so Duke could see it and pointed to the dozen or so projections of Garth's path. She saved one for last: the one that arced farther westward before turning sharply back to the east, sweeping directly into the resort.

As she traced that outlier, Savanah watched the young man who, like her, could trace his family lineage back to Hawaiian royalty. Where only Savanah's father had Hawaiian ancestry, both Duke's parents did.

"If Garth were to follow this track, what do you think would happen?" Savanah waited for Duke to study the various weather patterns showing on the screen.

"That's an unlikely track. The weather along the coast and the mountains bounce everything back out to sea."

"Normally, they do." Savanah nodded her agreement.

"It's moving slow and would rip apart before it got to us. We would get wind and rain. And surf." Duke ducked his head with a quick lift of his brows betraying his embarrassment of mentioning surfing in front of Savanah. He appreciated that even though she couldn't surf any longer, didn't mean she wasn't still addicted to the ocean. Just like he was.

"Monster surf." Savanah offered Duke the smile he'd withheld, then turned the conversation serious once more. "But what if Garth suddenly picked up speed? Like it had no intention of slowing down as it's supposed to do. That slow-down is necessary to allow our geography to do its job."

"If it came up far enough before turning, if it was moving fast enough, it might merge with the vacuum that comes across the valley," Duke spoke slowly as he studied the screen. "But that's the most unlikely thing I can think of. I haven't heard anyone else thinking that possibility. But maybe that's why you're asking the question."

"Would Haleakala, Maui, even the channel, act as a guide of sorts? Everything helping to shoot it straight into us?" Savanah began to imagine the outcome of that possibility, as if the hurricane were a murderous pinball, and the islands the bumpers.

Duke was already rising out of the chair. "I'll call my *Tata*. My grandpa will know if there are signs the weather people aren't looking at. Things that don't show up on the computer screens."

Savanah nodded. She didn't miss that Duke was rubbing his arms like she was. The chicken skin of intuition, what haoles called "gooseflesh," prickling their flesh.

"I was thinking of going to see Uncle Leroy. Thought I might ask how fishing's been the last few days," Savanah commented.

Savanah knew that Duke had grown up with the same stories she had. The "old wives' tales" that were such a big part of fish lore. Stories of fish jumping into the fisherman's boat before the coming of a storm were common. Savanah could hear her father's voice: "The wise man stays home to mend his nets and lives to fish the rest of his days, while the foolish man dies for the ease of the catch of a single day."

Like so many such tales, there were details based on fact. Centuries of fishermen had passed down the knowledge that the more intense the storm, the deeper big fish will dive to escape the roiling ocean. As a result, for a short period just before a storm hits, bait fish frolic at the surface, enjoying the freedom from predators. A phenomenon that would result in a huge catch for those who rolled the dice with the coming storm.

Duke nodded. This was the Big Island. Everyone knew everyone. Even if you'd never met him, you knew the reputation of a fisherman such as Uncle Leroy. Savanah wouldn't be surprised to find the man in his garage, his nets spread before him, and a cooler filled with beer rather than bait.

CHAPTER FOURTEEN

Race waited, looking at his watch every so often. It was a beautiful afternoon. Kids of all ages jumped off the pier into the sparkling water beneath. He cringed watching some of the more experienced ones doing summersaults or back flips as they launched themselves off the concrete pillars. From the tourists to the locals, there was a steady stream of bodies in and out of the water. Everyone was out enjoying the perfect weather of another beautiful day in Hawaii. But Race wasn't here for any of them. He was waiting for one special woman.

He had to admit, it had felt good to get in the water and work out some of the stress he hadn't even realized he was holding in. The waters on the west side of the island were pristine and crystal clear as they caressed the beaches of the sundrenched Kona coast—so different from the eastern side, where his office had been until two days earlier. There, the waters off the windward coast were muddied by the churning generated by almost constant wind and waves.

Looking around, Race could understand why people were so angry with his preemptive beach and park closures. There was no visible indication that Hurricane Garth presented any threat. The cerulean sky was almost cloudless. The sun beat down hot enough to drive people into the water for relief. Only at the southernmost point of the horizon was there a hint of the weather farther out to sea. A fine layer of haze almost obscured the line where sea met sky.

Race knew it for the lie it was. There was a reason behind the saying *the calm before the storm*. The bigger the storm, the more beautiful the days prior. It was one of the things that continued to concern him. Maybe that's what Savanah had been referring to earlier. Did she realize things seemed too calm, too perfect?

Race might not have gone through a hurricane in Hawaii, but he had survived enough cyclones, hurricanes, or typhoons in Australia and around the world to know the storm system was sitting out there growing stronger as it sucked up all the energy it touched. Merging every cloud, the smallest tendrils of disturbances, into the swirling behemoth that made up the massive system. Even if he couldn't physically see it, all the radar scans and reports told him the same story. The storm's low pressure even made his chest struggle to breathe.

Race knew something else. Being good at the job wasn't just about predicting the weather. That was for the pretty boys with their slick hair and young women in clothes and shoes that weren't meant for anything but the inside of a nice, dry studio.

Someone in Race's position needed to be able to stand in the middle of a swirling shitstorm without panicking and continue to think clearly. Because when the worst happens, everyone would be looking to him to tell them what to do to survive. If he didn't think he was up to that pressure, there was always that nice weatherman job. Race never could stand sitting inside.

Race's ears perked up at the voice he'd been waiting for. "Dad, I was talking with Duke today about Garth. I'm worried."

Race chanced a glance behind him. Sure enough, Savanah and the man who'd been with her the first time Race saw her swimming, were approaching the water's edge. He'd guessed the man with Savanah was her father. Her words, and what Race saw now that he was looking at the two of them up close, confirmed it. He had no trouble recognizing the piercing blue gaze, the same incredible eye color that Savanah had turned on him.

Savanah's father nodded. "Today will be our last day in the water until it passes. Tomorrow we will have other things to deal with. The water will not be a good place for anyone."

Savanah scoffed lightly. "I don't remember the last time you said anything took precedence over getting in the water every day."

A silent observer, Race watched the two of them. He noted how the conversation stalled as Savanah's father picked her up and carried her down the steps. Only once they were waist-deep did the man let his daughter's legs go. There was no rush to the movements as he lowered Savanah into the ocean. There was a clear reverence to the man's actions.

From where he sat unnoticed, Race was close enough to see every inch of skin that the scant bathing suit Savanah Jordan wore showed. He couldn't help thinking again that her body was perfect. Incredible that whatever had disabled her seemed to have left no visible signs. He remembered their first meeting when he'd been captivated by the sparkle of life in her eyes. She'd seemed so comfortable in her own skin and had seemed so genuine. Watching her as she sank into the water, he had the same thought: she looked perfectly at ease. As if her body was returning home.

Savanah turned as she prepared to sink beneath the surface and Race's mind recoiled with what he saw. Deep furrows ran diagonally across one hip. The deepest parts of the scars were still an angry red. Race was no stranger to reef burns. He'd seen his share, growing up in Australia and while traveling the world. Savanah's scars were so much worse than that. Over time, they might fade. But Race knew that the pain, and the memory of however she'd gotten them, would last much longer.

He hopped down off the wall and walked over to where Savanah emerged next to her father. Sticking out his hand, he met the laser blue eyes that left no doubt as to where Savanah had gotten hers.

"Good afternoon, sir."

Kyle Jordan didn't immediately take the hand being offered. He continued to hold his daughter steady.

"Race, what are you doing here?" Savanah looked around. "Where did you even come from?

"I would say waiting for you, but that sounds like stalking. And perhaps your father wouldn't take kindly to that." Race waited for the other man to finish looking him over.

Savanah blinked. "You're what?"

"I was waiting for you. I owe you an apology, and I'm determined to make it." He finally allowed himself to meet her surprised glare.

Savanah glanced around again in confusion. "Here?"

"You refused my request to meet at your office," Race reminded her.

"Okay. Apology accepted. Now you can be on your way." Savanah gave Race a quizzical look. "Aren't you supposed to be working or something?"

"I am. Doing some personal outdoor atmospherical testing right now." Race grinned.

"You just made that up. That's not even a real word." Savanah rolled her eyes.

"Doesn't mean it isn't a real thing." Race's smile was unfazed.

Savanah gave an exasperated sigh and looked heavenward. "Who have I angered enough that you're here with no intention of going away?"

Race held his ground.

She spread her hands in defeat. "Dad, this is Race Weston. The new Director of Civil Defense. Race, my father, Kyle Jordan."

Race returned the firm grip of Savanah's father. "Pleased to meet you."

"Director . . . what a coincidence." Kyle Jordan's eyes flicked to his daughter before going back to Race. "That's a big job you've got yourself."

"It is that." Race agreed solemnly.

"Great. Now that everyone has been introduced . . ." Savanah waved one hand toward the water and the other pointed Race toward the steps out of the water.

"I was wondering if by way of considering my apology, Savanah might agree to have dinner with me?" Race's smile was for her, but he maintained eye contact with her father. Race was sure she was keeping score. He hoped she realized he had just taken the lead.

"Dinner?" She gaped openly. "Are you kidding?"

Race nodded his sincerity. "Dinner," he confirmed. The smile on his face grew. He couldn't have asked for things to go any better.

"I'm sorry, but we are getting ready for a swim. It's required. Therapy. Maybe some other time." Savanah closed the issue.

"Oh yes. About that." Race turned his full attention to Savanah. "I was wondering if you could give me some lessons. You know, help me improve my swimming. You seem to be very comfortable in the water." Race had found himself mesmerized watching Savanah from up close as she moved in the water.

Savanah's father liked the way Race Weston hadn't flinched from his gaze. He also liked what he'd said about being determined where his daughter was concerned. It didn't surprise him to see Savanah had the young man on the defensive. That was typical of his daughter.

Things were getting more interesting by the minute. The man who'd just admitted to stalking his daughter happened to be the one who'd gotten the job she had applied for. Kyle found that entertaining.

He coughed to cover the effort it was taking to keep from laughing out loud. Kyle looked between the two of them. As hard as Race Weston was trying to get Savanah's attention, his daughter was trying even harder to ignore the man. Kyle Jordan found that extremely funny. His daughter had no problem ignoring people when she had a mind to. Which meant the man who only had eyes for his daughter had more than simply captured her attention.

Kyle knew Race saw the laughter that skittered across his face, his lips twitching to keep from smiling. His daughter might not think the new man was funny, but Kyle Jordan certainly did. Anyone who could rile his daughter enough to refuse dinner, deserved some help.

Savanah's father decided to throw Race a life preserver. "Why, of course she can. Savanah's an excellent swimmer." He knew his daughter well. Savanah could drown a man with her silence.

Savanah glared at her father. "Aren't you supposed to be on my side?"

Kyle gave his daughter's arm an almost imperceptible squeeze. "But something like that will have to wait, I'm afraid. As Savanah explained, we're about to start her therapy."

Savanah's face broke into a smile so wide it negated the need for a verbal "Thank you, Daddy." She looked back to Race with a triumphant gleam in her eyes.

"Of course. No problem. I'll just wait right over there until you're all done." Race indicated where he'd been sitting.

"You'll what . . ." Savanah sputtered.

"I'll just wait right over there."

Score another point for you, Savanah's father chuckled inwardly. "You do that. Waiting over there will be just fine."

Kyle watched as Race Weston nodded and nonchalantly walked back to the steps, where he climbed out of the water, grabbed his towel, and settled down on the seawall to wait. That his daughter Savanah hadn't moved and stood watching the Civil Defense Director, too, was telling.

He knew his daughter and how badly she wanted to voice some sort of opposition. All of which told him the underlying current of attraction he'd felt from Race Weston for Savanah wasn't one-sided.

Kyle turned and started walking deeper into the water with his daughter.

"What was that all about, Dad?" Savanah turned back to her father. Race had taken a seat as if he intended to watch and wait for her.

"I am wondering that very thing, daughter." Which only made Savanah sputter more. "It seems reasonable to let a man such as the Civil Defense Director take you to dinner." Kyle chuckled. "Do I want to know why he owes you an apology?"

Savanah stopped protesting. Seeing the curious light in the look her father turned on her, Savanah knew she needed to change directions immediately or face twenty questions. Then she knew what would happen. Her father would want an answer to his question. And Savanah did not want to tell him about what had happened in her office the first day she'd met Race Weston. Or that it had been the catalyst for what had happened after.

That didn't mean she had to like giving in. Something her father knew, which was the reason his face was filled with mirth at her expense.

"Come on, girl." Kyle eased her into the water. "Perhaps we shouldn't overdo things today. You might need that extra energy to survive the impending dinner debacle."

CHAPTER FIFTEEN

"You really are a great swimmer. Do you surf as well?" Race asked, trying to break the ice forming.

"I used to."

"I'm sorry. That sounded like a stupid question. I mean, given you're in a wheelchair. But you aren't paralyzed. You can walk." Race didn't like the way he was fumbling around or how crass his comments sounded. "I'm sorry. It's just that it seems unusual."

Race couldn't remember ever having apologized so much in his life. He looked over Savanah's shoulder and took his time studying the room behind her.

Most of the tables sat empty. Tourists and locals alike appreciating the last few moments of the sunset before they chose among the many restaurants like the rustic tiki bar he and Savanah sat in.

A few patrons sat at the rattan bar. It hadn't surprised Race when the hostess who'd seated them greeted Savanah by name. The restaurant was across the pier from where Savanah swam. She'd obviously been there before. And after one meeting, he knew she was hard to forget.

The tables and decorations could have come from any of the open-air restaurants along the waterfront on Alii drive. Vases on the tables held a single red, heart-shaped anthurium with its bright yellow stamen. Their gloss so perfect they looked made of wax. Along the two open walls, plastic sea creatures hung. Shells large and small accompanied crab, starfish, and tropical fish.

The side facing the ocean was plain, with only a half wall and short railing for safety. Bamboo shutters had been latched securely open to provide an uninterrupted view of the water. Race agreed that the ocean was enough decoration. He watched a server bring tiki torches at the corners to life with a long-handled lighter.

A soft cough brought his attention back to his companion. He'd ignored her long enough.

"You're asking very personal questions. Is this how you normally get to know someone you've just met? I imagine there's quite the potential to backfire," Savanah pointed out. "I thought you wanted to apologize for insulting me at our first meeting. Not take another crack at it."

Race turned serious as he looked at her. "Speaking of that . . . my comments in your office were inexcusable. I had no right to say those things in such a manner."

Race wanted her to accept his apology. He meant it.

The more he thought about things, the more he'd realized he wanted to start over. And then he wanted to find out everything there was to know about Savanah Jordan. Maybe she'd had a good reason for not following orders. He wanted to get to know her and find out.

"That implies, Mr. Director, that if you were to find a way to express the same sentiments but in a less offensive manner, you would." Savanah seemed surprisingly relaxed. "You don't need my help. You're doing a great job of shoveling all on your on."

Race kept his mouth closed in the hope of not shoving his foot even further in than he'd already managed to place it. Her interpretation of his words did not reflect how he'd meant them. He had the feeling that trying to talk his way out of it wasn't his best course of action. But he was damned if he knew what to do next.

"Shall I take your silence as consent?" Her words hung between them for several minutes before she finally sighed. "Look Race, it's fine. You wouldn't be the first person to look at someone like me and assume I'm less capable than a *normal* person, less capable than you even, simply because you think I'm different than you are. I have to admit I'm surprised that someone in your position would be so blatant about it. Typically, the higher up the food chain, the more that speaking politically correct is a requirement."

"Perhaps my silence is a sign of how confusing I find you." That was one hundred percent a true statement.

"All this really isn't necessary." Savanah waved a hand. "Save us both the time and the trouble. We can call it even."

"Let's start over." Race had never felt himself drowning on a date this fast in his life. He was normally much smoother than his present behavior was indicating.

"Start over? Exactly how do you propose we do that?"

He grinned at her. "Hi. I'm Race. Nice to meet you. Seems like an easy enough way."

Savanah didn't return his smile. "So, I'm simply supposed to feel sorry for you, accept your apology, and pretend you didn't say those things. Is that it? Let me explain the problem with that, Race. I think we both know you voiced exactly what you were feeling and thinking that day. Which, as much as I hate to say, is at least one point for you."

"From where I'm sitting, I'm not seeing it." Race wasn't sure he wanted to know, either. He had the feeling he wasn't going to like the explanation.

"At least we don't have to add that you're a liar, on top of being discriminatory and assuming." Savanah gave a short huff.

"I don't have a reputation of being any of those things." Race wasn't fooled by the beautiful smile and light laughter. He knew he should feel insulted.

He was thankful she hadn't thrown in egotistical. He'd been accused of that more than once, so arguing against it might have been a challenge. Still, he didn't feel like he was having much success disputing the things Savanah was currently accusing him of, either.

"I find that difficult to believe after what happened in my office," Savanah replied.

It was time for Race to go on the offensive. He was losing too much ground trying to handle things diplomatically. Obviously, Savanah Jordan, for all her petite size and ability to remain silent in extreme circumstances, didn't have a problem playing hardball when she had someone one on one. If the invisible scoreboard Race had congratulated himself on earlier was still operating, she was currently kicking his ass.

"Then why did I bother to come all this way? Why didn't I just accept your 'no' on the phone and skip the tongue-lashing?" Race forced himself to ease back from leaning over the table.

Savanah relaxed back in her chair and Race could feel her studying him over the top of her beer glass. "There's something worth considering. Maybe you're the sort who likes a good lashing?" Savanah felt her lips curve into the smile she couldn't quite hide. "Is that it, Director? You like a good lashing."

Race leaned forward. He could see the light returning to dance in her eyes like a wicked flame. There was the woman he'd met in the parking lot. "I'm afraid that would require you to get to know me better, Ms. Jordan. Much better."

A teasing smile tugged at the corner of her lips as her voice dropped to the sultry tone he hadn't been able to forget. Now, if he could just figure out a way to keep from insulting her again . . .

"Why should I want to get to know you better, Race?" Savanah's question was soft, even in the sudden quiet that had fallen over the restaurant. "Certainly, the lashing I experienced on your behalf wasn't that enjoyable."

"I assure you . . ." Race moved his chair closer to Savanah. His eyes serious. "That won't happen again."

Race placed his hand beneath her chin, keeping her face tilted to him. They weren't arguing. He wasn't going to miss the chance to kiss her. Something he'd thought about doing from the first moment he'd met her. Not being able to get a woman out of his mind wasn't a problem he was used to having. Usually, the only things that held Race Weston's attention had the power to lay waste to entire communities. That one small female could be so confounding and distracting was an anomaly. Maybe if he got this ridiculous, nagging urge out of the way, his concentration would return to normal.

But as his lips covered hers, their supple heat surprised him. There was no more contact than that, but it was enough to let him know he wasn't going to be able to simply forget it. Rather than let her go immediately as he'd planned, he found himself taking his time with the softness of her lips. He gave a small murmur of appreciation, at how her warmth began to infuse him.

Savanah was too shocked to pull away. Race's hand barely held her, but it was as if that simple touch had paralyzed her, allowing for no movement but her lips against his. She wanted to lean forward in answer to the call his body made to hers, but his touch didn't allow it. Instead, she found herself with her lips as the only outlet for the feelings that were suddenly running through her. The humid warmth of the Hawaiian air was nothing compared to the heat that blossomed at the unexpected touch of Race's lips.

When the kiss ended, they sat back in silence, both unsure what to say next. Energy pulsed in the air between them. As if the animosity had turned inside out to become a different kind of heat that reverberated through Savanah's body. Savanah bit her lip. She didn't want to feel anything nice for this man. Not when he'd made his thoughts so clear.

Yet she couldn't deny, he was infuriating in a way that intrigued her. As if the battle they were engaging in was an intricate dance. Her smile deepened as her eyes roamed over the width of his shoulders. If that was the case, she knew something he didn't. Race would lose. Savanah had learned to dance hula before she'd learned to run.

"I see humility is another of your qualities," Savanah ran her fingers through the condensation on her glass in an effort to cool the fire Race had so unexpectedly started in her.

"You said it yourself: I'm not a liar."

She didn't feel badly for pointing out the truth. It was his bad, not hers. She had to admit, it was entertaining to watch him handle someone being honest about his behavior. By his reactions, she guessed that didn't happen to him often. He seemed the type that people would be on constant alert around.

Race went on, "I'm not normally so difficult to talk to. I allowed another issue to influence our interaction and I shouldn't have. I'm sorry."

The feel of his fingers wrapping around hers interrupted her thoughts. The roughness of his hand as he held hers, as if it were a delicate shell he was afraid to break, brought her gaze to his. Savanah tried to martial the warmth that had flared as he'd kissed her. The emotional ground she found herself on felt unsteady.

"There is no excuse for my behavior in your office. I'm sorry for it," Race repeated.

Savanah debated silently. Up until the moment he'd started sounding like her boss, she'd found herself attracted to the man sitting across from her. She told herself it couldn't be for anything other than friendship. They couldn't be more than that. He wasn't from Hawaii . . . he'd taken the job she should have had . . .

She knew that wasn't fair of her. Race was selected. There were other applicants, just like her, who weren't. Granted, she was the only woman who had applied.

Her breath came out in a soft huff. He deserved a second chance.

Her internal war kept Savanah quiet as she worked through her issues with Race. She grimaced as she remembered the sting of that discussion in her office. It wasn't about Race owing her an apology. That wasn't the problem. The fact he'd believed the things he'd said. *That* was the real problem. Unless his thinking changed, all it would take would be the right set of circumstances and he would express himself in the same way. Believing the same things.

Race Weston didn't realize that it wasn't she who had to be understanding and accepting. It was him. And sitting there looking at him, it saddened her that she doubted he was capable of that.

"I want to accept your apology." She continued to gaze at him thoughtfully before admitting, "I'm surprised at how much I want it to be true. Enough so that I promise to keep in mind that you just can't help yourself."

Race sat back with a frown. "I just apologized. For most people, that means they don't plan on repeating the behavior that necessitated the apology. What do you mean, 'because I can't help myself?'"

How easily she believed the worst saddened Savanah. When had she become so cynical? She knew her feelings weren't all due to her boss's lies. Race had voiced his opinion before Clark had stepped into the room. It was a shock to realize she was treating Race like the storm: prepare for the worst, hope for the best. Except she was finding her ability to hope difficult.

She shrugged. "It appears I don't trust you any more than you trust me."

"I don't like the way that sounds. Trust is built by getting to know one another. But that is hard to do when everything I say makes me feel like I'm going backwards. Perhaps we could start by you saying why you don't trust me . . ."

Savanah shook her head vehemently. "I don't think we're ready for kumbaya quite yet, Director."

"*Hui* . . . Savanah."

She and Race turned simultaneously.

The call had been unmistakable, and her face lit up with a smile. Savanah waved at her cousin, Ikaika, who dodged between tables toward her. The two men with him she recognized easily. Colin and Mark were classmates from small kid time with her cousin. All three men bent down to hug her hello before turning to acknowledge her dinner companion.

"Director Race Westin, my cousin, Ikaika. These are his friends, Colin and Mark."

Race stood and shook hands with the men, then waved at the additional chairs around the table. "My lucky day. I met Savanah's father early this evening. We haven't ordered yet. Why don't you join us?"

Savanah looked at Race in surprise. *This won't turn out like you think.*

She considered offering the warning that came to mind. If Race Weston thought inviting Ikaika and his friends to sit down was a good idea, she'd let him learn his lesson the hard way. She'd do her best to ensure it didn't get out of hand and result in punches being thrown. If he made the mistake of disrespecting her in front of her cousin, things would get ugly fast.

"No thanks. We wouldn't want to interrupt," Ikaika responded.

"I insist." Race moved his chair closer to Savanah to make room.

The men took Race at his word and within minutes, conversation began flowing easily around the table. Savanah wasn't the only one smiling as the volume and laughter at the table increased.

The fact Race was watching her was too evident. Savanah knew just because Ikaika hadn't said anything didn't mean her cousin hadn't noticed. She took advantage of him ordering another round of beer to comment quietly to Race. "You're staring, Director. And looking awfully pleased with yourself all of a sudden."

Race leaned closer to her. "I felt like your father and I hit it off well. I think I've figured things out. The way to get to know you is through your family."

"Is that so? Be careful, that might be a slippery slope." Her warning bounced off Race's self-confidence.

Race wagged one eyebrow. "Given the smile on your face and the laughter in your eyes, you are enjoying yourself. Despite my still being here. Or could it be because I am here, and you've accepted the undeniable fact that I'm hard to resist?"

Savanah closed her eyes and shook her head. Race Weston didn't have a humble bone in his body. A body that, admittedly, she found appealing. When her gaze returned to his, the deep blue of his eyes sparked with the challenge for her to deny his words. She backed herself up from the table rather than accept it.

"Excuse me. I'm heading to the ladies' room." She declined the offers of assistance and began wheeling herself expertly across the room, calling over her shoulder, "Don't get into trouble, Ikaika."

CHAPTER SIXTEEN

Race congratulated himself as he looked around the table. Inviting Savanah's cousin and the man's friends to sit down not only caught Savanah off guard, she seemed more comfortable after they'd arrived. Even if she didn't want to admit it to him.

Disaster averted. He wasn't the damn CDD for nothing.

Conversation stalled as the four men watched Savanah wheel away. Race waited until she was out of earshot before he returned his attention to the table. He rehearsed several questions in his mind to ensure they didn't come out as offensive. Something he couldn't ever remember having to do before. Given his luck so far with Savanah, Race felt the precaution was warranted. The extra moments proved to be his undoing.

"So, how long have you known my cousin?" Ikaika asked.

Race turned to Savanah's cousin and the seemingly innocuous question. *He who asks the questions has control.* Race had made the mistake of waiting too long to speak.

Ikaika and his friends had been nothing but friendly since sitting down. Now that Savanah wasn't there, Race saw a protective light burning in their eyes. Ikaika's tone was suddenly far less sociable than what he'd been using in his cousin's presence.

"We met several days ago." Race stepped carefully into the verbal minefield. The less information he volunteered, the less chance of blowing things all to hell.

"You're the new CDD, right?"

"That's correct."

"You're not from Hawaii. You moved here when you got picked for the position."

Race couldn't argue facts. "That's right."

Ikaika's gaze was guarded when he leveled it across the table at Race. "Don't know if you're aware of it, but there's a hurricane just offshore."

Race nodded. "I'm aware."

"Maybe you should try worrying about that instead of showing so much interest in my cousin."

No one said anything.

The three local men finally began to laugh. Savanah's cousin glanced over his shoulder before turning back to Race. "Look man. I'm just trying to help you out. You're going about this all wrong. If you keep pissing her off, she's gonna lose patience with you and go all nuts. The macho man thing doesn't work on Savanah so much."

Race had a hard time picturing the Savanah that Ikaika painted. "I think I know how to handle this. And who said I've made her mad?"

"From what I see, you're about to have your ass handed to you." The young Hawaiian withdrew across the table, his tone losing its friendliness. "Like I said, the hurricane is a whole lot safer than messing with my cousin."

"I have no intentions of messing with your cousin."

There was a rumble from the other side of the table. "You got something against my cousin?"

Race had expected his first misstep to take longer. "Of course not."

"So why aren't you interested in her? She's a beautiful local girl."

Race cleared his throat. "I agree, Savanah is incredibly beautiful. My interest in your cousin—my interest isn't in *messing* with her."

"Sure, it is."

Race growled inwardly. Was it a family thing or was he just that far out of his element? He was losing ground to Savanah's cousin as fast as he'd lost ground to her. "The hurricane is why I'm meeting with Savanah. I wanted to get her insights on how it's behaving."

Race hoped that wasn't too much of a stretch. Just because the two of them hadn't gotten around to talking about Garth or what she'd meant with her warning yet, didn't mean he didn't still have it on his agenda. He hoped her cousin wouldn't check what he was saying with Savanah before Race had the chance to make good on it.

Ikaika and his friends laughed. "That's why you're sitting here having a beer and dinner with her instead of meeting her at her office? We aren't that dumb, Aussie."

"She wasn't able to meet me earlier in the day."

That was only slightly inaccurate. Not enough for Race to feel bad about saying it.

Ikaika gave an almost imperceptible nod as his friend Mike cleared his throat. "Sure thing, Race. Savanah's a good one to talk to. She's got a feeling for these things."

Race frowned. What was happening? The sound of Savanah's voice behind him explained the sudden change in topic.

"What do I have a feeling for, Ikaika?"

No one answered as they waited for Savanah to settle back at the table. Her gaze swept across the telling silence.

"Are you guys kidding? I was gone for five minutes. The tension between all of you is thick enough to choke on. I mean really, how personal could you get?" She directed the question at Race. "What did you say?"

He held up his hands. "What makes you think I said something?" Race was feeling seriously outnumbered.

"Hey, you know the rules. Never be the first one to pass out," Ikaika teased his cousin. "You were the one who left the table. Who else were we supposed to talk about?"

Even if Savanah hadn't remarked about the tension, Race had seen the writing on the wall. To her cousin and his friends, he was an outsider. They weren't about to trust him. And no matter how much Ikaika might say his cousin could hold her own, he was watching out for her. Which made his unexpected intervention on Race's behalf, even more of a surprise.

Race wasn't going to turn it down.

"Men are so predictable." Savanah shook her head. "So, is anyone going to answer? What do I have a feeling for?"

"Trouble," Ikaika answered. "I was just telling Race here that you've got a gut feeling about things. Whenever there's trouble, the whole family knows whatever you say goes. Speaking of which, Mom said to tell you she went and picked up all the supplies, just like you suggested."

Race's pulse had been on a steady uphill climb ever since her cousin had leaned over and started offering advice. But now, things were really getting interesting.

"Good," Savanah said. "You too, Ikaika. Even Dad said today, we won't be coming down tomorrow to swim."

"Uncle Kyle isn't getting in the water?"

Savanah simply shook her head.

"Wait . . . you're still making preparations? Why?" Race finally asked. "There's no sign Garth is going to turn this direction. It's almost completely passed South Point and should continue moving to the west."

You could have heard a feather hit the floor as everyone turned to Race. Their faces all mirrored the same disbelief.

"How the fuck did you get picked, bro? You do know you're responsible for the people of the Big Island, right?"

"I know what the responsibilities of my office are." Race was getting tired of people questioning whether he knew his job.

"This isn't about your office. This is our home." Ikaika shook his head. Finally, he turned his attention to Savanah. "I would say take it easy on him, cuz, but seriously, someone needs to help him before he hurts himself." Ikaika tilted his chair back on two legs as he looked back to Race. "Don't worry. Savanah here's real good with people."

Race felt vindicated, even if only slightly, at the scathing look Savanah shot her cousin. He decided to tread carefully when she turned her attention to him. "What am I not seeing? The National Hurricane Center is expecting to downgrade our watch in the next few hours."

Savanah hesitated. "Because that's what all the weather models are predicting. That Garth will continue moving to the west."

"You don't think they're correct?"

Everyone waited for Savanah to speak. "No. I don't believe that's going to happen."

The pressure in Race's chest agreed, but he couldn't walk around saying that. Which was why he was interested to hear her opinion. He needed something more to go on to keep the island on a higher alert. If things hadn't changed by the morning, protocols stated his office would cancel the voluntary evacuations and temporary shelters that he'd ordered opened.

"What do you have to support that?" Race's comment immediately setting off a round of disgruntled murmuring.

Amber-filled shot glasses arrived preempting a return of the earlier tension. Ikaika handed one over to Race.

"Bro, take this. You're going to need it."

Race took the shot glass. He doubted alcohol would clarify his confusion with Savanah. The others must have felt differently. There was the distinct clink as they emptied their glasses. Race noticed Savanah turned hers upside down before pushing it back to her cousin. A signal she wouldn't be doing another.

All eyes went back to him.

"Well hell, why not." He tossed the whiskey down his throat.

Only after Race returned his glass to the table, did Savanah answer his question. "None. I don't have any proof."

Chapter Seventeen

The whiskey-driven timeout had worked. Savanah watched as Race processed her answer. That he didn't immediately walk away made her think he might be willing to hear the reasoning behind her answers.

"Okay, so tell me why."

She took her time studying Race. Why should he believe her now? Just because they'd had a few drinks and there were other men backing her up? That was enough to piss her off if she dwelled on it. That thinking was exactly why Civil Defense was such a man's club. Savanah hoped Race would be open to what she was saying long enough that he could get past the subconscious hurdle.

"That question is harder to answer, Race. It's a feeling. Every time I look at the projections, my mind keeps going to only one of them. Along with images of what it will bring."

"Perhaps you're overreacting," Race suggested.

Anger flashed through Savanah. The grumbling from the other men around the table, said they felt the same.

"That's what Clark thinks. Seems like you and my boss are still on the same page." Savanah frowned. "Maybe you should be having dinner with him."

Ikaika broke in. "Oh, come on, Savanah, Dieter is a prick. Everyone knows it. Race here doesn't seem as bad as all that. Even if he is a haole." Ikaika turned to Race. "Unless there's something you've done that my cousin's not saying. Is there something I should know?"

"Clark's the CEO of a resort, 'Kaika. It isn't an easy job." Savanah felt compelled to defend her boss. Even as out of line as Clark had been when he spoke with her, she still owed him the respect due his position.

Race dismissed Ikaika's comments. "Clark Dieter isn't my concern. I'm asking you, Savanah." He pressed harder. "What's changed that has you thinking preparations are in order when only days ago you, didn't?"

"Race . . . It isn't so simple as to be only about what I think." Things were falling apart faster than a sandcastle with the tide coming in. Savanah could feel their tenuous truce crumbling, one grain at the time.

Ikaika interrupted before Savanah could go on. "Don't know where you've been, bro, but Savanah has been on everyone's ass for more than a week telling us to be ready. She's worried that fat bastard is going to turn and come straight at us." He turned at his cousin's small sound of surprise. "Duke called me after you talked to him."

Savanah's frown deepened. The feel of her skin prickling as if some unseen force were laughing manically in confirmation of her fears. "What else did Duke say?"

"He said to tell you his Tata agreed with you. Unlikely . . . It shouldn't happen, but... but he agreed. It is possible." Ikaika leaned forward earnestly. "Something tells me I don't want to know what Duke is talking about."

"I wanted to be wrong." Savanah rubbed her arms to rid herself of the premonitory feeling of doom.

"What are you two talking about? Wrong about what?" Race interrupted from where he sat, forgotten by the others. The climate at the table had bottomed out.

Savanah chewed her inner cheek nervously. She searched frantically for the words to convince Director Race "Know-it-All" Weston about something that she had no scientific data to back up.

"I know how crazy I sound," she started, her eyes pleading with him for some measure of understanding. "I just have this feeling that Garth isn't done. That it's going to sit out there gaining strength. Spinning and sucking up all the weather around it until it's big enough that it goes looking for something to prove how bad it is." She hesitated for a second. "Kind of like you, Mr. Weston."

Before Race could protest, Savanah turned over her napkin and pulled a pen from her bag. She made a quick outline of the island and its five mountains, then turned the crude drawing so everyone at the table could see what she was doing.

Using the pen to trace a path, she explained what she was thinking. "Once the hurricane gets big enough, the vacuum it created is going to start looking for somewhere to go. We all know the mountains aren't moving."

"You mean Mauna Kea and Mauna Loa," Race interjected. "I agree. They affect the weather around the Island. I may not be from here, but I know what I'm doing. I studied the role those mountains play regarding the weather here."

He frowned as laughter followed his statement. "Look, I spent countless hours studying everything about Hawaii, specifically the Big Island, before I applied for CDD. If you aren't talking about the mountains, what are you talking about?

There was the sharp crack of chair legs hitting the floor. Ikaika's friend Colin hadn't said much through the evening. Savanah was used to him not talking. Everyone else took it to mean the big man was an asshole. She knew it for what it really was. He was unbelievably shy. He'd gotten into powerlifting after high school to build strength and, he'd hoped, his confidence. Ten years later, he was built like an NFL linebacker, but he still wasn't comfortable talking in front of strangers. Savanah knew Ikaika and Mark were just as surprised as she was, as Colin stepped up to try explaining things more clearly to Race.

"No man. What Savanah is trying to tell you is, with a storm that big, you're either doing the fucking or you're getting fucked. And if that thing gets close enough to us, and gets on that path, all that power it's sucked up will have found somewhere to go. It will blow right through the middle of us. And then we're all fucked."

"Delicately put, Colin." Savanah wanted to laugh but couldn't. "But not wrong." There wouldn't be anything funny about Garth hitting them.

Savanah looked back to Race and used her pen to indicate the valley that ran through the middle of the island between the southern ridge of the Kohala mountain range and the northern slope of Mauna Kea. "If it comes through here, the pressure will combine with the lay of the land and bring not just the storm, but the eye of it. For the first time ever, our geography will suck it in and bring all that destruction sweeping right over us." She hesitated. Words were powerful and it suddenly felt as if she were prophesizing. "If that happens, the only thing we can pray for is that it's moving fast enough to leave some of us alive." No one drew a breath. Even the air in the bar was still, unwilling to be responsible for having unleashed Savanah's words and bringing Garth down upon them. "Because a monster like what that hurricane is becoming won't leave anything standing."

"There's no precedent for that." Race's eyes held Savanah's.

"I know that."

"That would be devastation like this island has never experienced." Something unseen brushed the back of his neck and Race looked over his shoulder, but there was no one there. He pushed back from the table.

"I know that, too. Race . . ." She reached out as if to take his hand but

109

stopped herself. "Race, that chill that just went down your spine . . . welcome to the club." Savanah prayed she was overreacting. God, she'd been praying for days.

"I don't understand." Race persisted. "If you think this is possible, why didn't you want to start emergency procedures at your resort when I suggested them?"

Savanah didn't look away. The way his eyes narrowed as he separated himself from them said it all. Race didn't get it. She tried again, desperate to get through. "This isn't about what happened in my office, Race. This is about what's coming—"

"Dude, somebody's fucking with you. Your 4-1-1's tossed," Mark scoffed.

While Colin had sat back most of the evening content to observe, Ikaika's friend Mark had no such reservations.

"My what—?" Race's face matched the confusion in his voice.

"As in, you've got your information wrong," Ikaika said. "Nobody is more cautious than my cousin. Didn't you hear me tell her my mom picked up the supplies? That's because Savanah texted the whole family days ago." Ikaika's frown deepened.

"Right after I spoke with her, it sounds like." Race's response made Savanah grimace. She was sure he didn't understand why.

That simply and that quick, the evening was over. Savanah knew it was time to go. The train wreck the evening had turned into was only going to get worse if they stayed. There had been that one moment when she'd begun to think she and Race were making progress. The moment was gone almost as quickly as it had come.

"What's your problem with my cousin?" Ikaika bristled.

Race opened his mouth as if to reply then stopped as if reconsidering his words. "Look, for whatever reason it happened, I'm glad she's finally getting on board with everyone else. Perhaps now she'll follow my advice that she make safety plans for herself, as well."

Savanah laid her hand on her cousin's arm. From the moment Race invited Ikaika, Colin, and Mark to sit at the table, the burden to earn their trust was on Race. With every word coming out of his mouth now, Savanah knew he was undoing any good that might have been accomplished. She could feel the anger flaring from her cousin and his friends.

She pushed back from the table with more force than was necessary, sending it skidding the other direction. The sudden noise got the attention of everyone in the room. She took advantage of the silence that followed.

"I appreciate you taking the time to hear me out. I'm sure you must be anxious to return to Hilo, Race. I understand you have a great many things in need of your attention. There's no need to worry about seeing me home. Ikaika can take me."

Savanah started moving. She knew if they stayed, things were likely to end up with her cousin teaching the arrogant Race Weston manners by way of fists.

Hawaiians were some of the happiest people you'd ever meet. They were also some of the most loyal. Happy shouldn't ever be confused with forgiving. They didn't take insults lying down. The response to even the hint of impugned honor was swift and usually long lasting. Savanah didn't need that happening here.

It was a no-win situation. She was caught between announcing that the head of Onimura Resort was a liar or being branded one herself. Savanah had tried to subtly guide Race into figuring out for himself what had happened.

Race got to his feet as Savanah moved quickly past him. She was at a loss as what she could say that might undo the last few minutes. Her brain had been telling her almost non-stop that he was trouble with a capital "T." There was no point to letting things get further out of hand now that he was back to thinking they were on opposing sides. The irony of the situation was that they weren't. Race only thought they were.

"Savanah, wait." Race reached to stop her.

"It's time I was going." If she could just get to the elevator with Ikaika and the boys.

"Look, all I'm trying to say is you need to be—"

Savanah didn't turn.

"Dammit Savanah. If you aren't going to be concerned for your own welfare . . . Why should anyone else be?"

That stopped her. She turned her chair to look at Race. "So, why are you?"

He stepped closer but stopped at the darkening face of her cousin. "At least we agree on one thing, Savanah. With there still being the possibility of a hurricane coming ashore, I have things requiring my attention. Things important enough I shouldn't be wasting my time like this."

She flinched at Race's statement. Comments like that were going to make it hard for her to keep Ikaika or the others from punching Race. Then again, maybe he was seriously starting to deserve it.

"But you are wrong about one thing. I'm not going anywhere. I've moved my office to this side of the island for the time being," Race finished.

"You did what?" She didn't know what to say. None of the other CD Directors had ever considered an office on the west side. They visited, and then went back to their offices next to the mayor until the next yearly visit was due. "Bet that didn't go over so well."

"I give the orders in my office," he retorted.

"Some of us don't have that luxury. We have people we answer to." Savanah felt an ache begin in her chest. Regret for how the situation was ending. There was no evidence he'd heard anything she'd tried to tell him. Race was still making all the wrong assumptions and believing the wrong people.

"Remember my promise earlier? Well, this is me doing my best to be more understanding with you, Race. I've tried to help you see the truth.

There's nothing more for me to say. Except maybe this: try looking back at the email I sent you. It might surprise you to find there's more information there than you seem to have noticed."

She turned and continued toward the elevator. She didn't have the time or energy to deal with him any longer. The prickling along her skin told her she had things to do and not a minute to waste. Garth was coming. Whether Race believed her, whether Clark believed her, or not. She was sure of it. And God help them all if she was right.

Ikaika spoke loud enough his voice carried easily. "I know you're just trying to keep us from kicking his ass, cuz'."

"It isn't worth it. And it would be easier for you to drive me home than to call someone." Savanah continued pushing her cousin in front of her. "I'm definitely not letting him take me home."

"One of us would be happy to teach him a lesson while 'Kaika gets you on home," Colin offered as they crowded into the elevator around Savanah. "What's his problem, anyway?"

"He thinks he knows everything," Savanah answered as she punched the button.

"Just because he's from the mainlan—" Ikaika started. Only to be interrupted by Savanah.

"Not just that, Ikaika." Savanah knew they weren't out of earshot as they waited for the doors to close and take them to street level. She met Race's eyes where he stood glaring at them. She knew that all Race saw was men standing protectively around her. The look on his face was clear. They were all just proving his point she couldn't take care of herself.

"Not just because he's from the mainland. Not just because we're *dumb locals*. Not even just because I'm a woman and I'm in a wheelchair. I think mainly he can't imagine anyone knowing more than he thinks he does."

Savanah didn't mind arguing with Ikaika about whether the Civil

Defense Director deserved the *dirty lickins* he was surely going to get if he continued insulting her. Her cousin's steady stream of insults against Race continued until the doors closed. The moment they did, Ikaika turned to look at her.

"So, you gonna tell us what he was talking about? What happened at the resort, Savanah? And why does he think you didn't want to do anything?"

Savanah should have known Ikaika had listened, even if Race hadn't.

Her cousin was going to be mad as hell once she explained what had happened. Savanah knew Ikaika wouldn't hold back on what he thought she should have said or done to her boss or Race. The sting of Ikaika's words would hurt far less than the comments from the overbearing Race Weston.

CHAPTER EIGHTEEN

Race poured himself another cup of coffee before returning to his desk to stare at the latest weather projections. After leaving the restaurant, he'd been restless and gone back to the new office he'd ordered setup for the west side of the island. He'd tried sleeping a few hours on the couch in the break room before giving up and returning to his computer. Going days with little or no sleep was part of the job. It was why he kept a "go bag" in his truck, another at his apartment, and a third at the office. Each had changes of clothes, protein bars, and other items he might need while in the field.

He set his coffee mug down in disgust. Instead of concentrating on what was in front of him, his mind kept replaying what had happened with Savanah. She'd seemed so sure of herself. Even her cousin and his friends had tried to convince him that she was the one telling everyone to get prepared. Their offense on her behalf had been genuine, when he hadn't believed them, as if that was her normal role. A stance that was at odds with her email and the opinion he'd formed of her as a result.

Race needed to ignore his personal attraction to her. It distracted him from his job, and that was unacceptable. He chastised himself. Being fair of face and form was not enough to counter the deficit of sense and ethics that Savanah Jordan had exhibited. She not only seemed unaware she wasn't capable of doing her job, but also that she'd been caught lying, as well.

What was it she'd said to him? That he'd find something more in her email. Race needed to send an email to Steve anyway. He switched screens and typed out a request for additional reports on floodplains and remote communities, then began a search for Savanah's email. He was determined to put the issue, and his concern for her, to rest once and for all.

The phone interrupted his search.

"You're up early, Director."

Race checked his watch in surprise. "It's five in the morning Steve. What are you doing in the office?"

"We have a hurricane out there, sir," Steve replied. "I'll get the additional reports you've requested put together and sent over right away."

"I couldn't sleep, so thought I would check for any changes that might have come about overnight. See how much the cone has changed." He didn't have to, but Race felt the need to explain.

"The cone is *all* about probability, Race. That's why we always give the disclaimer no one should consider the tracks shown in a cone a guarantee of anything." Steve hesitated, "But you already know that. You found something."

Race sat back in his chair, the squeak of the springs the only sound in the office. He raked his fingers through his hair in irritation as he contemplated what move his office should make next. There was still nothing that said Garth was going to turn. It had slowed its forward motion overnight but continued its gradual strengthening. The storm was coming dangerously close to being upgraded to a Category 4.

"Nothing I can put my finger on." Race finally admitted to his assistant. He rose and shut the door, maintaining the privacy of their conversation against any early arrivals to the office.

"Whatever it is you can't put your finger on, it's bothering you enough to have you emailing me before dawn," Steve stated. "Everyone knows jobs like these are a certain percentage gut feeling."

"We can't evacuate the island on a gut feeling, man."

Race traced the lone projection that brought the hurricane sweeping into the island. The one Savanah had been talking about last night. He'd told her there wasn't anything to indicate what she'd said was possible. Yet here was proof that at least one other person thought it was. Neither Race nor anyone else he was talking to had paid that one projection any attention. Everyone discounted it as ridiculously improbable. Everyone, that is, but a meteorologist on the other side of the world and one stubborn, confusing woman.

How can you believe that's possible, yet decide to sit back and do nothing? That doesn't make any sense, Savanah.

The latest update made that projection even more remote than it had been. "One of the projections is bothering me. The one hanging out there all by itself that has the damn storm dancing its way right over the top of us," Race told Steve.

"Hold on a minute while I pull it up." Race heard tapping through the phone.

"That projection is courtesy of our friends in Japan. They know what they're talking about when it comes to these things. The typhoons they deal with tend to be massive. Still, they are the only one predicting this curve," Steve explained.

"Get on the phone and find out why their interpretation of the data is so different than everyone else's. Or what data they have that we don't," Race instructed.

"Yes sir." Steve hesitated before asking, "How are things working out in the new office?" Steve added, "I'm not prying, Race. The decision to work from the west side is your call. It was just unexpected. Typically, the west side of the island enjoys quite a bit of protection from storms like this. Even now, the expectation is they'll feel little to nothing from Garth."

"There are at least a few folks over here who think otherwise. They believe that projected track from the Japan station is a very real possibility. I want to find out if they have a leg to stand on." Race appreciated his assistant's questions. They were a team. Knowing what the other was thinking would make them better.

"What's the reasoning?" Steve sounded surprised. "The West side generally seems more lackadaisical about preparations. Call it a benefit, or a curse, of having been lulled into a sense of safety with the mountains always standing between them and what hits the east side." There was a pause before Steve asked, "Who'd you talk to?"

"I met with the Safety Manager for Onimura Resort."

Steve responded with Savanah's details without being asked. "Savanah Jordan. Born and raised on the west side. Family is from down south, close to Kealakekua Bay. She's been volunteering with first responders since high school. Her degree is from Texas A&M. She's been at Onimura for several years. She's got a good reputation."

Race couldn't hide his shock. "She never mentioned any of that. What's her degree in?" In all fairness, Race hadn't asked her any questions about herself. They hadn't gotten that far.

"Meteorology and Atmospheric Sciences. There was a rumor NASA wanted her, but she chose to come home," Steve answered.

Race didn't know what shocked him more, the information Steve was giving him, or that the man was able to give such a play-by-play. "Do you know everyone on the island?" He was only half-joking.

Steve chuckled. "The Big Island may be bigger than the rest, but we are still very small town. I don't need to have met her in person to know of her. Besides, she's holding down a position that interacts with our office. That makes it part of my job to know about her . . . just in case the boss asks."

His assistant's attempt at humor was lost on Race, who recalled another conversation. "It comes with the territory . . ."

"Yes sir. It comes with the territory," Steve agreed.

Race hadn't meant to say the words out loud. Savanah had said almost the same thing at their first meeting as Steve had just now. "What else can you tell me?" Race barely kept from adding "about her" to his sentence. He reminded himself this was professional, not personal.

"Onimura is the biggest resort on the island. And that's saying something. Ms. Jordan's email to us put them at 97% occupancy, which translates to approximately 4,000 guests. Plus another 500 employees."

"What do you know about the CEO, Dieter?"

"The CEO of the resort has been at the job about the same amount of time as Savanah. This is his first job here in the islands. In a short time, he's managed to gain a reputation for not playing nice with others," Steve responded.

"What do you mean?" Race could hear Steve's reluctance to speak further in the silence that stretched through the phone. "Use my office and shut the door if you have to. This might be important."

"Look Race, I don't want you thinking I'm being unprofessional here. I'm telling you the truth as far as I know it. There are rumors Dieter's authorized things at the resort without going through proper channels or the appropriate State offices. No charges have been officially filed, but there have been more than a handful of accusations. If I were to guess, I would say that means he's been able to cover his tracks. If the rumors are true. And then there's the fact they are the only resort on the island that refused to go along with our suggested preparations."

That last part was something Race was more than familiar with. "I'm aware they declined our suggestions. The CEO and I straightened that out with Jordan while I was there last week."

"I don't think so."

"What the hell does that mean? I was there, Steve. I heard Clark Dieter tell Jordan she would start complying or jeopardize what was left of her job."

"I'm not talking about the first set of directives that you went to speak with them about. As of yesterday, they still haven't enacted any emergency protocols." Steve added quickly. "At least that's the last word I had. Things may have changed since yesterday afternoon."

Race trusted Steve. The man had no reason to lie to him. He was already proving to be damn good at his job. "The CEO himself assured me when I was there last week. He won't allow Jordan to continue refusing to act."

"I'm not questioning what happened at your meeting with them. I'm just telling you what I know based on the last update I received." A low whistle sounded through the line. "Jordan must be chewing nails."

"What's that supposed to mean?" Race felt like chewing nails himself if he didn't start understanding what the hell was going on.

Steve grunted. "She's known for running a tight ship. Before her accident, she worked 70-hour weeks. Because she *likes* to. The woman has a reputation of being extremely passionate regarding the responsibility of her position. For emergencies, she prefers to shut down all auxiliary departments and send working line staff home. She runs a managers-only scenario."

"That doesn't seem practical. She certainly won't be doing that now," Race interjected, his mind whirling at what Steve was saying.

"It makes sense, Race. Once the guests have been evacuated or centrally located, they are easier to care for. And with a lot less staff. Savanah is aware that most of the resort staff have a long distance to drive. That puts them at risk. Rather than putting people in a position of not being able to get to their families, she sends them home before things happen. She plans for the guests and for the staff both."

"My impression from the meeting was that Clark will be running things until she returns to her former capability."

A burst of laughter coming through the line caught Race off-guard.

"That would explain why they seem to have their heads up their asses over there."

"You're not making any sense." Race frowned despite knowing no one could see it.

"If Clark Dieter is in charge of emergency prep, that explains why they aren't doing anything. He may be able to balance a billion-dollar budget, Race. But the man doesn't know jack about something like this."

"That doesn't jive with anything I was told when I visited the resort."

"Don't take my word for it. You're in their neck of the woods. Ask around. Savanah's got a great reputation. I don't know anything about what former capability you mean, but we'd have benefited if she'd have gone to work for us." Steve finally added, "That's just my opinion."

"You know she's in a wheelchair?"

"Of course, I know she is. I don't understand your point." Steve responded. "Hold on . . . you don't mean . . . never mind. I didn't ask and I don't want you to answer that."

Race went on as if Steve hadn't tried to withdraw his question. "This is a matter of reality and practicality. If the woman has to move quickly, to save her life or someone else's . . . she can't. It's the truth of it. We're bound to protect the people who can't protect themselves.

"I'm not going to argue that with you, Race. And I won't be advertising your opinion on this. You're my boss. But I would suggest you don't make that comment too loudly or to anyone else. It will get you hung by HR. And you for sure won't be winning any popularity contests saying stuff like that."

A knocking at the back of his subconscious was getting louder. Race knew he was missing something about the situation. The information Steve was telling him contradicted everything that had happened in that first meeting with Savanah.

"Shit," Steve swore at his boss' silence. "You already did. Don't tell me who you said it to. I don't want to know."

Steve was right about one thing. Coming in and tearing down one of the homegrown girls didn't win Race any friends. Especially one who seemed to have Miss Congeniality for the island in the bag, if not the whole damn crown. Hell, Race had been drawn to her. He didn't get why it was so hard for everyone to see he was trying to provide for her safety, too.

Twisting his neck in a useless effort to release tension, Race let the topic of Savanah Jordan go for now. "The latest updates on Garth should be coming through any time. Get that Japan station on the line and see what they know. Anything you find out, let me know right away."

With only silence around him now, Race contemplated Steve's reactions to Savanah. His comments only added to Race's confusion. Who was the real Savanah Jordan? Something wasn't right. He just couldn't put his finger on what. Race dialed Steve's number to get the man back on the line.

"What did you mean when you said we'd have been lucky to have her?" Race asked the moment his assistant picked up.

"Exactly what it sounds like. In my opinion, she would have been a great addition to the Civil Defense team." Steve answered without a hesitation.

"Are you telling me she applied for a job in our office?"

"No."

Steve had been nothing but respectful. But Race could feel the underlying emotion building in the directness of his assistant's answers. "You just said . . ." Race stopped himself before his frustration found a new outlet. "Look. I'm just trying to understand what's going on here."

"No Race, I didn't say she applied for a job in our office." Steve spoke slowly. "Civil Defense Director Weston, she applied for *your* job."

"Jesus. No wonder she's undermining me. She blames me for getting her job." Race was thinking that explained a helluva lot.

"Race, you said you met with her, right?"

"I sat right there in her office. She didn't deny anything when I asked why she'd declined our suggested protocols." Even thinking about the exchange was enough to make him irritable all over again.

"Did she tell you it was her decision?" Steve countered.

"We've got her email saying it was." The hold on his patience slipped another notch.

"Just go with me here. Did Jordan tell you herself, when you were sitting in front of her, that the decision was entirely hers?" Race wasn't the only one losing patience, if the sound of Steve's voice was any indication.

"No, she didn't use those exact words. But—"

"You said Dieter was there, right?"

Race scoffed at what Steve was implying. "Are you saying the CEO of the biggest resort on the island lied to me?"

"Come on man. This is the big leagues. Everyone lies if it will save their own ass." Steve's laughter told Race how naïve his question was.

"If her boss was lying, why didn't Jordan say something?"

"We're old-school here. Five years behind the mainland in technology and ten years or more behind on everything else. Jordan isn't going to argue with her boss in front of someone. She's definitely not throwing him under the bus. Think about how that would have looked. That's not how we do things here."

"Not even if it meant her reputation?" Race asked.

"Like I said. No way would Savanah disrespect her boss in front of you. I already told you, word is she is passionate about what she does. If Dieter put her in the position you're saying, she wouldn't just jeopardize her job like that. Especially not to save her reputation to a stranger. That would be selfish, and weak. Protecting the reputation of the company, and even her boss, would come first." Steve took a breath before continuing.

"Squealing isn't the first choice, it's the last. Whistleblowers know the odds are no one will believe them, and nothing will change. What usually does happen? They lose their job and forfeit their reputation. It makes more sense she would do her damnedest to find another way to solve the problem rather than airing dirty laundry," Steve reasoned.

A cold fury settled in the pit of Race's stomach. Was it possible that Clark Dieter had lied about Savanah just to save himself?

"As of right now, I want you to make sure every one of the staff, top to bottom, understands something. If they lie to me, they're out. Is that understood, Steve?"

"You can't do that, Race. That's an empty threat, plain and simple. There are procedures. You're at the top of the food chain for Civil Defense, but even you answer to HR. And don't forget the unions," Steve argued.

"Then they can fire me. Until then, what I say goes. I find out someone lied, and I'll walk them out the door myself," Race snapped. "And Steve. If I've got my head up my ass, I damn well expect you to tell me."

"Is it out of line to say I thought that's what I was doing?"

"Keep it up. No matter who's standing there." Race snapped.

"Copy that."

"Answer one more question." Race forced himself to calm down. "If she's so qualified, why didn't she get the job?"

"Because you got it."

"That's not good enough." Race wasn't letting Steve off that easy. Not after everything else the man had said.

"Her accident happened right after applications went in. I don't know, maybe the review board wanted to fill the position sooner than they felt they could wait for her recovery." Steve hesitated.

"The truth, man. All of it."

"Or maybe they're just prejudiced . . . like you."

A heavy silence settled.

As angry as Race was now, it wasn't with Steve. "Call me when you hear back from the Japan station." The man deserved a raise. He'd stood his ground. Race respected that. "You're a good man, Steve."

Race hung up and sat thinking, his hands pushing through his hair as if the action would stimulate brain cells and give him the answers that seemed just out of reach.

So, Savanah was in her wheelchair because of an injury from an accident. That was a new piece of her puzzle. But try as he might, he found it hard to grasp the enormity of what Steve suggested. He knew if the roles were reversed in what his assistant had offered as a possible explanation of the situation with Savanah, Race would have stood up to his boss. CEO or not, Race wasn't about to let someone pin him with a lie.

He didn't have time for this. There was a hurricane coming. But he couldn't shake the feeling that surviving Garth was somehow tangled up with the mess he found himself embroiled in with Savanah Jordan. Ridiculous. Yet his insides continued to say it was all tied together.

If Race was going to believe the CEO of a major corporation had bald-faced lied to cover his own ass, he wanted proof. He turned back to his computer. When all else fails, go back to the beginning. He returned to his search for emails from Savanah and was surprised to realize she had sent only one. Race reread it slowly, finding nothing other than her straightforward response saying the resort would not comply. There was nothing to support a change of opinion. The email had come from her. She hadn't denied sending it.

So why the hell was everyone else so adamantly denying it for her?

The phone interrupted his thoughts again. Race pressed the hands-free option without taking his eyes off the screen in front of him. "Weston."

"I think you'd better look at the updates." The flatline of Steve's delivery enough for Race to know he wasn't going to like what he saw.

CHAPTER NINETEEN

It was early enough that the only guests strolling the resort's landscaped walkways were the few who like to view the sunrise. Everyone awake savored the quiet with a cup of the island's own Kona coffee. Staff nodded or murmured "aloha" or "good morning" in acknowledgment as guests passed, but otherwise continued the business of quietly preparing for the day. Arranging deck chairs. Replacing flowers. Cleaning before there were too many people to safely do so.

Savanah looked around. An unexpected warning rippled up her spine. Something was off. The resort went through the same motions every morning. The opening procedures completed like a well-oiled machine. She'd witnessed it hundreds of times. What was different about this morning? Stopping to study her surroundings, Savanah realized it was too quiet. As if there were a mute button for nature. And someone had pressed it.

The unnatural calm made her breakfast turn over in her stomach.

With a calculating eye, Savanah began to catalog the subtle differences. She should have been able to hear the steady sound of the waves as they caressed the sand along the beach. Even if the ocean was at peace, she could always hear it in the background. Today, there wasn't even a whisper.

Looking up, she noticed the parrots that usually decorated the morning sky were nowhere to be found. It hit her how little chatter there was from any birds. Their songs usually served as her alarm clock each morning. She watched as several small forms hopped through the sprinklers in the lawns, searching for insects that the water brought. The beautiful yellow feathers of the *amakihi* were easy to spot among the dark green grass. She could see numerous red-crested cardinals, dropping to the lawn before returning swiftly to the trees. Their brilliant plumage was a common sight in Hawaii.

As she looked closer, she saw dozens more yellow-and-green bodies. Multihued finches and sparrows. The dusty olive and soft pinks of lovebirds. There were even several pairs of the beautiful mejiro, her favorite. Their brightly colored bodies easily blending into the flora around them despite the tell-tale white ring around the eye, as they flitted from branch to branch.

The birds were all there. It was their chirps and squawks that were missing. Even bothersome mynahs quarreled beside a cluster of palms in an eerie pantomime. Savanah shivered with the sudden weight of the stillness. It wasn't tranquil and comforting. It was unnerving. She felt as if the silence was drowning her.

The sky was still a soft blue. The morning volcanic fog so unique to the island was an almost imperceptible layer of white.

Almost.

Unless you'd spent your whole life looking at it.

A normal morning would have the sun taking its time to heat up the land. Eventually that warmth would reflect into the air above. When that happened, the color of the sky would deepen. The *vog* would burn off, giving rise to descriptions of a sky so clear you could see forever. Savanah could still remember when every day started out that clear. Before the volcano started its decades-long rampage.

But not this morning. The vog lay like a fine veil that muted the colors and the very sounds of Hawaii.

Savanah turned to look toward the south, where Garth was passing. She knew the storm was too far away to be seen. So why did it seem there were faint traces of a murky promise on the southern horizon?

Please let me be wrong. She looked a last time to the trees, their motionless leaves contributing to the too-quiet morning. The sudden chicken skin prickling the flesh of her arms told Savanah it wasn't just her imagination. Garth was coming. She could feel it in everything around her. She could hear the storm's malevolent laughter in the silence.

A text from Leayne made her jump. But the request to stop in at the HR office was a welcome diversion. Thinking this might be the only time she had free for the next several days, Savanah replied she would be there immediately. She didn't know what Leayne wanted, but Savanah needed to talk with her anyway. There were some questions only Leayne could answer. Question number one, how quickly was Savanah going to lose her job for insubordination once she gave the unsupported order to evacuate?

"You're in early," Savanah said as she wheeled through Leayne's door.

"Hey, you're the one who keeps saying you think we aren't out of the woods yet. I'm trying to make sure I have my ducks in a row," Leayne answered. "Coffee or tea?"

"Coffee works." Savanah took the cup her friend offered, chuckling at the Halloween hula girl pattern. Leayne threw pottery in her spare time and what Savanah held was one of Leayne's creations. "This is new."

Leayne beamed. "You know me. Everything's better with a little Halloween."

"It's not Halloween for another five months."

"Shit. You're right." Leayne grinned. "Do you think I waited too long to put these out?"

"I'm gonna need one for my desk." Savanah turned the cup in her hands. "One of these days you should just open your own shop and say goodbye to all the corporate BS. Every new piece keeps getting better and better."

"Maybe. One of these days." Leayne's expression became serious as she shut the door. "I've been watching Clark. I think you should watch yourself, Savanah. He's been asking some strange questions about EEO law and what rights we have."

"Why would Clark be asking about Equal Employment Opportunity law? What did I do to be on his radar?" Savanah wasn't joking. Neither she nor Leayne had time for that. Instead, she hoped her friend had an answer. Maybe then Savanah could try to mitigate whatever Clark's sudden problem with her was.

"Do you remember going to Clark about an incident with some guests he authorized? The ones Duke caught drinking while they were swimming in the pool after hours. It was right after you returned to work from your accident," Leayne asked.

Savanah remembered. Clark had insisted he would take care of talking to his guests about adhering to resort rules. "My impression was he was more worried about his guests' feelings than the rules. He wanted us to blow the whole thing off. Even suggested I chastise my boys for overreacting. Wanted us to be more understanding about his guests having a good time in Hawaii."

It had been a shit show, and Savanah had finally explained to Clark her office had already looked the other way with the group. The swimming pool had only been the last straw. When Duke had found them, they'd been breaking numerous rules, not just one. They were drunk and still consuming. Savanah had been forced to explain in detail the danger their actions presented before Clark had finally agreed to speak with his guests.

When Duke had approached the group, it was to stop them from diving into the pool—something every resort feared because of the tragedy that often resulted. On this occasion, Savanah didn't think it was Duke's quiet confidence that had convinced them. She was willing to bet his imposing stature had gone a long way in making sure the rowdy, overly privileged group hadn't given him more trouble about going back to their rooms.

They'd given far less trouble than Clark had given Savanah when she'd gone to him about the situation. Savanah had been especially concerned with the guests' comments to Duke regarding how they'd felt some sort of entitlement, as guests of the CEO, to do whatever they pleased. Savanah had stood her ground with Clark until he agreed the behavior wasn't something they could allow to continue.

"Did anyone ever figure out who those people were? They weren't relatives." Savanah remembered breathing a sigh of relief when they finally checked out.

"Business associates of some kind was all Clark would say. He's the CEO. He can do that," Leayne answered.

"I wasn't questioning them being here, Leayne. Only why they didn't expect to adhere to the same rules as everyone else. As CEO, he can comp whomever he likes. Way above my paygrade to even care about. For me, it's all about the safety."

"He felt like you were questioning his authority. Questioning who his guests were and why he had them here. He spoke with me after you went to see him. Wanted to know if he could write you up for abusing your position."

Savanah gaped. "For asking him to speak to his guests instead of just throwing them off the property? You're kidding. First, I'm in trouble for doing my job, and now he's throwing me under the bus saying I'm not doing it. I don't get it, Leayne."

"I've had some weird calls from outside. Something's wrong and Clark seems to have settled on you to take his frustrations out on."

"To my knowledge, I haven't done anything wrong." Savanah frowned.

"Like I said, I don't think it's something you've done, Savanah. I think Clark has just settled on you as the one he's going to take everything out on. It isn't common knowledge, but we've had a couple discrimination complaints. When your accident landed you in the wheelchair . . . let's just say I think that was an opportunity Clark was grateful for."

"Sorry, but I don't get what you're saying. When I asked to come back to work, Clarke seemed genuinely happy about it. He didn't hesitate to authorize installing the ramp at the office."

"That's precisely what I'm saying. Having you here was visual proof the resort doesn't discriminate. That Clark doesn't discriminate . . ." Leayne's words hung heavy.

"There are a lot of different types of discrimination, Leayne. We local women aren't good for anything but housekeeping and desk jobs, according to people like Clark. He's no different than the rest of the management people who get shipped in from the mainland."

"I hire based on ability," Leayne stated firmly.

"And Clark has the final say if it's for management."

Neither of them thought anything of the intense conversation. They weren't arguing. They were trying to get to the bottom of what was going on. The only way to do that was by voicing their thoughts honestly.

"You've noticed he's treating you differently now. We've talked about it," Leayne remarked.

"It's confusing. He's made it clear that he won't accept my returning to work without my wheelchair until the company doctors release me. Even though I wasn't injured at work. This isn't a workman's comp claim. I've been getting the feeling he doesn't want me being cleared at all." Savanah slowed down as her mind struggled to make pieces fit that seemed to come from completely different puzzles. She continued almost as if she were talking to herself. "He keeps saying it's because he's worried about my recovery and doesn't want me to rush."

"But he's not saying that now," Leayne prompted.

"No. After last week, I'd almost say he wants to get rid of me. That he's gathering evidence to do so." Savanah agreed.

"You told me that you were beginning to feel like if you got out of the wheelchair, you were done," Leayne said.

"That's still discrimination, Leayne. Just of a different kind." Savanah was almost too shocked at what Leayne was suggesting to be angry. Why would anyone want her recovery to fail?

"I know. And now according to what you told me happened in your office last week, he's got what he considers to be proof you aren't doing your job," Leayne recounted, watching as Savanah processed what she'd said.

"You're telling me I'm screwed either way."

Leayne nodded. "From where I'm sitting, pretty much."

"Well that sure makes this easier." Savanah shrugged.

"Makes what easier?"

"If Garth intensifies at all, I'm going to start evacuating and shutting down the resort, whether Clark authorizes it or not. Whether he likes it or not. It will be the right thing to do. I'm sure of it." Savanah held Leayne's gaze, letting her words sink in.

"Making that call on your own would be enough for him to let you go immediately, Savanah. No questions asked. Whether you're in a wheelchair or not. You wouldn't have a leg to stand on." Leayne warned.

Neither of them flinched at Leayne's choice of words.

"Not if I'm right and it saves people. Not if it's the right thing for us to do." Savanah turned to leave. "I'll let you get back to your ducks and making sure they're all in a row."

"Fucking ducks . . . I wouldn't mind if the little bastards would just look the same direction for five fucking minutes."

Savanah knew what Leayne meant. The way things had been going lately, she felt exactly the same.

CHAPTER TWENTY

Savanah checked her watch. The updates from CD weren't due for another hour. After everything that had happened over the last few days, it was time for her to do some digging. She typed Race Weston into the search bar and waited for Google to shed some light on the island's new director.

The highlights, and the low points since meeting him, stuck with her equally. The memory of those first moments in the parking lot, before Race found out who she was, brought a smile to her face. How comfortable it had been for a time when they'd sat talking at the restaurant. When he'd kissed her and there'd been nothing but the warmth of his lips covering hers, and two beating hearts. Those few moments were enough to make her wish for more.

Then the evening had combusted. Perhaps not as badly as the first day in her office, but the result was the same. Race believing the worst. Savanah wished fervently things had ended differently. She sighed and leaned back in her chair, pressing the button that would start the electric pulses at her back.

It had been too much to hope that Race would hear more than just the words she'd said that night. She had needed him to hear what she *wasn't* saying.

As much as Clark had angered her, she would never disagree with her boss in front of someone, let alone a stranger. She certainly wouldn't lose her temper. Her parents had taught her there was a time and a place for emotions. The workplace wasn't one of them. Savanah had also been raised to respect authority. And as archaic as it sounded, male authority even more so. If she had a problem with her boss, it was up to her to find a way to solve it without suggesting the problem was anyone's fault but her own.

She looked up and realized her screen saver was on. She moved her mouse to clear it and went back to her search.

It was a surprise to find there was no shortage of articles on Race Weston and his parents. He was the only son of an American diplomat father and native Australian mother from one of the largest ranching families in the country. The articles mentioning the young Race centered mainly on his father. Savanah imagined that the privilege of diplomatic immunity would explain Race's expectation that he would be obeyed.

She continued her search until she saw a photo of Race rappelling down a mountainside. Savanah clicked on the link to bring the article up. *Diplomat's son risks life to save hiker.* The details she began to read told of a determined young man who refused to accept the victim couldn't be reached. Race had gone over the side of the cliff while everyone was still trying to think of a safer way to reach the hiker.

Savanah went to another article. *Last man standing.* In the picture, Race looked older than in the previous article. She saw the evidence beginning of that scowl of determination on his face she was already familiar with. The writer colorfully extolled the heroics of the college student who, despite the life-threatening flooding, refused to leave a local hospital until every patient had been safely evacuated. According to the journalist, when the young Race had been asked why he risked his life for people he didn't know, he'd answered simply, "They couldn't evacuate themselves."

There were nearly half a dozen such articles, all praising the brash bravery of Race Weston. He was somewhat of a disaster good-luck charm in the southern hemisphere, from what Savanah read. Always managing to turn up and save the day when all hope was lost. She didn't know what to make of his quasi-celebrity status.

According to the articles, Race's father had been offered an assignment allowing him to return home to the United States with his family. Race's life turned quiet it seemed with the move. She found no other references until the announcement of Race being selected as the Big Island's CDD.

Savanah checked her email. It was past time for the new updates from NOAA and the National Hurricane Center, the same updates that Civil Defense received. But she, and the others occupying similar positions on the island, followed information from their local CD office. Race and his team didn't worry about what was happening anywhere else. They were dedicated solely to what was best for Hawaii. So far, there were no new reports from any agency, so she returned to her search.

Google was far less helpful regarding Clark Dieter. Either his background wasn't as colorful, or he hadn't wanted to make the headlines. Most of the information seemed benign: prior employers, college. Savanah sat back in her chair as the electrical impulses ended and began doing the knee raises that were another part of her therapy, while she studied the screen in front of her.

Clark's employment history was impressive. He had worked for some of the biggest names in the resort industry. Savanah sat forward, holding a knee in mid-air. According to the last employer listed, his previous job had ended two years before he'd come to the Big Island. She wondered what he'd been doing for those twenty-four months. Maybe he'd simply taken time off.

Savanah bit her bottom lip as she dialed the number for the Colorado resort that was Clark's previous employer. Voicemail answered, instructing her to leave a message so that her call could be returned during normal business hours. Savanah hung up without leaving a message.

She should have known. The time zone difference meant it was early evening in Colorado. Management was done for the day. Crossing her arms, she considered her next move. She dialed the number again, but this time waited for the resort's directory and made the selection for the resort Safety Office. Someone answered on the second ring.

"Silver Bear Springs security, Fred speaking."

Savanah smiled triumphantly, "Aloha Fred. My name is Savanah Jordan. I'm with the Safety office of Onimura resort out in Hawaii."

"Whoa, Hawaii? I've always wanted to go there."

Saying you were from Hawaii was the ultimate icebreaker. "They don't call it paradise for nothing, Fred. Though I hear if I ever want to learn to ski, I need to come see you," Savanah laughed. "They say skiing's like surfing. Is that true?"

The man on the other end returned her laughter. "I've heard that. But I don't surf.

"If you ever get this way, I can take care of that." Even if Savanah couldn't, she knew a dozen people who would.

"That would be cool. So, what can I do for you?"

"I don't mean to bother you or anything, just wanted to talk story for a minute. Seems like the new CEO here used to work for Silver Bear. I was just hoping to get a feel for him." Savanah talked as if she and Fred were old friends. It wasn't a put-on. It was just how people from Hawaii talked. You were friendly until the person you were talking to gave you a reason not to be.

"No way? Who's the new man?"

"A guy named Dieter. Everyone says he's been around and really knows his stuff," Savanah answered nonchalantly.

"Dieter? Clark Dieter?" There was a moment of silence from the other end and Savanah wondered whether they'd gotten disconnected. "Yeah, I remember him."

She groaned loud enough for it to be heard through the phone. "Is he going to make my job easier or harder, Fred? You know what I mean. Some people think what we do is important, and others think we're just for show and to clean up puke in the pool."

"Right. I guess I thought someplace like Hawaii would be different. I guess it's the same all over. I hate it when they puke in the hot tub . . ."

Savanah wasn't lying. Guests were great. And awful. "Welcome to working with the public."

"No kidding. Sorry you've got Dieter. But not sorry we're rid of him. I was lucky. This has been my shift forever. I didn't have to deal with him much," Fred commiserated.

"That sucks for me, I'm not going to be so lucky," Savanah returned. "I'm on days."

"Maybe Hawaii will be better for him."

She didn't know what to make of that. "How so?"

"No casinos." Fred gave another laugh. "I always thought only losers skipped out in the middle of the night. Word here was he left before the auditors from corporate arrived."

"You're kidding? I guess that does make us lucky then . . . I mean since there's no gambling in Hawaii."

Savanah glanced at her watch. She'd kept Fred long enough. "You've probably got rounds to do. I should let you go."

"Yep, just about that time."

"I meant what I said, Fred. If you ever get to the Big Island, give me a shout and I'll hook you up. Personal tour guide and everything. Always better when you've got a local connection." Savanah rattled off her cell number.

"Thanks. I will." There was a pause and Savanah heard Fred talking but it wasn't to her. The sound was muffled as if he had his hand over the phone. "Hey, my patrol just asked, don't you guys have a hurricane or something coming?"

That made her laugh. "Or something."

"Well, be safe. Hope it goes the other way," Fred told her.

"Me too, Fred. Me too. Watch out for the chunks in the pool. Thanks again. Aloha and watch out for yourself."

"Roger that. Hey, you can keep Dieter."

That hadn't taken long. And had been a lot more than she'd bargained on. Savanah stared at her phone as she considered what she'd learned. Something in her was curiously relieved at the knowledge that there'd been problems with Clark before her.

The ding announcing a new email shouldn't have made her jump, but it did. She pulled it up immediately. Tension drew her body taut as she read the new update.

"Shit."

The morning's stillness made sense now. Garth had been upgraded to a Cat 4 and sat still, a mere one hundred and eighty miles south of the island. Everything and everyone officially now held their breath to see what the two-hundred-mile-wide hurricane would decide to do.

No one ignored it any longer.

Savanah forwarded the email to Leayne then dialed her number. She knew the quiet on the other end after the phone picked up was the HR director looking at the email.

"If it starts to move north, the projections show Oahu and Kauai taking the brunt of it," Leayne said.

"Except that one path that brings it around like a Sandy Koufax curveball." Savanah couldn't swallow the lump that had formed in her throat.

"You know I don't have a clue what that means."

"Leayne . . ."

"I see it. There's still that track that shows it coming through the middle of us. It veers out of the cone at almost a forty-five-degree angle, Savanah."

"I've got schedules and staffing changes for you to look at. I also have a draft of what I'd like the front desk to start telling the guests. I'd appreciate if you'd look it over for anything I've missed. But once I start this, you shouldn't have anything to do with me. I don't want Clark blaming you, too." Savanah needed help, but she didn't want to endanger her friend's job.

"I know what you're planning. I either turn you in now and stop you or I'm aiding and abetting. You're going to need my help. Send over what you've got, and I'll start looking at it."

It was old-fashioned mutiny, plain and simple. Savanah was implementing shut-down procedures and telling the guests to get off the island, while there was still time. If they were smart, they would get out of Hawaii completely. If Clark stopped things once Savanah put them in motion, the responsibility, and the lives lost, would be squarely on him.

"Any way this goes, it's probably going to suck royally," Leayne said.

"Have you not noticed how much fun I've been having lately?"

Savanah wished things were different. She wished Garth weren't there at all. She would have more than appreciated Clark calling all of them for a meeting to discuss what was happening. That's what a CEO was supposed to do. Be a leader. But there wasn't any more time. Savanah knew all their energies needed to focus on getting people as far from harm's way as possible.

"This will either get you a promotion or a pink slip." Leayne didn't mince words just because Savanah was her friend. "I have to warn you. It might not just be about losing your job. You might be legally and financially responsible for repercussions. It would suck and it wouldn't be fair. But it could happen."

It didn't matter to Savanah. She wouldn't sit idly by if she felt she could prevent loss of life or property. Either way, it was going to end badly. For Savanah, or for them all.

"What do you want me to do first?" Leayne asked.

"Look over the evacuation plan, especially the locations I've listed and how people are going to get there." Savanah waited to give Leayne a chance to open the attachments she'd just sent to her.

"Since when do we evacuate people to Puna?" Leayne laughed at the absurdity of it. Hilo and the Puna district were always getting the crap kicked out of them by even the smallest passing storms.

"It's as far away as we can get people who are left here, and I'm hoping by then, Mauna Kea and Mauna Loa will be making a difference and disrupting things." Savanah knew how crazy she sounded. This was one time she wouldn't mind losing her job for being wrong. "If the valley catches it, the mountains will just act like a funnel for all that energy and bring it right over the top of us."

"Waimea and Waikoloa should be evacuating, too. Even Honokaa if that happens. Isn't your uncle a retired fireman from Waimea?" Leayne asked. "You should call him."

The suggestion proved talking to Leayne had been the right choice. "I'll do that as soon as I hang up. Maybe he can talk to PD and Fire over there. I know they have their own plans for this, but until Civil Defense starts saying so, no one is going to worry."

"Speaking of that . . . maybe you should call the CDD and try talking to him."

"We spoke yesterday. That won't get me anywhere," Savanah said with a grimace.

"Yesterday? He was here again . . . what for? You didn't tell me that." Leayne was surprised.

"I didn't invite him. He tracked me down in town. Said he came looking for me to apologize for that first meeting. This one didn't fare any better. I'm pretty sure he left convinced more than ever that I don't know what I'm talking about. Except now he's added crazy to his list." Savanah should have still been angry, but there was something in all the articles she'd found. There was more to Race, too. Just like there was more to her than he was willing to see.

"We need to talk with Pinky and her staff at the front desk first and get them working on contacting the guests and suggesting they leave with no penalty for changing their reservations. The airlines are still offering to change flights and are waiving the fees. They haven't rescinded that yet." It was all-or-nothing time, and Leayne was all in behind Savanah's plan.

"I want it put out to the managers, once their area is shut down, for them to leave as well." Savanah went on. "By tomorrow night, I want as few people here as possible."

"Protocol is all managers stay, no matter what." Leayne corrected.

"This is different, Leayne. If we don't need them, they should be home. They need to be home." Savanah hesitated for only a moment. "You need to go home when the time comes. Your department will be empty. You don't have to be here."

"Hate to burst your bubble, but some of my department will be here. *You* will be here, and as head of HR, every employee is technically my department." Leayne paused. "I'll leave when you do. As a matter of fact, I'll be happy to drive us both home. We can ride together."

Savanah knew it wouldn't do any good to try and talk Leayne out of staying. She didn't waste any more time on it. There were more important things Savanah had to do. Like finding somewhere she could take everyone to safely shelter the storm. The problem was, sheltering in any building would be like sitting in a grass hut against one hundred and seventy mile an hour winds and thirty-foot waves. That's what Garth would hit them with when it came ashore.

"There's something else...something I've never seen before in a warning." Savanah tried not to show her own fear, but her throat didn't want to work.

"The Central Pacific Hurricane Center just added tornadoes to the list of advisories." She failed to hide the gulp that sounded as she tried to swallow. Her words trembled despite her efforts.

"Now we have to worry about fucking tornadoes. Are you kidding me?"

"Your house is in a good place. You should go home." Savanah tried again.

"If you're here, I'm here. That's in my job description." Leayne sounded adamant. "Did you think it would be that easy to kick me off the fucking island?"

Savanah couldn't help it. She started laughing, and Leayne joined in. A wave of relief washed over her. She no longer felt completely alone.

Chapter Twenty-One

The moment he got the notification upgrading Garth to a Category 4 Hurricane, Race jumped into his truck to drive to the main office in Hilo. He wanted to meet with his staff personally one more time.

As he drove along Saddle Road between Mauna Kea and Mauna Loa, he mentally reviewed the notification. Garth continued to sit south of the island, creeping along at barely eight miles per hour, absorbing every bit of energy that the unusually warm waters had to give. It might as well have been standing still. Race felt like Nature had put them in her very own escape room. Except there was no way to know how much time was on the clock. They could do nothing but wait for the behemoth that was Garth to make up its mind about how badly it wanted to crush them.

The drive passed quickly. Saddle Road was empty so early in the morning, and Race was able to cross the island in half the time it usually took. The roads on the windward side were another story. They teemed with the normal traffic of a beautiful day like any other. Overhead the sky showed no sign of Garth or the vog that plagued the west coast of the island. There was nothing but blazing blue all the way to the horizon.

Race went straight to his office when he arrived. He stopped as the radar and satellite images on the huge screens that hung across from his desk in the main Civil Defense compound came into view. It didn't take much of an imagination to think of the long tendrils on the back side of the storm as claws. Meteorologists called the back side the *dirty* side, and Race agreed. Garth's dirty side appeared to be dragging a sheath of razor-sharp fingers, as if the storm were trolling for anything unlucky enough to be caught in its path.

Hundreds of screens and monitors around the world watched for any indication of what the hurricane would do next. They all showed the same thing: Garth was not moving. Orbiting satellites saw it only as a lazy mass of white. But Race knew there wasn't anything lazy about Garth. Thinking that would be like getting in the water with a Great White and telling yourself if you closed your eyes and couldn't see it, the shark wouldn't see you, either.

In the past six hours, the storm had moved a scant forty miles north—too little to change the hurricane watch that had been issued for the island.

Race considered the clear lines of the eye in the image before him. He tried to visualize the width and breadth of the storm along each of the projected storm track possibilities. So different than the thin lines that represented them in the illustration. The cone of probability traced the projected movement of the center and didn't take into account the massive size of a storm.

There was still the one lone arc that suggested the storm would sweep up the valley across the top of the island. The geography glared at Race as if it had something to say.

Race pushed the other possible tracks aside and concentrated on the track that presented the greatest threat: what would happen if Garth came head-on into the island. The front side, where the rotation was strongest, showed a tight, clean edge. In his mind, he could see the storm clouds compacting down upon one another, forced by the mass of Mauna Loa and Mauna Kea to choose an alternate path. He couldn't help thinking the mountains decided who would live and who would die.

Not anymore, Race resolved.

It was his job to stack the odds in favor of everyone living. Race sat at his computer and drafted the email to his counterparts on the other islands. It explained that the Big Island was officially taking the next step. He was ordering the island to prepare for the hurricane to make landfall directly.

Race couldn't officially change the hurricane watch to a warning. That was up to CPHC and NOAA. But he could begin to tell the people of the Big Island they should expect the hurricane to make landfall and not wait for a warning to be issued to prepare. It didn't matter that the current radar didn't support his warning. Race was sure that it would—in a matter of hours.

Race hit send and rose from his chair. It wasn't yet mid-morning, but the outer office teemed with two dozen staff. They had a right to know what was going on. A right to understand the decisions he made. He went to the center of the room, in front of the biggest monitor situated where the entire office could see and waited for everyone to look up from their screens. Conversations trailed off and a hush fell.

"I know the data doesn't support my decision yet," he began without preamble. "But I believe the storm is going to turn and come directly ashore on the Kona coast. I have notified the other islands we are moving forward. I want the shelters on the west coast emptied and closed if possible. I want those towns evacuated. Get HPD and Fire on the phone and tell them we think this thing is going to come straight at us."

Race held up his hand at the rush of air that sounded. The collective breath of surprise of a room full of people, all wanting to ask questions.

"That lone track . . ." He tapped the screen to bring the light orange line of the model that bisected the island to the forefront. "That track was predicted by one station. A weather station in Japan. Someone there thinks that given the perfect conditions, Garth could gain enough power and boomerang straight into us." Race paused to look around the room. "This is a Category four hurricane hitting our island head on."

If there was anyone who hadn't been paying attention before, they were listening now.

"While we've sat here waiting, Garth has been sitting out there eating up every raindrop, every cloud, every ounce of pressure it can get its hands on. I believe we need to be ready for the worst, ladies and gentlemen."

"If that happens . . ."

Race wasn't sure who started the sentence, but he finished it. "We're in trouble."

The room was silent, as if raising his hand had not only kept them from talking but had stopped time as well.

"As of right now, we prepare for that track. It's the worst of them." Race pointed again to the line highlighted on the screen. "If we prepare for that and Garth takes one of the others, we'll still be ready."

He pointed to the words behind them on the wall. *Prepare for the worst. Hope for the best.* "This time, hoping for the best won't be enough. I suggest we start praying for anything but *this.*" Race circled the track on the screen.

"You all know what to do. I want a notice out to the people of this Island in the next ten minutes. Let's hope it's not too late to do what they pay us for and help guide them through what's coming."

Race thanked them and let them get back to work. Now that he'd made his decision, there was plenty to do. He hoped they'd all slept well over the last few days. It would be the last they were going to get for quite some time.

Race approached Steve. "Get the conference room set up and alert the radio stations so I can get on the air. Then meet me in my office. You and I need to go over how things will work before I leave for the other side. A hurricane coming in on a track like this is a new scenario. It's unlike any hurricane strike this island has ever prepared for."

Steve nodded, reaching to answer his already ringing phone. "Civil Defense." He looked to Race in surprise as his hand covered the mouthpiece. "Onimura Resort is on the line for you."

Race pointed at his office, telling Steve to forward the call there. He wondered who would be on the other end. Was it possible the CEO wanted to shed some light on what was really going on? Perhaps offer an explanation why they still hadn't made any preparations despite his assurances otherwise? It didn't matter. The moment the update went out telling residents to prepare as if a hurricane warning had been ordered, things would no longer be up for debate. By Onimura, or anyone else.

Race would have preferred it be the raven-haired Safety Manager on the other end. But he couldn't think of a single reason why she would call.

"Race? It's Savanah," he heard as soon as he picked up the receiver. "I just wanted you to know the resort will be evacuating and we are beginning shut-down procedures."

"I don't know how you already found out we are upping the warning levels. The notice isn't out yet. But that's what everyone is being instructed to do," Race replied.

"What do you mean, you're upping the warning levels?" Savanah's voice caught. "I'm calling because your office needs to know the status here at the resort. So you can mark us off the list of things to worry about."

"Everyone is on the list for this office to worry about," Race corrected.

"Jesus . . . I should have just sent an email."

"You heard what we're doing. Isn't that why you're shutting down?"

"No. The last update from your office says everything is still holding. When things change, it's going to be too late to do anything. Which is why we aren't waiting any longer. We are getting as many people out of here as we can in the next twenty-four hours. After that, I don't believe anywhere on this side of the island will be safe."

"Someone didn't call you and tell you about the emergency update going out?" Race heard Savanah groan. Though whether in frustration or defense, he wasn't sure. There was the sound of both in her words.

"No, Director Weston. No one called me."

"But now you're evacuating the resort? Who decided that?" Race had to know.

"Look, I never ignored your warnings . . ."

Race wasn't sure he'd heard correctly. He opened his mouth to ask her to repeat what she'd said but she continued before he could. The bite in her tone replaced any softness he thought he heard.

"This may come as a shock, but I made this decision all by myself."

"It's about time you started doing the right thing."

"I could say the same thing . . . Look. I'm glad your office is coming out with the increased warnings. When the time comes, it will have helped."

"I don't need you to tell me my job," Race replied.

Race stared at his phone. The line was already dead. Savanah had said she'd made the decision for the resort. What had she meant when she said she hadn't ignored his warnings? Or by her odd comment, that his decision would help? Help what? He growled but was forced to put her to the back of his mind as Steve walked in.

"Steve, no matter how this plays out, I will be running things from the West Hawaii office until it's over. I'll be leaving within the hour."

"With what you think is going to happen, people will expect you to stay here and direct things," Steve countered.

"This isn't debatable. It's my call. I need to be there myself to know what's happening. While it's happening. Not after."

Steve tried again. "Someone needs to be here giving us directions."

"You're right. That's why I'm leaving you in charge here. As the Assistant Director, you have the authority and you're more than qualified. Don't worry, we'll be in constant contact. If I get cut off, you will take over keeping in touch with the other agencies." As he spoke, Race looked around for anything else he might need.

"And if everything does go to hell like you're expecting?"

"Power will go out and communications will get jammed. The 9-1-1 system is going to go down or be severely compromised." Race held up the satellite phone that went with his position. Having one wouldn't mean a thing to all the people who didn't have that advantage. He clipped it to his belt anyway. "Start educating the public now to expect those things to happen, what they can do to help and the alternatives. Make sure HPD is putting on extra dispatchers to take care of the emails and texts that will start flooding in. This will be the first time since those systems have been implemented that they're going to be put to the test. Start reminding people that phone service may be out, but text messaging and email can be used to call for help or let loved ones know they're okay."

Steve gave a short nod of understanding.

"When the time comes, emergency personnel will be ordered to stand down. Then all we can do is wait until things clear. People need to understand that's why we do as much as we can now," Race continued. Then he thought of something else and stopped to look at the young man furiously taking notes.

"Call your family and bring them here. Use my office. I don't want you having to worry about them. Any of the other staff who feel they need to be home, tell them to go. If it isn't safe for them to go home, they can bring their families here as well. Just like what I'm telling you. For what it's worth, this time I don't think we're going to be the ones needing help. But still, I want you to make sure everyone knows taking care of their family is their first priority. People won't be any good to us here if they are worried about their family."

"No one's going home. We'll be here for whatever you need from us," Steve assured.

"Let's get a move on. Once Garth starts to turn, we've got twelve hours at most before the edge of it reaches the coastline."

Race heard the repeated tone of email notifications. He wasn't surprised to see the names of the directors from the other islands in his feed. They would want to know what had made him jump the gun.

He couldn't tell them it was because of his gut. And the goosebumps of one petite Safety Manager. Someone who had been at odds with him from before they'd even met. Race knew he'd have to come up with something better than that. Even to him, it sounded crazy.

Steve announced that he was ready to start the recording to go out to the radio stations via the emergency broadcasting system. Race didn't hesitate. He didn't need to write it down. He picked up the phone. "This is Race Weston, Director of your Hawaii County Civil Defense. Our office is issuing a hurricane warning effective immediately. We believe Hurricane Garth is going to turn and come ashore, moving directly through the South Kohala valley. Make the necessary preparations for yourself and your families immediately. All beaches and parks will remain closed until further notice. Follow all instructions of the emergency personnel in your area who will be directing coastal evacuations. Plan to shelter your family for the next forty-eight hours . . ." Race drew a steady breath. They were going to survive this. He refused to accept anything else.

"I want you to know we are with you. Until this is over, I will be at the office we have opened on the west side. This will allow me to know exactly what is happening, as it happens. I am going to be right there, on the ground, with you. We will get through this. And we will do it together. God bless you and be safe out there."

He felt the chilling caress of fate as the echo of his words carried through the office from the radios whose volume had been turned up. Race realized that he and Savanah Jordan were finally walking the same direction. Squarely into the path of a category 4 hurricane.

CHAPTER TWENTY-TWO

Things were going better than Savanah expected. Clark hadn't come down to fire her yet. Savanah could hardly believe it, even though she knew the reason didn't have anything to do with her. The CEO was AWOL. Not even his secretary had a clue where he'd gone. While her job was easier without him around, Savanah still didn't like not knowing where he was. It would be just her luck for him to show up right in the middle of things and blow up her plan for shutting down the resort and evacuating everyone out of there.

Once she had the updated warnings from Civil Defense in hand, Savanah went full force to put her plans into action. She had the front desk send a message to all guests to evacuate. Leayne helped reassign staff to assist Pinky and her lobby crew with the mass check-out. Manny had the landscaping staff assist him directing traffic out from the parking lot.

The resort's main dining room would remain open as long as possible to feed any remaining guests that were unable or unwilling to evacuate, and remaining staff as well. Once the danger was past, Savanah's plan was to have the resort begin feeding anyone in the area that needed it. The resort had thousands of pounds of stored food that wouldn't keep for long without electricity. Even though the resort had emergency generators, Savanah wasn't banking on being able to use them. Supplying the community, first responders and guests with food would be just one way they could work together.

In following her schedule, Maintenance would do a final walk-through in the morning to ensure that all gas valves had been closed before shutting off the mains. That would remove any danger of a gas leak or fire—unless one of the main lines ruptured. God help them if that happened.

Maintenance would also secure the dozens of individual propane tanks used in grills and tiki torches around the resort, to a safe area below ground. Savanah was sure they would need the tanks when the storm was done with them.

Everywhere she looked, people worked at a furious pace to complete the preparations she outlined. It wasn't just about the job. The staff wanted to get home to their families.

"Savanah, did you hear?"

Savanah turned to see Leayne walking toward her. "Did I hear what?"

"Civil Defense, well Weston anyway, has moved its base to this side until Garth passes." Leayne handed a bottle of water to Savanah. "Drink it. I'll bet you haven't had anything since I saw you last. You need to stay hydrated."

"You know, that's funny. I'm betting forty-eight hours from now we'll have more water than we know what to do with." Savanah took the bottle and swallowed half at once. Leayne was right: getting dehydrated wouldn't help anyone. "And yeah, I actually did know. Doesn't mean I know what Race is thinking, though. The CDD usually keeps his butt safe in the bunker in Hilo. That way he can keep giving orders from somewhere that's nice and dry and where he won't lose power to all that fancy equipment he has. All those computers to tell him what's going on right outside his door," Savanah added sardonically.

"According to his message a few minutes ago, he's decided he wants to be able to see for himself what's going on when the hurricane flattens us. That he is one of us and the island will survive it together." Leayne pursed her lips as she mused. "Fine line between brave and stupid, it would seem."

"He's going to find out firsthand what it's like to be one of the local folks trying to survive. Rather than the white knight riding in with the sunrise."

Savanah didn't think there was a snowball's chance that Race Weston would ever understand what it meant to be Hawaiian or to be connected to the land like she was. She still felt that was something extra she had brought to the table when she'd applied for the position. The experience of having grown up living through the disasters the same as the people she'd be responsible for protecting were trying to do.

None of that matters now, as long as he does his job. Savanah cast her eyes skyward. *Please God, let him be as good as we need him to be.*

The general population didn't have the benefit of a bunker where they could weather the storm. A privilege Race had surprisingly given up with his sudden desire to personally staff an office on their side of the island. She wasn't sure how she felt about his decision. Everything to do with running the island had always been done from the east side.

When it came down to protecting people, it shouldn't matter where you lived or who your district representative was. The CDD's job was to protect the island and everyone on it.

She didn't know if he was ready for what was coming. She doubted any of them were. She did know it was time they all start thinking and behaving like they were on the same side. Race had gotten the position. The best Savanah could hope for was that all those articles about him were true and he truly was the best one for the job.

"Are you going home tonight?" Leayne asked.

"I don't think so. I wouldn't be able to sleep, anyway. I might as well be here."

"Use one of the rooms. We're doing a good job of clearing them. Pinky says occupancy is down by thirty percent already. Which means you've got your choice. She says the penthouse guests have been the only ones who haven't responded at all yet."

"Pinky and her staff have done an amazing job." Savanah was impressed with how fast people were deciding to leave after learning the Category four hurricane they'd written off was now potentially heading straight for them. "Do we know where the penthouse guests are?"

The top floors had been rented by a movie crew filming on location. It was one of the things that had caused such a problem when Clark had given his directive to use only the hotel safe. The female lead had brought enough jewelry to fill a store front. A second manager had been called to assist Pinky in checking the items in. The safe in Pinky's office was filled to overflowing.

"They left yesterday for a remote location, and no one's seen or heard from them since," Leayne said.

"You're kidding me. With a hurricane coming, they thought that was a good idea? There isn't anyone who has any idea where they went?" People still surprised Savanah.

"The valets helping them load up yesterday suggested they stay close to the hotel and wait things out. But from what Kimo said, the director was convinced the storm had passed far enough to the south that we were in the clear," Leayne explained. "He thought, if anything, they might get some good storm footage to use."

"Oh no. That doesn't sound like Iniki at all." Savanah could only shake her head in disbelief.

"Maybe it will be a blockbuster and make us all famous." The irony of the similarity with the thirty-year-old hurricane wasn't lost on Leayne, either. "Some of the staff talked about hiring on as extras. I'll keep asking."

"We need to find them and get them back here."

"I'll let you know if I find anything out. You need to try and get some sleep tonight." Leayne added one more question before leaving. "And because I'm your friend, how's the back holding up?"

"It's good."

"I heard you had a seizure last week. You haven't had one in a while."

Savanah didn't know how Leayne managed to hear everything. But the woman did. It made her extremely effective as the head of HR. And sometimes a huge pain in the neck as a friend. "I overdid it while I was out swimming with Dad."

"It's better to know what caused it. Rather than like before, when they would just happen out of the blue."

Savanah agreed. This knowledge could help her avoid future seizures. She hated feeling like she had to be treated like an infant for fear of bringing on such a painful event. Her doctor promised it wouldn't always be like that. It wasn't too much to ask for a little patience to allow her body and spine time to heal. Especially given the original prognosis had been that she might never regain control of her legs.

"And you don't think this is overdoing it?" Leayne didn't look away.

"I'm not planning on doing anything stupid."

"Hah. If only it were that easy. Just because you aren't planning on it . . ."

Savanah loved that Leayne never babied her because of her accident or being in a wheelchair. Instead, Leayne expected her to be honest about what she could and couldn't do. Based on that, Leayne expected she would hold up her end at work and at recovering. Savanah wished more people could look at her like her friend did.

"Get out of here. I'll see you tomorrow." Savanah would miss having Leayne on property. Having her there brought a measure of comfort even if Savanah would have preferred her friend stay safe at home.

CHAPTER TWENTY-THREE

Race was driving himself crazy. Checking the satellite images every ten minutes was like waiting for water to boil. He finally decided to get out and start assisting with evacuations along the coast. That would get him out where he could see and feel for himself what was going on. He promised Harlan, the man assigned to assist him in the new west side office, to stay in areas with cell phone reception in case anyone needed to speak with him.

No sooner were the words out of his mouth than Race wondered what was happening in the areas he'd just promised to avoid. During a disaster, or potential one like what was happening now, there were too many areas without reception. Visitors loved Hawaii for its rugged, wild beauty. Until they needed saving and couldn't call for help because of it. How many were out there right now, cut off with no idea about the change in the threat to the island—and them? Race sent a message to Steve that he wanted a report listing all the outlying areas where it was possible for people not to have heard yet.

He had to admire what he found at Kona International Airport. The check-in lines were long, but from what he could see, everyone was keeping a cool head. There was no sense of panic. Race attributed that to the numerous emergency personnel walking about. Their presence helped give a feeling of security. Anyone who had a question only had to turn around to find someone in an official capacity to talk with. Even the airport fire department personnel had come out of their station at the far end of the airport terminal, to assist with the crowd attempting to flee Garth's impending wrath.

Race found Sam Masuna, Keahole Airport's Director of Operations, meeting with the Fire Chief and the head of airport security. They wasted no time in updating Race on the airport's timeline for shutting down if Garth turned to come ashore.

"We're on open, flat land at sea level. We have two concrete bunkers that could withstand something like Garth, but none that could accommodate the number of people that will flood the airports in an evacuation," the airport manager stated. His face creased with concern.

"Don't wait until it's too late to get people out of here," Race advised. But he wasn't talking about flying people out. He was talking about what to do with them when getting a plane off the ground was no longer an option.

"You really think this is happening?" the Fire Chief asked.

"It's a possibility we can't ignore any longer." Race nodded. "And we wouldn't be doing this if I didn't think so."

"We're working with the airlines and the owners of the private planes to get as many out of here, with people on them," the airport director assured Race.

Race left a short time later, confident Director Masuna would keep him updated on the state of the airport. Transportation of people wasn't the only concern. Transportation of goods was a major priority. Race had spent an hour on the phone with the Port Authority and captains of the two ports that served Hawaii Island. They'd given immediate orders for vessels over 200 tons to leave port and head for safe water until conditions no longer presented a risk to life or cargo.

The drive through town was vastly different from a few days earlier, when he'd waited for Savanah. There were far fewer people walking along Alii Drive through the center of Kailua-Kona. However, the vehicular traffic on the town's main thoroughfare was almost bumper to bumper. People assumed they were safe in their cars as they checked on the storm preparations being taken by the businesses that lined the coast.

Race stopped at the pier to watch people continuing to play on the beach and in the water, disregarding the danger so they could enjoy the still-clear blue skies. The mood was tempered compared to the last time Race had been there. Gone was the easy laughter that he'd heard from the busy sidewalks. The crowds now thinned by half with the increased warnings his office had sent. Most of the businesses along the waterfront had taken the time to board their windows.

Race knew this wasn't the first storm preparation for most of the business owners. He could see the brackets already in place for the plywood coverings to protect the abundance of glass windows and doors. The existing fixtures meant the plywood could be hung and secured at a moment's notice. It was a matter of pulling the materials from wherever they lay in wait for the one day of the year they might be necessary. He knew the businesses would stay open to the last minute, on the chance Race and the predictions were wrong.

He watched cars pass by. Locals and visitors out doing the same thing he was. Looking at the changes. The locals trying to gauge whether the threat was real. The tourists just passing the time as they found themselves in paradise with activities suspended and itineraries that no longer mattered. What else was there to do but drive around to take stock of how effectively Mother Nature could ruin your vacation?

There were far fewer sandbags than Race expected. The few he did see lining the storefronts seemed old and worn. He verbally instructed his phone to text Steve to check whether there were enough on hand or if more needed to be flown in.

Race was surprised when he realized that several of the hotels only appeared to be boarding up the areas facing the ocean. He drove slowly along several alleys where the smaller businesses seemed content to disregard preparations altogether. He growled in irritation. Those business owners and managers frustrated the hell out of him.

He knew they needed every dollar of revenue. But refusing to do anything was inviting disaster. There were many things that they could do while remaining open.

Race returned to the pier and parked. The Department of Land and Natural Resources had their office open at the entrance of the popular Kailua-Kona landmark. The unlucky officer on duty was overrun answering questions from tourists and locals alike. A police officer stood next to her car, using it to control vehicle access to the pier. She, too, was being inundated with requests for the latest information. Both officers continued to encourage people to avoid the beachfront and low-lying areas and get to safety. Race resolved to remember to thank the people on the front lines who continued to inform and encourage the visitors to stay out of the water and make plans to get somewhere safe.

Race thought about the day he'd waited for Savanah and gotten in the water to swim with her. The day he'd somehow found himself making an even bigger mess of things. He sat there, the memory his only company, and watched the activity around him until well after dark. As he prepared to leave, he admitted to himself he had been hoping she would appear.

"Why did you tell me to look at your email, Savanah?" Race queried the empty air of his SUV.

It was a question he'd asked a dozen times over. The words of the email she'd sent that day weren't going to change. What did Savanah want him to find? What she'd written spoke to incompetence and poor decision-making. Not to mention directly disobeying her company's mandate by way of the CEO's directive to comply with Civil Defense. Why then would she seem so confident when she'd told Race to go back and look at it?

Race swore under his breath. He couldn't get the damn situation off his mind. Picking up his phone, he pulled up Savanah's email. Sure enough, the words hadn't magically rearranged. There was no hidden message suddenly becoming clear. Not a single thing to indicate Race had been wrong in his interpretation of what she'd said.

"Onimura Hotel and Resort will not be taking any steps to prepare for impending inclement weather. It is the resort's opinion that emergency protocols are not warranted at this time. It is the decision of this resort that such action would be premature."

There it was in black and white. Sent to him and copied to her boss. Both men had the evidence of Savanah's poor choice in their inbox.

Race searched his memory of that day in Savanah's office when Clark Dieter had come walking in. The CEO was adamant he'd agreed with everything Race said. The man's attitude had professed concern that an employee in such a position as Savanah had disobeyed a direct order. As a result, she'd misled not only her boss but the entire company.

Race continued replaying the events in his head. The CEO had been unaware of Savanah's email to Race's office, stating that the resort would not comply with the suggested preparations. Clark had said he'd told Savanah specifically to follow Civil Defense recommendations and had assumed she'd done so. The CEO had made it clear that only Race's presence that day had brought Savanah's actions to his attention.

Race looked back at the email. This time, Clark Dieter's name as a recipient jumped off the screen. *That* was what Savanah had wanted him to notice. The CEO had lied about having no knowledge of Savanah's email or her actions. Steve's words came back to him, that even a CEO would lie to save himself. If Clark Dieter had lied about that, what else had he lied about?

How many other things had Race misjudged about Savanah based on the lies of her boss?

He sighed in relief as the puzzle pieces settled into place. Now that he'd cleared up the one thing that made everything else inexplicable, the rest of the picture of Savanah fit together. Race was sure he knew where he'd find her. He suddenly felt as if he knew exactly who Savanah Jordan really was.

Chapter Twenty-Four

No one noticed the milestone of Savanah's release from the confines of her wheelchair. Not with an impending Category 4 hurricane. Maybe it was better this way, she mused. No one to fuss over her. She could just begin getting back to something that resembled her life. Like being able to do things so simple as walking beneath the glittering stars of a clear Hawaiian sky.

Savanah loved the resort property at night. She walked slowly, double-checking the lists each department had given her for what had been accomplished during daylight. The resort staff had done their best to prepare without causing a panic. Not for the first time did Savanah think that Pinky and her staff were grossly underappreciated and underpaid.

A wave of sweet scent enveloped her she stopped. Gardenia bushes heavy with their snow-white flowers spilled their unmistakable scent into the air. She closed her eyes and breathed deeply. Even with the threat of Garth's landfall looming, Savanah appreciated the beautiful Hawaiian evening. A million stars twinkled down from the sky, as if she shouldn't have a care in the world.

The hurricane continued to hold a tight formation, refusing to release even small amounts of energy to form stray clouds over the island. That, along with the lack of light pollution, meant the night sky was exceptionally clear. The stars were to the sky what the grains of sand were on the ocean floor. A shimmer of refracted light was the only indication when her hand broke the water's surface as she watched, transfixed by the ebb and flow of the sand around her fingertips.

Savanah was tempted to reach her hand up into the inky blackness of the night. To sink her fingers into the darkness and swirl her hand in the Milky Way. Her fingertips tingled as if she could feel the stars dancing through them.

She noted that the unnatural stillness of the air, which she'd found so unnerving that morning, yet remained. It felt like the molecules were suspended, growing larger, heavier with each passing hour. The weight of them against her skin slowly becoming too much to ignore.

"I knew I'd find you here."

Savanah didn't look away from the sky. Funny how after only their few meetings, she recognized Race's voice. She'd have recognized it anywhere. "What are you doing here?"

"Where's your wheelchair?"

Savanah gave a huff that was supposed to have been a laugh, but the only funny thing about it was how badly it failed. "My doctor cleared me this afternoon." She gave a small motion of her head to dismiss the importance of it. "In the excitement of the day, it seems I forgot to mention it to anyone."

"You just told me. Congratulations."

"So I did. Now maybe you could tell me why you're here," Savanah countered.

"Your boss said he didn't know you'd sent me that email and what it said. But you copied him on it. He lied that day in your office."

"You finally went back and looked at it."

"Why didn't you just tell me that?" Race asked.

"Because *just* telling you what was going on with my boss sounds far

163

simpler than it would have been." Savanah gave a long, exhausted exhale. The situation with Clark was anything but simple.

"What is going on with him?"

"That's a good question. I don't know. Neither does anyone else."

Race frowned, "Still, I wish you would have explained things to me."

"I doubt you would have believed me. Actually, I'm sure you wouldn't have."

"That's not true. I would have believed you."

"Race." Savanah shook her head, giving another tired sigh. "If you aren't a liar, then be honest with yourself. Whatever your problem is with me, you don't want to trust anything I say. From the first, it seemed easier to believe I was lying—"

Savanah found her words cut off by Race's lips meeting hers. There wasn't time to protest or question. Heat and longing instantly bloomed at the contact. Like the first time he'd kissed her, she was totally unprepared for everything about his kiss and could do nothing but melt into it as he held her captive. His hands at the sides of her face, creating a barrier against anything but the feel of his mouth to hers.

It occurred to Race that the only time there wasn't the underlying resentment and angriness between them was when his lips were on hers. That was fine with him. If it took kissing her to burn through the layers of indignation he'd unwittingly raised, so be it. He held her still in his hands. Silently commanding her to look past his words and accept the attraction that was a mutual flame between them.

As the kiss deepened, he brought his body to hers. One hand tracing a path down her shoulder to tuck at the small of her back. Her lips parted in surprise, and he hesitated, wondering if she were about to protest. Or if he'd hurt her in some way. He suddenly needed to know everything about her injuries.

Instead, her lips softened. That was all the invitation Race needed to deepen the kiss. His tongue stroked her lips. He reached up with one hand and pulled the ornate wooden stick from her hair. There was no sound as the heavy locks tumbled down her back. A shimmering black cloud that enveloped his arm against her.

Savanah shivered at the release of her hair. Race sank one hand into the thick of it as he pressed her close enough to feel her heart racing. Her lips followed his as he pulled back.

"I didn't mean to sound so severe when I asked about your wheelchair. To say I am happy your doctor cleared you is a colossal understatement." Race pressed his lips back to hers. "That news, seeing you walking trumps the impending doom headed our way. I'm glad you could share it with me."

"Race . . ." she said.

"That's what I wanted. To hear you say my name like that." He stroked the soft skin beneath his fingers in appreciation. "Much better than when you're swearing at me."

"I have never . . ."

"Right. Calling me an egotistical ass isn't technically swearing." Race chuckled. He leaned down to press his lips to hers again, to assure himself he hadn't imagined what they'd felt like. "I've wanted to kiss you from the first moment I saw you. I thought it would be enough when I kissed you at the restaurant. It wasn't."

"You have a funny way of trying to make friends, Race." Savanah drew in a deep breath. How long had the kiss lasted?

"I don't have that many friends. And I don't kiss my friends," Race replied, letting his hands drop as Savanah stepped away.

She laughed briefly. "One of the more easily recognizable signs you aren't from Hawaii. We kiss everyone."

"I don't think I like that."

Savanah tilted her head to give him a wistful smile. "It's part of how we say hello. Physical contact is a part of life in Hawaii. Shaking the hand of anyone other than a business associate is almost offensive."

"I think shaking your hand has been one of my least offensive actions where you're concerned," Race conceded.

"Agreed, Director. How nice to finally agree on something." Savanah said archly.

That made him grin. "I'd like to suggest from right now, that we operate on the premise I believe everything you say. That seems like a fair place to start given I've been . . ."

He searched for something that didn't paint too bad a picture. After all, he felt he deserved some leeway given Clark Dieter was the CEO of a major resort and should have behaved better. God. That sounded lame even to him. Obviously, Savanah had the same thoughts.

"Given you've been an ass."

"I was looking for something nicer. But if you insist, we can go with I've been an ass."

"A difficult, maddening, and perhaps sometimes charming, ass." She offered a smile. "Better?"

"Much."

"Now we have two things we agree on." Savanah laughed lightly at the pained look on Race's face. Only to gasp as he put his hand beneath her chin so he could tilt her face to his.

"We agree on something far more important." He took her lips beneath his to prove his point. The immediate leap of her heartbeat along with her unconscious sigh of approval at his kiss confirmed his words.

"That I find kissing you to be a pleasurable experience? Press conference for that seems premature." Savanah reminded him of those first few minutes when they'd met in the parking lot. When she had smiled at the easy banter with a total stranger. Just like she was doing now.

"A pleasurable experience? I'll have to try harder. I think I'm the one who should feel insulted now."

Race picked one of the fragrant yellow and pink blooms from the tree overhead. He tucked it behind Savanah's ear, thinking the delicate blossom was the perfect complement to the beautiful woman it decorated.

"I'm still surprised you decided to run operations for Garth from an office here." Savanah commented as they began to walk.

"I don't like being safe and sound underground while the people I work for are in the thick of the fight. I felt we needed to have someone here. A means of getting out the information about what is really happening."

"There are several staff from the CD office stationed on this side. I meant you personally, Race. That seems a bit extreme." Savanah chanced a glance in his direction. "It puts you in danger. But the fact you're willing to do that . . . it says a lot about who you are."

"The same could be said for you, Savanah. Why are you here tonight? I don't see anyone else that looks like a manager." Race appreciated the easy rhythm their conversation fell into as he walked beside Savanah.

"Maybe they're here and you just don't see them."

"Maybe that's the first lie you've told me," Race replied smoothly.

Savanah held up a hand in surrender. "I'm the MOD, Manager On Duty, for the night. I volunteered. There was no need for anyone else to be here. As you can see, it's quiet. The others will be here when, if, needed."

"Which means I'm here for the exact same reasons you are." Race finally felt like his imaginary scoreboard was beginning to even out. He'd been almost entirely in the red. He refrained from saying *I'm here because you are* aloud.

"What do you think tomorrow will bring?" Savanah asked quietly.

"I'm hoping it doesn't curve like you seem sure it's going to. But there's a station in Japan that says the air trough that runs through the corridor between the mountains will pull Garth in rather than pushing it away. If it comes close enough to interact with it."

"If it's gotten big enough."

"That's right. If the system has gotten big enough."

"Size matters." Savanah couldn't help herself.

"It would appear so." Race responded dryly.

His body's awareness of her jumped up another degree. The danger of a Category 4 hurricane suddenly seemed miniscule compared to the danger the woman next to him presented. Her calm quiet belying the risk of trying to get to know her. From the moment they'd met, it had been explosive and exciting, and nothing had been what it seemed.

That realization made Race smile. He was an adrenaline junkie, just one who didn't get his thrill from bungee jumping or skydiving. The position he held on the island's Civil Defense team was about danger and saving people. His job was to outguess the dangers he saw coming and find a way to beat the ones he didn't. Those were the things that gave him a thrill. Which explained his attraction to Savanah Jordan.

Whatever her handicap, he'd thought she was predictable and that he knew her. He now saw how wrong he was. The more curves she threw him, the more attracted to her he became. The thought that she was his kind of adrenaline somehow made it easier for him to accept that attraction. And that she'd had him second-guessing himself from the moment they'd met.

"Would you like to share what's behind that self-satisfied look on your face?" Savanah asked.

"No. I don't think I would."

"Secrets don't make friends, Race. Didn't your mother ever tell you that?"

Race leaned down. Putting his head close to hers he asked softly. "I'd like to hear your secrets, Savanah. If you want to share. I think I'd like being your partner in crime."

"Who are you and what have you done with the stuck-up Race Weston?" Savanah gave him a look that said he was crazy.

The gentle warmth of the breeze brought Race back to the approaching danger of Garth. "I really would like to know your thoughts on what's happening. And I'd be interested to know your plans."

CHAPTER TWENTY-FIVE

Savanah shivered with the way his words had whispered across her skin. But in the blink of an eye, he was back to business. She found herself admiring his ability to switch mental gears. She needed to keep her thoughts focused if she wanted to keep up. She watched him for a moment, trying to decipher more of who he really was. It made her realize she hadn't really looked at him in all the times they'd met before. She'd been too busy defending herself. A situation she decided to solve immediately.

Savanah stopped and took a step away from Race. Her gaze grew thoughtful as she began her assessment. In response, he stepped back and did a slow turn, holding his arms out, giving her a better view.

She amended her early description of his character to include smart ass. But Savanah didn't let his attempt to make her laugh stop her. Resisting, she studied him harder.

He had the lithe build of someone who'd grown up outdoors. The strength she could see in him was born of activity in the real world, not inside a gym. He'd asked her to help improve his swimming. Savanah wasn't fooled. She was sure Race Weston swam well. Since he had been born in Australia, it was highly unlikely he didn't swim. He'd probably tried surfing, as well.

But it was how he carried himself that spoke to her. He stood before her evaluation with a calm arrogance, waiting patiently for her to announce he'd passed whatever exam she was making. The look on his face saying he was sure that he would. Confidence. Arrogance. Sometimes the two were inseparable. But Savanah had to admit—they were part of what attracted her to him.

"Did I pass?"

"Yes. I think you do."

"Any chance you'll let me in on what I've finally done right?"

"You're dressed for the job. Your shoes, for example. You've got on boots meant for muck and mud. I can see a flashlight and a utility knife on you." Savanah reached toward Race's pants pocket, stopping just short of touching him. "And I'm guessing this is a protein bar of some sort. I like people who are prepared."

His gave a slow whistle as her hand dropped away. "I have news for you: this is how I dress every day. I don't understand what you find so unusual about it. Since I passed, does that give me access to what you're thinking about the storm?"

"Sure. Since you seem so interested in my opinion all of a sudden. Everything was quiet this morning. Even the trees were afraid to make any noise. As if every living thing were trying not to catch Garth's eye and attract it to us. Was it like that in Hilo?"

Race shook his head as if Savanah had just confirmed something for him. "An observation like that is the simplest explanation as to why I'm here. Why I wanted an office to work out of on this side."

Savanah raised her brows in confusion. "Because it was quiet here?"

"Yes. No . . . No, because I can't answer you. I was inside looking at the radar and satellite images and talking to the people who were doing the same thing. We knew the temperature and the cloud density. I could tell you wind speed and direction. That's what people use to predict the weather these days. Talking to you has reminded me there's more to it than that."

"Those things are great," Savanah answered. "No one said they aren't. Used properly, technology should be able to provide earlier warnings to people. But you shouldn't discount the other things. Like looking out the window to be able to say if it's raining. Or your intuition, for example. Listening to that little voice in your head will save you. But here in Hawaii, we are also blessed with generations of knowledge that's been passed down. It just requires someone willing to listen and give it the credit it deserves."

"That's why you started evacuation procedures without your CEO's approval," Race said.

Savanah knew what she was trying to explain could be difficult for an outsider to understand. Hawaii was unlike so many places where natural disasters and storms had such predictable behaviors. The only thing that could be said for disasters in Hawaii, was that they were predictably unpredictable. She'd been hell on her instructors in college as she'd questioned things, looking for explanations that went beyond the textbooks. "Yes. We have to be able to look beyond the numbers. To put all the information together."

"You do realize Hawaii isn't the only state that uses a Farmer's Almanac," Race told her.

"Uses a what? I don't even know what that is."

"Farmer's Almanac. A book that has information about planting and fishing and weather. All based on the patterns of what's happened in nature over hundreds of years. It's obvious you think Hawaii is the only place where people record such things and use that information. But you should go visit the Midwest some time."

"I doubt it's the same—" Savanah started to protest.

"Have you ever been in a tornado?" Race interrupted gently. "Do you know anything about them?"

"Thankfully, no. We get waterspouts here. They seem a far cry from their land-based cousins." Savanah didn't think what she'd learned in school was what Race was asking her about.

"You've heard that the sky turns green and the leaves of the trees turn upside down right before the funnel cloud appears." Race prompted. "I was visiting family in Illinois one summer when one came down on top of us. It was one of the most terrifying experiences I'd had at that age. I remember thinking tornadoes were killers from the sky. All that swirling mass of power unleashed as a deadly, demented finger dragging destruction across the land as easily as a child would drag their finger through icing on a cake."

"I knew about the sky color . . . I've seen it . . . in movies," Savanah admitted. "I know about the leaves, too. That happens here before certain storms. But not always."

In her time at college, she had been fortunate not to have experienced a tornado firsthand. Something she had been thankful for, since tornadoes were common in Texas. "I noticed the newest warnings from your office included the possibilities of tornadoes. I've never seen that in one of our hurricane warnings. Is that why you asked me if I knew about them?"

"If Garth comes ashore, the conditions will be more than what's needed to spawn them." Race confirmed as they went back to walking.

"Because a Category 4 hurricane isn't bad enough," Savanah added ruefully.

Race continued with his story. "The leaves turn over because of the humidity and barometric pressure of the storm cell."

"I studied basic meteorology, you know." She doubted he knew that about her.

"The point I'm getting at is this. We were in the cellar long before we heard the warning over the radio. My aunt and uncle had known not just that a tornado was possible, but that one was going to touch down. My aunt used to swear up and down that Uncle Bill could tell if it was going to be a hot summer just by the way the birds pooped. I thought it was funny, the way my aunt made fun of her husband. But he knew with utter certainty. If Uncle Bill said they were getting in the cellar, Aunt Cami followed him without question."

"So, you're a bird poop whisperer like your Uncle Bill. Cool for you." Savanah couldn't help teasing. Maybe there were some island qualities about him after all. Her grandfather probably read chicken poop signs.

"If that would help, damn straight I would be," Race chuckled.

"In Hawaii, when the trees turn silver, it is Kū`ula, the god of fishermen, warning his followers to stay off the ocean."

Race stopped as the hair on his arms rose. He began to look around. Savanah was doing the same. The air was suddenly alive with electricity.

"When the sky above you rolls like the water below, take heed. Wākea, the sky father, is angry," Savanah chanted as she looked for signs of the clouds beginning to tumble over themselves.

"It's coming." Race muttered.

"He is."

They saw the small flashes at the same time. From this distance, there was no definition to the lighting. There was only a sudden, muted orange glow in the far-off clouds. The colors reflected wildly due to the ash in the air along the south coastline from Kilauea volcano's continuous eruptions.

There was no need to say anything as they stood side-by-side, watching. The sight made their hearts speed up.

Garth had finally decided to make his presence known.

CHAPTER TWENTY-SIX

"I don't know anything about what god is or isn't out there. What I do know is two days ago, my gut started telling me this wasn't over," Race told her.

"I'm glad you listened. It isn't just your gut." Savanah said, glad they were finally able to talk freely. "Here in Hawaii, there are other things that speak, too."

They continued to watch as Savanah led them through the resort, stopping periodically to watch for the faint flickers of light. Yet, the clean smell of ozone remained absent from the air, which told them the lightning wasn't that close, yet. Garth was letting them know he was out there but was guarding his might like a jealous lover. The storm was unwilling to show his hand and waste even a precious drop. Instead, the hurricane continued to feed its energy back in upon itself.

"Savanah . . ."

Something in Race's voice made her turn to look at him. His face was written with worry as his eyes tracked her every move. "It's not going to hit tonight."

Savanah ran her key card through the lock and opened the door they'd come to, inviting Race in behind her. She waved toward the open balcony while she went to get some bottled water before joining him. The suite she had chosen faced out, over the ocean. The balcony had a clear view to the beach below but was high enough that they could continue watching the lightning at the edge of Garth's massive reach. She had picked it specifically for the view it would afford her of the ocean. Leayne had been right. There had been plenty of rooms to choose from.

"Do you mind me asking what happened?" Race asked.

Savanah settled into her wheelchair and triggered the electric unit to massage her back. She wasn't stupid. Just because she'd been cleared didn't mean she should run a marathon or disregard how much the electric pulses contributed to aiding her continuing recovery. She'd been walking for the last few hours. The therapy the chair still provided was necessary. She didn't think anything of it as she wheeled onto the balcony where Race was.

"I was surfing one morning. A wave got the better of me and sent me to the bottom. Only the bottom was far too close. I was caught between the power of the water and the unmoving ocean floor below. The ocean won. Or maybe the ocean floor did. All I know is, I lost."

The story was devoid of emotion. Savanah had repeated it many times. It was her way of working through her fear, by talking about what had happened, over and over in the middle of the night when she woke drenched in sweat. Her throat aching from the screams made in her nightmares.

"I saw the scars from where you hit the reef." Race admitted.

Savanah simply shrugged in confirmation. The parts she didn't remember had been filled in by those who'd rescued her.

"What was the injury?"

"Think a stinger on a football player. Except mine wasn't at my neck. It was in my lower back. I was lucky. Luckier than I should have been. The damage wasn't permanent, but we didn't know that originally. The fluid gathering around where my back had been injured continued to put pressure on the spinal cord. The doctors weren't sure what would happen."

Race reached for her hand.

"Everyone was ecstatic when the doctors announced that my back wasn't broken. I mean, that's the worst thing that can happen, right?" Savanah exhaled slowly as she recalled the day the doctors had realized what was happening.

"That party didn't last long when the doctors had to explain there was no way to safely drain the fluid that was pressing on my spinal cord. There was no way to relieve the pressure. All we could do was wait to see if my body would begin to repair itself . . . or not."

"The wheelchair was precautionary, then." Race looked down at Savanah's legs.

"Wow. Why does that sound like you almost don't believe me?"

"You're misinterpreting what I said. I'm relieved you weren't more severely injured."

Savanah gasped in shock. "Insulting someone because you don't take the time to consider how your words sound before you say them is no excuse. It just means you're rude along with being inconsiderate."

She moved to the rail. She needed to get away from the sudden feeling of suffocating. Race Weston was like Hurricane Garth. Savanah couldn't get near him without feeling like he was sucking up all the air around her. She groaned at how irritating Race could be. Just her luck she also found him charming enough in other moments, that she couldn't shake her attraction to him.

Race moved beside the wheelchair. He turned it, giving Savanah no choice but to face him.

"Despite how good I seem to be at doing so, I don't mean to offend you. The thought of you being hurt and forever in this chair . . ." Race closed his eyes as he chose his words. "It affects me more than I'm prepared to admit." He swept the heavy shawl of her hair off her shoulder. "It appears the only time I'm not offending you is when I'm kissing you."

"And yet, you're still talking . . ."

Race moved forward to cover her lips. She could not help responding to his kiss.

Savanah was shocked by her actions. She'd never thought of being attracted to anyone who wasn't from the islands. Race Weston was a perfect example of why she'd always felt that way. Judgmental, sexist, egotistical . . . an outsider. So why had she goaded him into kissing her again?

The subtle tightening of his grip made her shiver. She could feel how careful he was being every time he put his hands on her. Treating her as if she would break. It came as another shock for her to realize that wasn't what she wanted. She was hungry to feel the strength his body promised.

Savanah gave a gasp of surprise that wasn't a protest as Race's arms slid beneath her to lift her from the wheelchair. Her arm went over his shoulders automatically as he tucked her body closely against his. He sat down on the cushioned lounger, still holding her securely.

"I like the way your arms feel around my neck." His breath teased across her skin.

"I've had a lot of practice." Savanah's eyes opened as Race withdrew his lips.

"I'm sorry. And because you told me to stop talking." Race pressed his lips back to hers. "I want to know the rest . . ."

Savanah couldn't believe she was going to give in. She thought about it for long moments before deciding she was willing to share more with Race. "My doctor used the wheelchair to keep my spine stable. In the beginning, there was the concern that even the slightest jarring might result in permanent injury or undo any progress we were making. They assured me that was all normal for a spinal injury."

She let out a long breath as she thought about everything that had happened since the accident. There had been so many people helping her. From the men who'd pulled her from the water to the doctors and nurses at the hospital. Her family had been by her side constantly, as had her friends.

It took a while for her to go on, but Race didn't rush her. He just kept his arms around her. "It was the unexpected that caused the biggest problem. I suddenly began having spasms around the area where my spine had been injured. As if the traumatized area had PTSD or something and was reenacting the injury. The tissue would just . . . go berserk." Savanah shivered with remembered pain.

"There was no way to predict what was happening. It would happen in any position. At any time. I could be awake or sleeping. Nothing made a difference. There was no rhyme or reason to it in the beginning."

She didn't add that it had been a daily occurrence. At times, she would just start to recover before another round would hit. Savanah tried hard not to remember those dark days.

Race drew in a breath almost as ragged as hers. "That's what happened to you on the pier last week."

"You were there?"

Savanah didn't remember seeing him. Then again, once the spasms started, she didn't remember anything that was happening around her. Her focus consumed by what was going on inside her body.

"I was having dinner across the street. I saw the wheelchair and thought it looked like yours," Race explained.

"So, you watched." Savanah thought she'd done a decent job of coming to terms with the humiliation of the seizures, or whatever they were. Somehow though, the thought that Race had seen her when she was vulnerable . . . Savanah realized she hated knowing that.

"I did."

Lowering his head, Race rested his chin against the soft silk of her hair and they sat in silence.

Savanah sat motionless in Race's embrace. Her stomach clenched when she thought about him witnessing her at her most vulnerable. She tried to tell herself it didn't matter. The effort it took to let go of the humiliation she was feeling, said it did. She exhaled slowly. There was nothing she could do about it now.

She let a few more minutes pass before she went on as if she hadn't just learned Race had watched her. "My doctors were primarily concerned with the injury to the sacral spine. The trauma to the surrounding tissue had been overlooked as minor compared to the sacral injury. Yet that is what's taking the longest to recover."

Savanah peered at Race. "Are you sure you want to hear all this?"

"I'm sure." He told her. "You know, rainy day information."

"Okay. You asked . . ." Savanah continued her narrative. "The theory is the nerves were shorted out either when the ocean crumpled me or when it decided to play whack-a-mole with my body on the rocks. Now they're like a bunch of wires with a faulty connection. Sometimes they work fine. And then one of them shorts out, and suddenly they go off like blinking lights on a Christmas tree. Except in this case, every blink is a stab of pain. Until they reestablish the connection and everything smooths out, the pain doesn't stop."

Savanah tried to distance herself as she answered Race's questions. But even so, trying to describe what her body went through brought flashes of unrealized fear skittering across her. Race must have felt them too, because he tightened his arms slightly. It made her feel safe enough to continue.

"There are electrodes in the seat back of the chair. They're meant to deliver shocks to specific areas determined by my neurosurgeon. Originally, the timing was at regular intervals and then, as I improved, only as necessary. I can trigger it myself when I feel it's needed. The whole thing is still considered to be experimental. Being cleared means I'm no longer required to use the wheelchair fulltime. Though he suggests I continue to do so any time I feel the need."

"Is this okay? To hold you like this?" Concern laced through Race's words.

"A little late now to be asking." Savanah teased the fingers of one hand along Race's collar as she considered undoing a button of his shirt.

"I meant, does this cause you any pain?"

"No." Savanah gave a low laugh. "I knew what you meant."

"Would you tell me if I was hurting you?"

Savanah considered his question. She hadn't expected him to ask something like that. It was a mystery to her why she wanted Race. The mystery made it no less true. Maybe it accentuated what she felt for him. "Does the ache that I have because I'd like to feel more of you count?"

Race captured her gaze with his. There was no indecision. Savanah searched the depth of his gaze only to see the same desire she knew was in hers. Her arms went around his shoulders as he cradled her and got to his feet, walking back inside the suite. He didn't stop until he reached the bed. Savanah held her breath as he carefully laid her down upon the pillows.

He tucked a pillow beneath her knees as well. "Tell me if something isn't good for you."

"Okay . . ." She paused. "I don't think you're good for me, Race Weston." Savanah settled against the pillows as he laughed.

"You must have been quite the patient." He shook his head as he laid down on the bed beside her.

"I was told I was the model patient, thank you. It would seem you're the only one who thinks I'm difficult to get along with."

Race chuckled. "So I've been told. You've got quite the reputation. I'm not making friends by giving you a hard time."

Savanah had decided undoing the buttons of Race's shirt was necessary now that they were lying on the bed. She took her time, enjoying exposing the lean muscles of his chest an inch at the time. "So, stop giving me a hard time." She said without looking away from the task she had given herself.

Race put a hand beneath her chin and brought her starburst gaze to his. "I'm not giving you a hard time on purpose. You seem to be easily offended."

Savanah put a finger to Race's lips to keep him from saying anything else. "You should stop talking now." She pulled his lips back to hers. "Why don't you find something else to do with your mouth that doesn't offend me."

"I'm worried something I do might hurt you," Race finally admitted.

"So don't do anything that does." Savanah's lips curled devilishly. "I really am stronger than you think." She laid a hand to his smooth cheek. A thrill going through her at the warmth he exuded beneath her touch. "And I promise to say if something seems too much for me to handle."

Race started to respond but stopped.

He lay to one side, so his weight wasn't pressing down on her as he explored her body. He returned to kissing her, one hand lost in the energetic waves of her hair while the other found the curve of her waist. Her hand made to pull her shirt from her waistband, but Race stopped her, his fingers encircling her wrist to put it back on the bed beside her.

"Oh no you don't. I heard you loud and clear the first time. The only thing you get to do now is tell me if you want me to stop. I get to do the rest."

Savanah moved her wrist slightly to test his grip. He didn't tighten his fingers, neither did he let her go.

"I'd tell you that's an order, if I thought it would make any difference," he added.

He placed his lips to the skin exposed where her shirt had begun to lift, and she felt him smile against the softness. She also felt her heartbeat beneath his lips. He took his time, lingering on the sensitive area. Race sent a warning glance with his eyes up her body and released her wrist. He had other things to do with his hand. Like wrap it to her hip so he could bring it closer.

Now that one hand was free, Savanah sank her fingers into the sun-kissed waves of Race's hair. Thick and luxurious beneath her touch, she curled her fingers through it in appreciation. She used the light hold she had to encourage his exploration. She squirmed at the unexpected warmth of his breath as he blew a kiss to her skin from where he had his mouth pressed to her clothes. The separation caused the small gesture to be erotic in a way Savanah would never have guessed. Her hips lifted, wanting to get closer to the pleasure.

There was a sudden moment of panic and Savanah hesitated. For all the therapy and hours spent in the ocean or at the gym since the accident, she was unsure. Moving her body as she wanted to do now with Race was something she hadn't done or even considered doing for a very long time. Race's grip interrupted her thoughts. He was letting her know he'd meant what he'd said.

CHAPTER TWENTY-SEVEN

He hadn't been sure what would happen when he'd picked her up from the chair. Race had just known he needed her in his arms. He needed to ease the knot that had formed in the pit of his stomach as Savanah described her accident. Her body broken and bruised as she lay in a hospital bed. Holding her and touching her helped to reassure him of the life in her now.

Now that he was lying beside her, he wasn't quite sure what to do next. A position he'd never been in before with a woman. His gaze roamed over her before returning to her crystalline eyes. Race's blood quickened at the blue flames of desire that burned amid the starburst of white.

If the grip Savanah had on his hair was any indication, she was enjoying what he was doing. There was no way to know whether it was his touch eliciting the small movements of her body, or reflex responses. She hadn't said anything about areas that might still be recovering sensation. Race decided he was going to go on the assumption she could feel everything he was doing. Everywhere he was touching. But he wasn't about to relinquish control of her body. Instead, he took over the movements for her. Lifting her hips, he blew another heated breath in greeting.

Sliding his leg between hers, he used it behind one knee to replace the pillows he'd placed for support. He smiled as his hand began a slow trek down her side. With the same pace, he stroked over the curve of her hip to her thigh, where he tucked his hand behind her knee so he could press it to his waist.

Savanah held her breath as Race fingered the zipper of her slacks. Agonizingly slowly, he began to drag it down.

Race took his time. Not everything was meant to be rushed. He didn't think there'd ever been a time he'd put so much thought into touching a woman as he was doing now with Savanah. It was proving to be incredibly sensual. He found himself wanting to do things to evoke more than just a reflex. Every touch was important for the sensation it would give her. It was giving him a sense of control he'd never considered. The realization he was responsible for everything she was experiencing called to something inside him. He didn't want things to be any other way.

Race had made it clear that Savanah wasn't to do anything but absorb what he was doing. He had taken control of the smallest movements of her body. His hands guiding her. Moving her body so her muscles were spared of expending the energy.

Race slid his arms around her to raise her from the bed, sliding her shirt from her shoulders. He'd seen all of her body before, when she'd been swimming at the pier. But it was different now that she was in his arms. He trailed his fingers over her reverently. As the yellow of her bikini that day had glowed against her skin, the powder blue of the bra did the same. He cupped the lace-covered swell of one breast. Practical yet enticing. Just like the woman wearing it.

"I'm not sure if this is in the safety catalog as recommended apparel." Race teased as he lowered his head to replace his hand at her breast.

"It stopped you—"

The rest of her retort was lost in the moan that escaped her. He let his laughter slide hot across her. Savanah's desire bloomed to life where his lips pressed to her skin. She tried to rise to meet more of his kiss, but Race held her still as he concentrated on following the erotic tempo of her pulse.

Race was reluctant to leave the captivating swell of her breasts. But there was more for him to discover. More for him to pleasure. Laying her back on the bed, his lips and finger trailed down the exposed flat of her abdomen, reveling in the delight of Savanah's body. Tracing places as they searched for the sensitive areas that would continue to have her gasping with growing desire.

Rising onto a knee, Race teased his fingers beneath the edge of Savanah's waistband. He pulled it just enough to see the blue he'd known would be there, matching the bra. His fingers played on the skin exposed to his touch. Skin silken as the petals of a flower quivered beneath his fingertips. Another inch and Race had to remind himself this wasn't something to rush. The only sounds in the room were Savanah's soft moans and the rush of his blood in his ears.

Race couldn't keep his eyes from devouring her. The glow of her skin through the blue of the boy shorts she wore was like the promise of gold shining in the sand of a miner's pan. Her natural beauty mesmerized him as he uncovered her inch by inch. Race pushed Savanah's slacks down her hips, his hands lifting her so he could clear the tight curve of her butt. He let his fingers sink gently into her backside, kneading softly as he reminded himself to be conscious of anything that might cause her pain.

"You don't voice your feelings much." Race uncovered the rest of her legs.

"I've had a lot of practice keeping quiet." She shook her head as if she was having trouble staying focused. "You told me I could only say stop. I'm just following orders."

He ran a finger over her toes as he uncovered them. Perfectly painted nails with bright flowers. "Pretty. I like this."

"It's Hawaii. We spend a lot of time with our feet bare." Savanah only wore shoes when she had to. At home, at the beach, never.

Race moved back beside her. The tan lines proved how often she wore the bikini he'd seen her in. The lines were perfectly defined. Outside of the office, she must live in her bathing suit.

"Do you ever swim naked?" God, he hoped she did. He would find a way to be there.

Savanah's shock was audible. "No."

Race chuckled. "Why not? Your water is amazing. It's perfect for it. And don't tell me you're worried about sharks." Even Race knew sharks weren't the biggest threat in Hawaii. Not when you compared it to somewhere like Australia.

"Of course not."

"Okay then, why not?" Race was enjoying the feel of Savanah tucked against him. His hand lazily stroked her skin as he watched the expressions going across her face. She wasn't hiding from him. For the moment at least. He was picturing her rising from the water, with no suit to hide behind.

"That's just not a thing here." It was the best Savanah could come up with.

"It should be. I can imagine how breathtaking the sight of you would be somewhere like the beach at *Kīholo* or Makalawena." Race fingered the tan lines. "You wouldn't have these, though."

It was her turn to ask. "How about you? Is swimming naked a thing in Australia?"

"It's different when you've got nude beaches. Of course, if you're the only one naked, that's going to land you in front of the judge."

"That's not an answer. Have you ever?"

"Me . . . no." He rolled her slightly beneath him, his arms bringing her closer. "And I'll not be sporting a *budgie smuggler* either."

His answer made it sound as if her question was ridiculous. "Double standards then. A budgie smuggler?" Race rubbing against her answered her question more pleasurably than words would have done. Speedos.

"Men aren't supposed to swim naked. Our dangly bits are too tempting." Which wasn't a problem now. Race wanted to feel Savanah naked against him. Skin to skin.

A flush suddenly colored her cheeks and she gave an embarrassed laugh.

"I like that surprises you." Race released the clasp of her bra. "We'll go together one of these days when we aren't fighting . . ."

"A hurricane."

"Right. Fighting a hurricane," he responded, his voice distracted as he focused his attention on Savanah beneath him.

There was a whispered "yes" as her bra followed her discarded shirt, but it was impossible to tell whether the single word of longing had come from him or her.

For a moment he was sorry to see the bra go. The color perfectly complemented Savanah's skin. Raising his eyes, he pulled the flower from where he'd tucked it in her hair. He planned to explore every inch of her. Race accepted the responsibility of helping her remember the good things her body could feel. Dragging the petals down her neck, he could smell the fragrance being released as it contacted her skin. As fragrant as the flower was, it was nothing compared to Savanah. Race breathed her in as he continued stroking her skin with the delicate flower. She was an intoxicating mixture of sun, ocean, vibrant life.

Race discarded the flower, swirling his tongue around the taut nipple he'd been tracing. Pulling with his mouth, he bit down softly as her hips rose from the bed. She was already quaking with the orgasm that came so fast neither of them was ready. Race didn't let her go. He pressed her to his body. He increased the suction of his mouth until her hands flew to his hair. Her fingers pulling to let him know she couldn't take much more.

Sitting up, he removed his clothes, quickly returning to the bed. His need for her was becoming a drive he couldn't hold off. Sliding the sexy blue from her hips, he caressed the lean muscles of her thighs. Fitting himself between them he brought her knee to his hip.

He entered her slowly. Watching with satisfaction as her head burrowed back into the pillows. The encouragement of her hands to quicken his pace was hard to resist. His body wanted to answer the insistent need of hers as she pressed him closer with the leg he held.

Race leaned down to kiss her. Her eyes opened with a sensuous flutter as her body responded. The cool mask that she kept her emotions hidden behind burned away by the flames of need flickering over her skin. She writhed with pleasure beneath him. It was so much harder to keep control than it would have been to let go. But he knew his need to be inside her would have meant he'd have been thrusting into her with everything he had. He wasn't willing to take the chance of hurting her. Not when she had come so alive in his arms. He burned into memory the sight of her body, her face, glowing with pleasure as he made love to her.

"That's it. Come with me. Let it all go and let me take you there," Race whispered against her skin.

There was something about the way Race touched her. Turning even the simplest caress into something that left her breathless. The feel of the buttons of her shirt falling away beneath his fingers sent shivers across her in anticipation of his next touch. The hunger in his gaze had her falling helplessly beneath his spell.

She'd meant to sound more sophisticated as they'd traded words. But the sensuous tickle of Race's laughter as he gave his undivided attention to her breasts proved too wicked. Need coursed hot and bright through her at the sudden pull of his mouth on her sensitive skin.

Her hands slipped from his hair as he moved down her body. She sank her fingers into his muscled forearms, enjoying the journey down to his wrists. She held onto him as his skillful touch brought sensation after sensation rolling through her. She drew a ragged breath as he cupped a cheek in each hand. An appreciative squeeze goodbye before he continued on his way.

The silken petals sliding against her skin were her undoing. She began to tremble as he traced the definition of muscles in her arms. From there, he made his way to the light lines where her bathing suit hid her skin from the sun and began with renewed effort. His touch already enough to have her body running toward an edge she hadn't known was so close. Her hands gripped his shoulders and she sucked in the corner of her bottom lip as a cry threatened to break free.

The release of her breasts to the humid air and the heat of Race's hands and mouth wound her tighter. Her body blazed with the need for more and Savanah cried out with relief when Race fit his hips to hers. His body was a sweet weight as he slowly entered her. She pushed against him as he held himself above her. Her breath was coming faster as he guided her to meet the pleasure of each slow, purposeful thrust.

Savanah wrapped her arms around Race's shoulders. Her hold tightened as she rode the rising tide of his body sliding in and out. Heat and desire twined together, gripping them both. The urgency of her need pushed her body to grip him tighter. Savanah felt Race thrust deeper and she responded without thinking.

Her body was reaching for release, and she tightened around Race. He faltered and Savanah's lips parted in a soundless cry as he gave a short, unexpected thrust that sent her spiraling into the orgasm that took control of her. She moaned softly as the flood of her heat convulsed around him, sending Race's body over the edge.

He gave a last thrust that locked them together and Savanah pressed into the pleasure that swept through her. His release joining hers. Every movement he made coaxed another ripple of her orgasm that left her gasping for air with its intensity.

Her body refused to let Race go. Selfishly wringing every pulse of his body for her own pleasure. From the first orgasm he'd brought as he'd teased her skin with the flower, her body had been in ecstasy. She couldn't tell where one climax ended and the next began. She only knew she wasn't ready for it to stop. She sank her fingers into the tense muscles of his butt. Reveling as he flexed in response. A movement she immediately felt as he slid deeper inside her.

She lay still as her heart slowly made its way back to normal. As her lungs remembered how to breathe for a purpose other than begging Race to touch her. He was quiet beside her, and Savanah was content to let him take his fill with both his eyes and his touch. Whatever magic had taken them, he wasn't the only one unwilling to disrupt it.

Savanah was glad Race didn't say anything. She had no words to describe what she was thinking or feeling. A flicker of lightning in the distance reflected off the mirrored surfaces in the room, beautiful and frightening in the same breath. The inadvertent comparison was too close for comfort.

Savanah closed her eyes against the darkness. Tomorrow, and whatever it would bring, would come soon enough. A shiver danced across her skin where she lay beside Race. They'd left the lanai door open and there was a diabolic chill to the breeze that swept the room. She cuddled closer as Race reached across her body and pulled the comforter over her cooling skin.

CHAPTER TWENTY-EIGHT

Savanah drew a deep breath, holding it for several seconds before letting it out slowly. She felt incredibly good this morning. She had done the *Reiki*, not out of a need to direct her inner energy to heal, but rather to just gather it and hold it to her for the peace it offered. Reiki was a common energy healing practice in the Islands. It was one of the things her doctor had embraced to use every available method to give her the best chance at recovering. One method on its own hadn't worked. Savanah's doctor believed the success was the result of different methods working together.

She didn't need to open her eyes to know Race was awake. Her senses tingled with awareness as a result of the Reiki, and she felt the influx of vitality as he left the oblivion of deep sleep behind. She remained sitting on the balcony, enjoying the energy that danced through her for a few minutes longer. Only when her body told her it was ready did she execute the kata to bring the Reiki session to a close. She held her hands together and whispered the silent prayer of thanks before opening her eyes.

Race was watching her. Just as her senses had said he was. "I'm sorry. I didn't mean to wake you."

"You didn't. But you could have." He glanced down where she'd slept beside him. "Waking to an empty bed isn't all it's cracked up to be."

"I'll keep that in mind." Savanah swallowed trying to ward off the tension breathing to life between them.

"You showered. I'm sorry I missed that. I could have helped."

Savanah reached up to her damp hair. The comfort she'd enjoyed from knowing Race was with her began to evaporate. Not because of him. She didn't know what to say. She rose and came into the room, where she'd placed her clothes before getting in the shower. Turning her back to Race, she began to dress, pulling her clothes on beneath the bath towel she'd been sitting in with practiced ease. She hoped the simple act would stave off the nerves threatening to take hold of her.

There was an uncomfortable weight to the silence growing between them. She knew Race's eyes had been on her when she sat outside. Too bad she couldn't discern his thoughts as easily. She chanced a glance at him. He was pulling his clothes on, no longer watching her.

"I'm beginning to realize I prefer our verbal sparring and the sound of your voice mocking me to the quiet calm you use to hide your feelings," he said, his tone guarded.

"I was sitting in a towel. That can't be considered hiding." Savanah groaned as she realized she'd just proven his point. "I wasn't hiding . . . I was just thinking."

"So was I."

Savanah could discern nothing from Race's voice. His back was still to her, so she didn't have the benefit facial expressions might have offered. None of this was how she'd intended the morning to go.

It occurred to her, the night hadn't either. Race's arrival at the resort had been completely unexpected. Sleeping with him wasn't on her agenda.

"I was wondering, did you being cleared from your wheelchair include what happened last night?"

Savanah paused, then continued buttoning her shirt to cover the tremble of her fingers. "I'm not sure. I don't think I asked that question."

"Maybe you should have."

"Called my doctor before having sex with you?" Savanah nearly choked. She thought she'd steeled herself for talking with Race and how badly it always seemed to end. "Are you sorry about what happened?"

"Yes." Race frowned at her. "No. Dammit, Savanah!"

Her fists clenched to keep her from flinching at how badly Race's words hurt. "Got it. You don't have to say anything else. Besides, it wasn't your fault. I instigated everything." Savanah hoped her face held its mask against the humiliation flooding her.

Race growled as he rubbed the day's growth of beard on his chin. "Jesus, Savanah. We're less than two feet apart. The sun's barely up. And just like that we're back to talking two different languages. You make it damn hard for a man to say he cares about you."

Savanah went back to the balcony. Race was right. The comfort they'd shared last night burned off like dew in the morning sun. She thought she should bring the chairs inside, or Garth's winds would turn them into projectiles. She wouldn't be coming back to the room, anyway.

Race's phone rang, but Savanah didn't bother to turn around. She fixed her attention on the sky beginning to lighten overhead. Grey clouds roiled as far as the eye could see. Savanah began to shake. The last thing she'd seen as the ocean slammed her down into the sea floor was the endless churning water above her. Giant swirls cascading one on top of the other, down the perfect line of the wave that was crushing her. To see the clouds overhead mimicking the frothing formations that killed her, froze her in place as she watched in horror.

It was an eerie déjà vu that made her heart pound.

She had never doubted the stories she'd been told since birth. But as Savanah stood looking up into a sky she'd never seen, she couldn't breathe.

If what she saw was any indication, the sky god was angry enough to kill everything in his path.

"It's picking up speed. The path is changing. I have to go," Race said from behind her. "My office is waiting for me. What are you going to do?"

"Yes. You should go. You shouldn't be here with me. The people of the Big Island need you to do your job." Savanah had things to do as well. She needed to get down to the front desk. She felt her phone vibrating in her pocket.

"I know my job," Race told her with heat in his voice.

"Let's hope you do, Director Weston."

"You don't sound like you believe that. Why? You didn't get the job so you're sure whomever did can't possibly be qualified?"

So, he knew she'd been one of the candidates. That was the first time he'd said anything about it. Savanah wondered how long he had known. "I'm just tired of you thinking you're so much better than everyone else. You might not believe this, Race. I hope you are better. We need you to be. But I'm afraid. I'm afraid because I'm not sure you understand that." Savanah reached forward, imploring him to understand. "We need you. But you need us, too. This time it isn't about you being the lone hero riding to the rescue."

Her hand dropped at the frown he gave her. "You don't want the help of the people around you," she continued. "What is it? We don't have anything of value to offer someone in your position? Isn't that why you moved your office on this side? So you'd be down low enough to find out?"

Savanah hated that her breath was coming fast enough she could feel her chest heaving. This was her home. Right now, the danger approaching was scaring the hell out of her. She tried to shake it off, get a handle on it. Being afraid wasn't going to help anyone. But for the first time since she'd woken up in the hospital, Savanah was. Except now it wasn't for herself. It was for everything and everyone she held dear.

"You need to get somewhere safe." Race put his hands on her arms. "After last night—look, it's okay to be afraid. That's why I need to know you're safe."

Savanah shook his hands off and stepped away from him, determined to hold on to what strength she could. Fear wasn't going to make her run away when people were counting on her. "Everyone needs to get somewhere safe. As soon as we've swept the hotel and accounted for everyone, that's the plan." Savanah nearly laughed at how ridiculous it sounded. There wasn't going to be anywhere safe from what was coming.

"Let someone else do it." Race told her.

"Is that what you're going to do? Let someone else be put in harm's way?" Savanah felt her emotions rising, threatening to spill over. "That's not how we do things here. That's not how I do things."

"God dammit. You are so stubborn. You're twisting what I say."

"You are wasting valuable time."

"And you still can't see I'm not wrong!" Race almost yelled. The first crash of thunder outside absorbed his emotion as Savanah flinched and stepped further away. "Don't wait too long, Savanah. I've given the order that once Garth hits, emergency personnel won't be allowed to respond."

Savanah made sure to wait until the door had closed behind him before she replied. "Don't hold your breath for me to call, Director Weston. It would be over my dead body."

CHAPTER TWENTY-NINE

Leayne found Savanah in the resort's Ocean Tower, going room to room to ensure that all guests had been evacuated. Manny and Charlie were doing the same in the Mauka towers. So far, they'd found fewer than 50 people to be evacuated down to the ballroom kitchens.

Savanah couldn't help being surprised at the people she did find. Their expectation that the storm would disappear was mind-boggling. They seemed unaware that their refusal to evacuate endangered not only themselves, but those who had to look for them, as well.

Savanah knew she couldn't force anyone to do anything, up to a certain point. If she had to, she would explain the same thing Race had said to her: there would come a time when no one would be coming to the rescue. Anyone unwilling to do as they were told now would be taking full responsibility for their decisions. So far, she hadn't come across anyone who hadn't been willing to follow her directions once she explained what followed rescue was recovery . . . of the bodies.

Harsh? Maybe. But true. And it got the point across.

The kitchen beneath the giant ballroom was the safest place Savanah could think of. There were no windows, no roof to blow off. As it was tucked away in the bowels of the main hotel, the storm would have to destroy the layers of building above them before it could harm them. It was the next best thing to having a storm cellar. There would be food and water and walls of steel that had been built to prevent a fire in the kitchen from spreading to any other part of the hotel. That safeguard would offer at least some protection against the dangers Garth was going to unleash on the island.

"I know where the film crew is," Leayne said to Savanah as she joined in knocking on room doors.

"Security. Is anyone in there? The hotel is being evacuated," Savanah called out as she knocked on another door. "Please tell me in California," she answered Leayne.

"We couldn't get that lucky. They're supposed to be filming somewhere close to *End of the World*. They found someone to take them to caves down there," Leayne answered.

The cliff jumping at End of the World, as it had come to be called on the Internet, had grown more popular than the sacred grounds it sat upon. Far fewer people were aware of the history. One of the final battles among the Hawaiian people had taken place on the barren lava field. Its outcome forever changing the course of Hawaii and her people. More than three hundred warriors had perished, along with the sacred practices they'd been fighting for.

Savanah knew there were numerous caves at the water line and in the rugged hillside above. The cliffs, which had become so famous to jump from, marked the beginning of the trails to get to the caves.

"Could it get any worse?" Savanah grimaced, sorry for the words the moment they left her mouth. Things could always get worse.

"Since you asked . . . I saw Clark's car in the parking lot."

"No one's seen him for days. Why bother to show up now?"

Not that Savanah cared. Clark and his issues had taken a backseat. The whole world was watching as Garth headed straight for them, picking up speed along the way. Meteorologists around the world scrambled to alter their forecasts. Savanah had known from the moment she looked at the sky that morning what would happen. Garth was going to unleash his full fury upon the island.

"Did you see the clouds this morning?" she asked Leayne as they continued down to the next floor.

"Fucking scary. I got some great pictures of it."

Savanah laughed at that. Of course, Leayne would have taken the time to snap a few photos.

"Is there anyone who knows where those caves are that we can send after the film guys?" Leayne asked after they'd cleared another set of rooms.

"Any staff left who do, need to stay here with everyone we've evacuated down in the kitchens," Savanah replied.

"I should be able to find it. I've been there once or twice."

"No." Savanah rejected her friends' suggestion. "*Trying* to find something in this weather isn't an option."

Feeling a sudden twinge, Savanah put a hand to her back.

"Are you okay?" Leayne stepped forward.

"Fine. Just a little more out of shape than I realized." She saw the concern in her friend's eyes. "I haven't done this much walking in a while. I'm fine, though. Really."

"Okay. What's the plan?"

"We finish clearing the towers and everything here first. Once we have it all shut down and everyone is safe down below, I'll go get them."

"Why you?" Leayne argued.

"I've got the best chance of finding them. I know the coastline better than anyone here. I grew up climbing those cliffs."

"If you can't get them, you can't. At some point you need to admit that."

Savanah pictured Race's worried face as he told her the same thing. She wasn't accepting the words any better from her friend. "Don't worry. I'll find them and get them back here in plenty of time. We can all hold hands and sing campfire songs while the whole world goes to hell above us."

That had them laughing, despite knowing it wasn't going to be that easy.

"Is your family safe?" Savanah didn't look back. She knew Leayne was right behind her.

"I've got them downstairs. We decided not to separate. How about you?"

"They're all together. Dad isn't happy I'm not with them, but he understands. I know he'll take care of everyone." Savanah trusted her father more than anyone in the world. When he'd said their family would be okay, she believed him.

"Any idea where Clark is?" Savanah asked as they cleared another floor.

"Not a clue." Leayne shrugged. "Speaking of our fearless leader though, he'll be losing his job when all this is through. I've been keeping Corporate up on things since he disappeared. It won't matter what excuse he gives to them. They're aware of his severe dereliction of duty. They are also aware of everything you've done."

"I'm glad they know about Clark." Relief filled Savanah. "And thank you."

"It's only right." Leayne gave a satisfied look to Savanah. "I wanted you to know in case you were still thinking you might lose your job. If we survive . . ." Her laugh didn't have anything to do with funny. "I'll expect you at work."

CHAPTER THIRTY

Race hadn't stopped moving or talking since he'd left Savanah and Onimura Resort that morning. The good news was that no one was questioning his orders anymore.

The fact they'd started evacuating yesterday had given them a small advantage. He marked areas along the coast on the map before him as updates confirmed they were clear of people. He'd already confirmed with the Coast Guard, the National Guard, the heads of both airports and both port chiefs that once the hurricane cleared, they would assess damages, make necessary repairs, and begin bringing in emergency supplies.

Race took a call from the Governor, who was watching things unfold from the safety of Oahu. He assured Race that, no matter where the hurricane came ashore, the state would weather the storm together and help would be immediately available. The base commanders of every military branch on Oahu echoed the sentiment, putting all their personnel on alert.

The small Army detachment from the Pohakuloa Training Area, at the center of the Big Island between Mauna Kea and Mauna Loa, had already mobilized. The extra people and equipment assisted in evacuating the hard-to-reach areas and extending the reach of emergency services already stretched thin. Race couldn't help but be impressed by how seamlessly everyone had begun working together once there was a direction to go. Everyone was poised and ready. It had been a matter of him pointing the way.

Which made him think of Savanah. He hated to admit it, but everything that had happened with her, the things she'd said to him, had influenced his decisions. If it hadn't been for her pushing him, he might not have acted so preemptively. He wanted to call her. He just didn't know what he would say. As if on cue, his phone rang.

"We've got a media disaster in the making."

Race grunted at Steve's comment. "Tell me something I don't know."

"I'm not talking about the hurricane. Police just got a call from someone saying they belong to a film crew, and they've just realized they're in trouble," Steve explained.

"They've just now realized they're in trouble? Seriously—" Race fell silent momentarily. "How many people are we talking, Steve? Where are they and why is this the first we're hearing about it?"

"From the information they're giving dispatch, 'somewhere south of Kona.' I know, descriptive, right." The normally controlled assistant made a disgusted sound. "They were booked at Onimura but have been out on location filming the last few days. Seems like the film's director wasn't worried about a storm that wasn't happening."

"Guess he's worrying now."

Race should have known it would have something to do with Savanah and her resort. From the moment things had started, everything about the hurricane coming at them had been linked to her. He had given up trying to understand how or why. It just was. If he didn't know better, he'd think the world revolved somehow around the woman he found so attractive, and so very frustrating.

"The director wants someone to come and get them." Steve hesitated, "It sounded like he plans on filming their rescue."

"They'll be lucky if it's a rescue. Tell HPD to keep them talking while I get someone on the phone at Onimura and see what they know about it." Now, he had a reason to call her.

As he listened to her number ringing, Race wondered what the odds were she would see who was calling and not answer. He was surprised how relieved he was when he heard the call connect.

"Race?"

"What can you tell me about a lost film crew?" Race asked immediately.

"We've been looking for them since yesterday. We just got word on their location. As soon as we finish clearing the rooms, I'm heading out to get them."

"Send someone else. It shouldn't be you. There has to be someone closer."

"Barking at me like I'm one of your employees isn't going to work, Race." Her voice sounded more distracted than angry.

His mind whirled trying to come up with an option they could both live with, and that she would accept. "You should continue running the evacuation at the resort. It's your emergency plan. Delegate. You can't do it all and your responsibility is there."

"Race, I don't think you understand. They aren't somewhere you can find by simply saying '*Hey Google, take me to this secret spot in Hawaii.*' Where they went isn't on the map. The film crew hired someone to take them there. So, no, I can't just send someone to try to find them. Even if I could, I wouldn't. I don't know if you've looked outside, but we're about an hour from getting the crap kicked out of us."

"Which is why you need to send someone else, Savanah."

"I'm the best chance they have at getting back here."

"I'm the Civil Defense Director for the island. If I say you aren't going, then dammit, you need to do as I'm telling you and send someone else while you keep your ass somewhere safe," he snarled as frustration got the better of him.

Savanah gasped, "Race Weston, you did *not* just say that. How is it you are such a control freak with everything but your feelings? I mean, don't hold back, go ahead and hang it all out there. If I didn't think you were a jerk . . ." Savanah stuttered to a stop.

"Just stay put." There wasn't a chance in hell that Savanah was going to do as he asked. The sound of subtle laughter drifted through over the line.

"Sure thing, Director. I'll just sit my happy ass down and do as you command."

"Savanah . . ." Why did he have the feeling his life depended on hers? Race forced himself to calm down. "Please."

Her reply was barely audible and for a moment, Race thought maybe he'd gotten through to her. "You'd better get going, Race. Don't worry about this one, I've got it," was the last thing he heard.

Race stared at the ceiling for long moments as he weighed his options. He had no doubt that Savanah Jordan was the most maddening female he'd ever met in his life. His mind made up, he got Steve back on the line. "Relay to HPD to tell the film crew stay put. Someone's coming for them."

Race started to hang up but brought the phone back to his ear. "And Steve. Pass along to that damn director, if anyone gets hurt rescuing them, they'll be answering to me. I'll end up owning the studio they work for."

He grabbed a radio from the charging rack. If Savanah headed out into the storm before he got there, she had better hope there was someone around who could point him in the right direction. Otherwise, Race would tear the island apart looking for her. He knew her well enough already to know she'd go alone.

Well, she should know him well enough by now to know he was going to come looking for her.

Race hesitated, the door of his SUV hanging open. Could it be possible that soft laughter she'd sent back through the phone, her refusal tempered by her teasing, had come from knowing he would follow her? Jumping in and shutting out the rain, he started the engine.

CHAPTER THIRTY-ONE

Time slowed down as the sound of the hurricane intensified outside the resort's walls. The eerie calm of the preceding days was gone. In its place was something worse. A fury that defied reasoning. As if Garth was angry at anything that dare stand against it. Its wrath vibrating in the air with a violent turbulence that Savanah had never experienced. Even in the hallways, Savanah could hear the constant beating of wind-driven rain against the building. An incessant, varying whistle of ever-changing pitch made her flinch continually. She knew it was a result of the gale winds forcing their way through every crack and crevice.

The morning breeze had brought the smell of rain, a scent that Savanah would have savored on any other day. Something she couldn't bring herself to do, knowing the floods that were sure to come.

Hours of steady rain had drowned the comforting smell of soil washed clean by nature's hand, replacing it with the suffocating thickness of mud.

A huge clap of thunder sounded. Even muffled by the walls, it was enough to back her against the wall. Savanah stared down the hallway. The air reverberated as if the building had been struck. The lights didn't flicker, so she knew it hadn't. Still, it had to have been close. An almost too pure scent flushed everything else away, seconds before the air turned to the acrid scent of sizzling electricity. The hair on her body stood up as white light flashed from the bottom crack of every door in the hallway. The immediate boom that sounded confirmed the lightning was directly over them.

"That one was close," Savanah said to no one in particular.

"Yeah. No kidding," Leayne agreed.

"Am I the only one feeling like the floors are repeating themselves?"

"I've seen what comes next in that movie. If a guy in a fedora and red striped shirt jumps out, I'm gonna scream worse than when I see a gecko."

"Don't I wish this was a bad dream we could wake up from," Savanah responded.

Both women jumped at the sound of Manny's voice over the radio.

"Charlie and I are all clear here. We are making our way down to the kitchens with the last of the guests we found and the staff from the front. Other than your tower, the resort is clear."

"Roger that, Manny." Savanah sagged with relief. His news took another thing off her list of concerns.

"I think this was our last room," Leayne chimed in.

Savanah looked up and down the hallway at the room numbers. Leayne was right. They'd made it to the bottom floor.

"We're done here as well," Savanah said into the radio. "Leayne is heading for you. Until you get an all-clear, no one leaves."

"I should go with you to get the film crew," Leayne said firmly.

"No. You know as well as I do there needs to be a manager down there. You're the highest-ranking person here." Savanah wasn't kidding. She was being practical.

"Clark might be in there," Leayne offered.

"I'm not sure if I hope you're right or wrong." Savanah hadn't given

Clark much thought over the last few hours. "We aren't taking that chance. Get going. Besides, your family is down there, and they'll be waiting for you. You should be with them. I'll be back as quick as I can."

They hugged, their arms holding on an extra few moments, in case it was the last time. Nothing more was said as Leayne went one way and Savanah went the other. There was no sense in arguing. That wouldn't accomplish anything but waste what precious time they had. Savanah's chances of making it to the film crew in time to get them to safety were ticking away.

Savanah watched Leayne cross the main floor toward the underground tram that would take her to the ballroom and the kitchen where everyone was waiting. Knowing she would be out of harm's way was another relief.

Lightning streaked across the sky, and the lights flickered this time. Savanah dropped to a crouch and froze, waiting in case the backlash of thunder blew out any of the glass. Brilliant streaks fractured the air outside again and the crackling of three hundred million volts blended with the immense detonation that followed. She held her breath waiting to see whether the power would remain on.

In the moment of deathly quiet that followed, as Savanah waited for the next strike, she heard a sound that wasn't supposed to be there. If the lightning hadn't stopped her, she wouldn't have heard it. She listened harder. The sound of things hitting the floor was unmistakable.

There wasn't supposed to be anyone left up here. Manny had said he had gathered all the remaining staff to safety. She looked over to the ornate front desk at the sound of swearing. It didn't matter who it was, Savanah needed to get them out of there. She went around the desk toward Pinky's office.

"Clark, what the hell are you doing?" Savanah stood in the doorway looking at her boss in shock. He sported a black eye.

Clark turned at the sound, keeping one hand behind him. "I thought you were with everyone else."

"Leayne and I just finished checking the rooms. The film people haven't been here since we started evacuating and someone needs to go get them. I'm heading there now while Leayne stays with everyone else in the lower kitchens." Savanah moved farther into the office, trying to see what Clark had been doing. The way he mirrored her movements made her uncomfortable.

"Why aren't you in the wheelchair?"

Savanah ignored his question as she craned her neck to get a better look behind him. The resort safe was open. "What are you doing, Clark?"

"You were the proof I don't discriminate. You didn't have to do anything but sit behind your desk and be handicapped. But you couldn't do that, could you," he hissed.

"I was never handicapped, Clark. I was recovering. I got my clearance yesterday." From the wild look in his eyes, Savanah didn't think her words got through.

Clark pulled his hand out to point a gun directly at Savanah. "You couldn't just mind your own damn business and keep your ass in the wheelchair." He kept the gun trained on the center of her body as he reached behind him to pick up the bags he'd been filling.

"You're robbing the safe?" Savanah didn't believe what she was seeing. "You ordered the guests to use the resort safe instead of the ones in their rooms . . . so you could steal the contents?" She stared at him dumbfounded. "There was no way for you to have known the hurricane would turn."

"You're right. I didn't. But you did. You kept telling anyone who would listen what you thought was going to happen." Clark gave her an evil smile. "I'll give you this much, Jordan. You were dead-on about that. Look at it this way. I believed you enough to put my plan into action. It really is a compliment. You should thank me."

Savanah sputtered in disbelief. "For what? Using me?"

"I knew you'd eventually hit the panic button and empty out the place.

You're too obsessive to leave anyone behind. All I had to do was wait and let you and the hurricane take care of the rest."

"You're the CEO of the largest resort on the island. You're not some thief." Savanah's mind was reeling with the shock of what she was seeing.

"There are people who don't care about anything but getting their money back. If you'd have left things alone, this might not have happened," Clark threw at her.

"Left what alone?" Savanah was thinking back to what she'd learned about Clark having left his last job under suspicious circumstances.

"I tried to tell you let them do what they wanted. But not you. You couldn't do that, could you."

Savanah hoped that if Clark talked long enough, he might not notice his arm tiring. The end of the barrel began to drift lower. There would be less of a chance he would hit something vital if the gun was pointing down. Savanah didn't want to think about him shooting her while the gun was pointed at her chest.

"Take whatever you came for. I'm not going to stop you." Savanah didn't have a choice.

"You couldn't stop me if you wanted to. But I can't just leave you here, either. And that's a problem. Instead of the hurricane being blamed for everything, you'll tell the police, and then I'll be on the run for the rest of my life. Either from the mob, or from the law. I don't have a mind to do either."

Clark waved the gun at her, motioning for her to turn around. "Let's go for a walk."

"Why don't you put the gun down. You don't need that." Savanah swallowed hard against the fear creeping over her. "I'm cooperating with you."

Clark broke out with a laugh that bordered on hysterics. "I'm not putting the gun down. I'm not that stupid."

"Where are we going?" Savanah walked sideways, keeping Clark in view. She wasn't about to turn her back to him.

Savanah's radio beeped and they both jumped as Leayne's voice came through.

"Made it to the basement. All good here. Cozy even. No sign of Clark. Get out there and find that film crew and then you get back here Savanah."

Clark waved his gun. "Tell her I found you as I was making sure everyone was evacuated. Tell her I am going with you. That I won't let you go out there alone."

Savanah stared in disbelief at the crazy man who used to be her boss.

"Tell her," Clark hissed, taking a step closer.

"She won't believe me."

"Make her believe you," he threatened.

Savanah raised the radio to her mouth. "Clark's with me. He's worried for my safety and insists he's going with me to help." Savanah didn't look away from where the gun still waved in her direction. She let her arm drop, praying Clark wouldn't notice the lack of beeping that would have signaled her release of the transmit button.

"Let's go." Clark pushed her forward with the gun barrel.

"Where are we going first?" If she could just keep him talking long enough for the others to hear . . .

His mouth twisted to begin a retort, but then he stopped. He leaned toward her as his eyes narrowed. Savanah's lips thinned as his gaze went from her face to the radio at her side. Clark bared his teeth, and she wasn't sure if it was a horrible smile or a silent howl. He motioned toward the desk and mouthed silently, "Put it down."

She had no choice. The beep as she let go of the Talk button, closing the open connection gave her away.

"You think you're so smart." Clark gave a triumphant smile. "The last everyone will know is I was out there helping you. It will be a shame that just when you were doing so well with your recovery, you have another accident. But I'm sure you won't be the only person this storm kills. Either way, your body is getting buried. If I'm lucky, I won't even have to shoot you. That damn hurricane outside will do the work for me."

Race pulled up to the resort's wide-open lobby. He wasn't surprised to see the bellman's desk was empty. The space that usually teemed with staff and visitors, was vacant. He walked farther in, searching in vain for someone who could direct him to Savanah. There was no sign of life other than the ever-increasing volume of Garth's malevolent chorus overhead. He turned to leave.

The sound of Savanah's voice stopped him: "Why don't you put the gun down. You don't need that. I'm cooperating with you." He ducked down behind the end of the counter and froze.

Seconds later, she walked out of the back office, followed by none other than Clark Dieter. Race leaned carefully around the counter trying to get a better view without being seen. Fear for Savanah gripped him as he saw the gun the CEO had pointed straight at her.

"Keep walking. We're going to take a little ride, you and I." Clark told her.

"I already said I won't stop you. Why don't you just leave?" Savanah said. Her voice broke and lost some of its bravado. Race's gut clenched as she pleaded with her boss. "That film crew is waiting for me. I'm only interested in getting them to safety. Clark, even you don't want to just leave them out there to die."

Clark stepped closer to Savanah, poking her with the gun as he growled at her. "It would be a shame for me to shoot you in the back just when you're walking again. Now move."

Savanah angled away from him, trying to put room between her and the gun. "What difference does it make, if you're just going to kill me anyway?"

Chapter Thirty-Two

"I told you. I'm not going to kill you. The hurricane is going to do it for me."

Race couldn't let them get outside. The further away they walked, the greater the chance Clark might turn and shoot him. It was now or never.

He launched his body across the floor and straight into the CEO.

Savanah turned at the unexpected movement from the shadows. As Race's body slammed into Clark, Savanah jumped for the gun in Clark's hand. The force of the men colliding knocked the gun loose and sent Savanah hurtling toward the floor. Race didn't let go at the sudden dull crack that sounded. It was drowned out by a deafening boom that shook the open lobby as a bolt of lightning struck the center of the courtyard.

"Get out of here!" Race yelled to Savanah.

Their bodies tangled together, the two men rolled across the floor. Instinct drove Race to get Clark as far away from Savanah as possible. Race used their momentum to lock his legs around Dieter's waist. By the time they came to a stop against one of the couches that decorated the lobby, Race had one arm threaded beneath Clark's and another locked securely around the man's neck. The grip of his legs around Clark's midsection allowed Race to tighten his arms in the sleeper hold.

He didn't give Clark Dieter a chance. Didn't ask for an explanation. He kept his arms locked tight until he was sure the man was no longer a threat. The moment Race saw the gun pointed at Savanah, the only thing that mattered was eliminating the threat to her.

Race flexed his arms to see if there was any answering movement. There wasn't.

Still, he released Clark cautiously, watching for any sign of the man regaining consciousness. He quickly unraveled the paracord from his wrist, and within seconds, tied Clark Dieter's hands securely behind his back. Only once he was sure the CEO wasn't going anywhere once he woke up did Race feel a sense of relief. He turned his head and look for Savanah to let her know it was safe to come out.

Seeing her still form on the floor, he dashed to her side. His heart thundered in his ears as he slid down beside her. He brushed the hair from her face only to find her lashes lay against her cheeks, her eyes closed.

"Savanah, can you hear me?" he asked gently. "Open your eyes if you can hear me, Savanah."

Relief flooded him when he saw her eyelashes begin to flutter. "That a girl. You can do it. Just open your eyes for me."

She gave a soft moan and slid one palm to the floor as if to put weight on it. Race felt relief turn to terror. "Don't move. I've got you." He held her more firmly to prevent her from causing further injury.

"Hold still. Just hold still," Race told her as she stirred again. He wasn't sure how to help her, but he was sure her moving would only make things worse.

"Why can't I get up?" Savanah asked him. "And why is my leg burning?"

"There was an accident. Your boss looked like he was going to kill you. It will be okay. I promise it will be okay," Race reassured her as he kept his arms tight.

"What are you talking about?" She tried to move her head to bring Race into view. "Race, you aren't making any sense."

"When you fell, it looks like your back . . . your legs aren't moving." Race hadn't wanted to say it. She should never have been there in the first place. He should have forced her to get somewhere safe. It was his job to protect people. Especially when they couldn't protect themselves. Even when they didn't want to protect themselves. He couldn't even protect one. The one that suddenly mattered the most.

Savanah turned her head slowly, first in one direction, then the other.

"Stop it. You shouldn't be moving." Race told her firmly despite the anguish filling him at what he'd done.

"Maybe Clark isn't the only one who's crazy. My neck seems to be working okay," Savanah said. She rolled her neck again slowly despite his protests.

He watched as she gingerly moved her arms. She was able to take her weight and raise her shoulders from the floor.

"You shouldn't be trying to move. I'm going to lay you down and call an ambulance." He lowered her body slowly back to the floor, releasing his hold on her one finger at the time.

"Race, wait. Help me turn over first," Savanah stopped him. "If I'm paralyzed like you seem to think, Race, I might need your help." He didn't return her tentative smile. "Hey, I'm not screaming in pain, so maybe your assessment is overly cautious."

"You haven't tried to move your legs yet." He regretted the words instantly and reached out to stop her from doing so. "God, I'm sorry."

"Maybe you don't have to be. I can feel my toes."

Relief flooded his face. He checked the hope that bloomed in his chest. "That's great. Now stop moving until we can get you to the hospital and get you checked out."

"Why do you think I'm hurt?" Savanah asked pointedly.

"I found you on the floor."

She nodded, as if remembering. "When I realized it was you jumping Clark, I tried to knock the gun away." She wet her lips. "By the way my leg is burning, I think it might have gone off."

Race looked down in surprise. Blood soaked through the leg of Savanah's pants and dripped to the floor. "Wait a minute . . ."

"Maybe you should find something to stop the bleeding, Race," Savanah suggested.

"Are you saying your legs, your back, that you think you're okay?"

"Other than I think I've been shot, yeah, I think I am." She beamed up at him.

"I'm going to stand up but we're going to go slow." Race got to his feet carefully. He kept Savanah in his arms and carried her toward the counter. "Does anything else hurt? How bad is the pain?"

Savanah nodded. "Not nearly as bad as it would have been if Clark had shot me in the chest."

He swore again under his breath, wishing he were close enough to land a fist on the still unconscious CEO. Race returned his attention to Savanah. "We need to get your pants off."

"You're kidding. Now. Here?" Savanah tried to joke.

"I need to see your leg so I can bandage it." Now that it looked like her back hadn't been reinjured, Race was thinking more clearly. He didn't realize how serious he sounded until he heard her teasing.

Savanah's hair had come loose and was blowing around them both as wind whipped through the open doors. He fell captive to her gaze, hopelessly ensnared in the blue depths with their blazing ring of white. He couldn't remember ever having seen anything more beautiful in his life.

"We really do need to stop the bleeding and I need your pants off for that," Race tried again, only this time he cupped her cheek with his palm and returned her smile. He could see the blood soaking further down her pants leg.

Savanah agreed. Race held her, taking her weight easily so her hands were free. She released the zipper and began to wiggle them over her hips.

"A little help here, Director Weston, would be much appreciated."

Race bent so she could lean on him while he used both hands to push the material past the curve of her hips. His hands didn't linger. His attention focused entirely on her legs as he lowered her slacks.

"God dammit." He couldn't help himself as he saw the furrow the bullet had made just above her knee.

"I'm not an expert, but this looks like it's just a scratch. All we need is a little superglue and I'll be fine."

Race rolled his eyes up briefly at her words before he continued examining the wound. The woman was incorrigible when she wanted to be.

"We're lucky the bullet wasn't an inch the other direction." Race leaned her against the counter so she could keep herself upright without putting weight on her leg. "Where's the first aid kit?"

"In the office." Savanah pointed to the door she and Clark had come from.

Race vaulted over the counter rather than walking around. He didn't have any trouble locating the kit. Walking back to Savanah, he spied a roll of duct tape behind the counter and grabbed it as well.

Savanah held still as Race pulled things from the kit. She wasn't surprised he knew first aid. It would have been more of a surprise if he hadn't.

"This is going to hurt," Race warned as he ripped open an antiseptic wipe. He knelt in front of her, bringing his face level with her thigh.

"You may not have noticed, but pain is one of the few things I'm good at," Savanah replied with a half-smile.

Race gritted his teeth as he gently wiped the blood off her skin. He didn't waste time, making quick work of cleaning the area. Then he surprised Savanah by blowing across her skin, as if to ease the pain.

"The bandages in there aren't going to be big enough," Savanah said.

"I was afraid of that." Race nodded to where he'd set the roll of tape.

"Wondered what that was for." She tried not to cringe.

"Now you know. I didn't see any superglue," he explained. It didn't seem fair for him to make light of the situation, given it was Savanah doing the bleeding.

He opened several packages of sterile dressings and pressed them to her leg. "Hold these in place."

Savanah complied as Race ripped several pieces of tape. They worked together to quickly cover the bandages. Savanah bit down on her lip as Race taped the skin together.

"You okay?" Race asked when he was done. She was right. She was good at pain. He'd only felt her flinch once, and she hadn't made a sound.

"I've had worse." Savanah breathed out slowly.

Race brought her pants up from where they'd pooled at her feet, so she wouldn't have to bend down. Moving her leg would pull the tape, and then her skin where the bullet had torn through her flesh. He'd had to make the dressing tight enough to stop the bleeding. It wasn't perfect, but it would do for now. He held her steady as she fastened her pants back over her hips.

"Thanks. That doesn't feel as terrible as I was expecting. It just has to hold until we're out of this mess," Savanah remarked as Race rose to his feet in front of her. She put a hand to his chest and inclined her head toward a spot behind him. "And thank you for saving me. You know. From the crazy man over there on the floor."

Race saw the spot of blood on her lip and the swelling from where she'd clenched it between her teeth. He passed his thumb over the tender area. "I thought you were good with pain." He stopped the retort he knew she'd make with another gentle sweep of his thumb.

Bending his head to hers, he apologized with a kiss.

Chapter Thirty-Three

"We need to go get the film crew. They aren't going to survive where they're at," Savanah reminded him when his lips released hers. She didn't mind that Race continued caressing her neck with the hand buried beneath her hair.

Savanah's hand rested against his cheek; she didn't remember putting it there. Seeing the lines of concern that creased his forehead, she brought her other hand up so that she could massage his temples. He had a lot on his plate. Maybe if she quit fighting so hard, Race wouldn't have to fight back so much. If they worked together, they could accomplish so much more.

There was a sigh on the wind that had nothing to do with the storm as the universe drew a breath of relief. The awareness of it kissed her skin, catching Savanah by surprise with the sudden thrill that coursed through her. It made her smile to think perhaps they'd finally joined hands and were jumping off the cliff together.

"No one should be going out in this," Race answered in a tone that said he had hoped she might have changed her mind.

"We can't just leave them out there, Race. Not when I know we can get to them."

Rather than reply, Race pulled up the latest satellite images of Garth on his phone. The storm was almost directly on top of them. "We'd never make it back in time."

Savanah laughed. "We don't need a satellite to know where the hurricane is, Race." She pointed past the lobby doors. "That jet-engine scream above our heads would be Garth."

He grimaced. "You just proved my point why no one should be out there."

"Why don't you quit arguing for once and trust me. I can get us to the film crew, and we can save them." Savanah glanced outside and for a moment, her confidence wavered. "But our time, and theirs, is running out."

"You can't get . . ." Race stopped. "Us? You're asking me to go with you?"

Savanah stared wide-eyed. "Isn't that why you're here? So we can go get them? Unless you plan on staying here while I go find our lost director and his people."

He glanced over his shoulder. "We should do something with him."

"Manny and Charlie are downstairs with Leayne. They can handle him with the way you've got him trussed up." She looked around. "My radio is in the office. Clark made me tell the others he was going with me to help. When he realized I tried to leave the channel open so they would hear everything, he made me get rid of it."

"Stay here. I'll get it," Race told her. He disappeared back behind the counter, returning with the radio moments later.

"Savanah to Security, over." She watched Race double-check the paracord he'd tied Clark with.

"Go ahead Savanah," Manny responded.

"I don't have time to explain. Dieter is in the lobby and needs to be evacuated to your location. Bring Charlie and someone else with you." Savanah stopped but then pressed the button again quickly. "And Manny, keep him restrained until I return. No matter what he tells you."

"Copy that."

"One more thing, Manny. Tell Leayne Race is with me." Savanah looked up at Race. "Okay, that's taken care of. Can we get a move on now?"

Race picked her up and strode purposefully out the front door. "We're probably going to die." He carried Savanah out to his SUV, parked on the sidewalk.

"I could have walked out here."

"I know." Race deposited her on the passenger seat and closed the door.

Savanah looked out the window. The way he'd pulled onto the sidewalk, he might as well have driven all the way into the lobby. She waited for him to settle in the driver's seat. "Nice park job."

"I thought so," Race shot back. "Which way?"

Savanah pointed south. "End of the World. If we don't run into anything blocking the roads or flooding, we should be there in twenty minutes. Then we start looking and with a little luck, we find what rock they tucked behind for shelter." Savanah knew they were going to need more than a little luck. "Let's hope we find that sooner than later."

Race groaned. "From what I remember of my island tour when I arrived, the cliffs in that area are pretty sheer. I don't remember seeing anything flat enough to walk on, let alone use for shelter. I do remember thinking those thousands of acres of coastline would never be inhabitable. The area was too dangerous and too remote."

"Some things you need to be up close and personal to see. Native Hawaiians walked the trail to Kealakekua Bay along those cliffs for centuries. Without the benefit of fancy footwear or gadgets to guide them," Savanah reminded him.

"Up close and personal on fifty-foot cliffs in a C4, I think I'll stick to my first prediction." He tightened his grip on the wheel.

"You really should try being more optimistic. We aren't going to die," Savanah said.

"And you know this because you have a crystal ball . . ." The wind was so powerful, Race struggled to keep it from pushing the heavy SUV across the road.

"No. I've done it before. This isn't what it feels like," Savanah said.

"Done what before?" Race's eyes never left the road.

"Died." Savanah laced her fingers through his. "It isn't anything like this. This is called living."

Reaching the entrance to the End of the World took longer than Savanah expected. Not because they'd seen another vehicle on the road. Just them and a Category 4 hurricane, which slowed them to a crawl as they did their best to avoid the branches and rubbish littering the road from the winds whipping about them. Anything not tied down could become a projectile.

She could almost feel Garth's fury at their continued defiance. As if the storm took a personal affront to their audacity in believing they could walk unscathed through his might. Savanah knew it was stupid to be out. Since she was the one who'd insisted on going to rescue the film crew, she kept that to herself as Race pulled onto the access road for the popular cliff-diving spot that was their destination.

"Now what? There's a gate and it's locked." Race pointed in front of the SUV to the heavy galvanized gate that looked more like it was for livestock than vehicles. Several locks had been strung together at the ends of a thick chain that secured the gate to a chunk of lava the size of a Volkswagen. "Maybe you're wrong and they aren't here. They wouldn't have gone past a locked gate."

She looked at him dumbfounded. "Really? Don't even tell me you believe that. A locked gate only stops people who follow the rules. Rules don't seem to be our Hollywood director's thing. Besides, from the information I've gotten, this is the way they went."

Savanah told him the combination and waited. When he didn't make a move to get out, she looked at him. "Do you want me to open it?"

"What I want is for you to tell me we can turn around and get the hell out of here. I don't know if you noticed, but we only got this far by using the braille method of driving. The sound of us running over the reflectors on the road was how I knew we were still on it." He flexed his fingers where he was still gripping the steering wheel. "But I know that isn't going to happen."

"Race—"

"Look, we aren't going to make it much farther, Savanah. And there's nowhere out there to hide for them, or us . . . how far from here do you think they are?"

"I can't say for sure. Hopefully, only a mile or two. They should have started back this way once they realized the weather wasn't going to get better."

"A mile or two. You say that like it's nothing."

Savanah watched as Race weighed their options. Her hand clamped down on the door as another gust buffeted the SUV and rocked it hard enough that she felt the wheels on her side leave the ground. Race's arm shot across her and pinned her to the seat as the wind screamed in fury. She wanted to ask Race to shut the windows and seal out the earsplitting whine as Garth roared around them but didn't. The gap was necessary to keep the intense pressure of the hurricane from blowing the glass out.

"We can't see anything out there but rain. Look at it, Savanah. It might as well be the ocean trying to swallow us."

"It's nothing like the ocean," Savanah corrected, even though she knew what Race was trying to say.

In Hawaii, the daily afternoon cloudbursts brought rain so thick and heavy it formed a solid curtain that brought traffic to a standstill. The line of rain so defined, it would move over the land with the precision of a carwash conveyer belt.

What was happening outside was the opposite.

The huge raindrops pelted them chaotically. One minute the wind drove them like shrapnel from a bomb exploding in every direction, only to gather them together with its next breath, hurling it outward like a giant net.

"You saw the downed poles we passed. Electricity has to be out." He waved his phone in her direction. "The cell towers are probably gone, too." Race squinted through the windshield. "There's nothing out there but cliff, Savanah. Unless you want to call that dirt path ahead of us a road.

"The last text said they were in the vehicles and trying to drive back to the gate. They stopped because they couldn't see to drive anymore," Savanah explained, desperation seeping through in the ragged edges of her voice.

"But you think we can."

"All hell is being unleashed on the Gold Coast of the Big Island. We expected these conditions. They are what you've been warning people to prepare for."

"And here we are, driving through the middle of it."

"They aren't going to be safe for much longer." Savanah felt the grip she'd kept on her fear slipping. Who was she kidding? They weren't safe now. Not the group. Not she and Race. Not anyone.

She tried to imagine things from Race's eyes. There was nothing but lava rock on one side and pounding ocean on the other. Savanah grabbed her door handle.

He frowned, then cursed, pulling her back into her seat and cinching her seatbelt for emphasis. He repeated the combination to the gate, then jumped out himself.

By the time Race to returned to the truck, he was soaked through his rain gear. He might as well not have been wearing anything. Savanah turned on the heat as Race put the SUV in gear.

"How many are there?" Race kept his eyes focused on the road that was no wider than a goat path, and had turned into a shallow, rushing stream.

"A couple dozen or so. Depends on how many extras they took with them for the shoot." God, she hoped that was all.

"That wasn't something you thought you should mention sooner?" Race muttered. "My information was a crew of five, maybe six. We can't fit two dozen people in here."

"Let's just find them, Race." Savanah was working on a plan. But it would require more than a little luck. It wasn't up to her. They'd need permission. No sense making him worry any more than he already was.

The silence as they both concentrated for any sign of the crew competed against the roar outside the vehicle. Savanah screamed as forked lightning lit up the sky and rent the air.

"Race, stop. There they are."

The group had been smart enough to pull their two vans high and tight to a rock overhang. It offered a small amount of protection.

"Can you still get up-to-date satellite images on your phone?" Savanah asked as they proceeded slowly.

"They're out. I checked when we were at the gate. There wasn't any signal."

"Try again. That area is known for being a dead spot. We're higher up now and not sitting in a basin," Savanah encouraged. Being a dead zone added to the danger of cliff-jumping at End of the World. When someone was in trouble, calling for help was almost impossible. "You said the group *called* for help. It's why I was sure they were still inside the gate. But they couldn't have made that call if they were within a mile of it. It wouldn't have gone through."

He grunted at her explanation. "That's handy to know."

Savanah nodded toward his phone. "I've lived here my whole life. Those are things you know. Try again." She knew right know her optimism had to be enough for both of them.

"I've got a signal."

Savanah wasn't going to waste it. "How far away is the eye?" That would be their best chance.

"No more than an hour." He told her as he displayed the images she'd requested. "It will still be ugly. Only marginally less ugly than this."

"When the eyewall passes over, we need to move."

"That van isn't going anywhere." Race pointed at the tire on the lead van that was obviously flat.

"I'm not talking about driving."

They both flinched as a rock the size of a wheelbarrow bounced like a basketball off the hood of their SUV. The boulder rocked the vehicle like it was a little red wagon instead of six thousand pounds of metal. That was all the proof Savanah needed to know the eyewall was getting close. The wind was reaching deadly strength. They weren't safe in the vehicles. They wouldn't be safe outside. But her plan was the best chance they had. It was the only chance they had.

"Secrets don't make friends, Savanah," Race prodded. "Care to share what you're thinking?"

"As soon as the edge of the eye clears us, we start climbing."

"Climb where?" Race waved toward the hillside above them that was nothing but endless black lava, barren of vegetation thanks to its unforgiving sharp lines and density.

"If we don't die from the debris, we won't survive being picked up and tossed on those rocks. Savanah, the wind is gusting up to 170 miles per hour out there . . ." Race was almost shouting.

"We're just as likely to fall into one of those crevices and die as we are to be hit by the boulders being tossed around, or tossed back into the ocean," he went on. "You've already gone through that once. I don't want to watch you go through it a second time. Even if we survived the injuries, no one will be able to find us for hours, maybe days. I'm not letting anyone go out there."

"We aren't letting anyone do anything. We're going to tell them if they want to live, they have to go out there," Savanah corrected calmly in the face of Race's desperation. Just because she wasn't yelling didn't mean she didn't understand why he was.

"You're crazy if you think I'm going to send people out in that."

"You already know I'm crazy so that isn't much of a surprise now, is it. We'll make it." Savanah didn't waver.

Race tried again. "Look. I agree about using the calm when the eye comes over us to get moving. We need to get everyone in the two vehicles that are running and try to get out of here. There was a low point a couple of miles back. That should offer more protection than here."

"We don't want a low point. We need to get to higher ground. The vehicles can't take much more," Savanah reiterated as he shook his head in denial. "We wait for the lull and then we go."

"There's nothing out there Savanah. There isn't anywhere to go." Race forced his hand through his hair.

"You're wrong." Savanah took Race's face in her hands and pressed her lips to his to shut him up. She was scared, too. Giving in to her fear wouldn't help. She turned his face so he was looking out the window at the mountainside. "There are caves up there. Lava tubes that run deep into the island. If we can get to them, we'll be safe."

"You want to climb that?" Race asked, his mouth falling open.

"I need you to trust me. Just this once. We can make it." She kissed him again, a desperate plea for him to see past the image of her he had in his mind. She needed him to quit trying to save her. She needed him to help her.

"Race, I can't do this without you. Please."

CHAPTER THIRTY-FOUR

Race didn't answer. There was nothing else for him to say. He stuffed extra batteries and anything else he could get his hands on into his pockets. He pulled his go bag and first-aid kit from behind his seat.

"Pull alongside the van. As close as you can." Savanah indicated where the group had crowded into one van. *There's safety in numbers* wasn't going to help them. Not now. Not through this.

Now that she didn't have to waste time convincing him to follow her, she could concentrate on other things. Like telling the people they were trying to save to get ready. She motioned for the occupants of the van to roll down their window.

"We're going to make a run for it. Get ready. When you see us get out, you know it's time to go." Savanah tried to yell loud enough they could hear her. It was impossible over the incredible rushing that filled their ears, as if the hurricane were a mechanical monster and they'd been dropped into the middle of its engine.

"Run where?" Savanah barely heard the voices ask as one, before the wind fractured the sound. She could see them arguing as they rolled the window back up. She knew the fear in the van would be so thick she would have been able to feel it against her skin if she were in there with them. She didn't blame them.

Race still hadn't said anything. He held the bags in one hand as he waited for Savanah to give the word. She looked over and took the straps of his go bag.

"I'll carry this one."

"I've got them."

"If I sling it on like a backpack, it will help me balance. And it will offer some protection at my back," she explained.

"Are you sure about this?" he asked, handing her the bag.

She nodded. "I'm sure."

"Okay then. Get ready." He'd kept the two vehicles close, so they were shielding one another. No one would be able to open the doors until he moved. Thunder sounded and lightning fractured the sky. The eyewall was making land. Race threw the SUV into reverse.

As soon as her door was clear, Savanah jumped to the ground. Even though she was expecting it, the energy in the air was enough to push her against the vehicle and take her breath away. She stood upright just as Race took her hand in his and pulled her toward the other vehicles where people were spilling out.

"Follow me. Watch your grip on the rock and make sure you have your footing. It will be a tough climb. But we can make it," Savanah told them.

They all looked skyward as intermittent sunlight began to dot the landscape. The wind and rain fell off abruptly. The temperature rose quickly, returning to an almost too-warm tropical heat. The sudden change felt scary and surreal, compared to what had been happening only moments before. But the eye was over them. Size was on their side—even Garth's eye was huge.

Time, however, was not their ally. Savanah figured they had no more than twenty or thirty minutes to reach the lava tube and safety.

"Make it to where?"

Savanah didn't know which one of the group from the van asked the question aloud. It was a collective question.

"There's a lava tube entrance up there. We'll be safe inside." Savanah adjusted the bag at her back, tightening the straps so it wouldn't slide around.

One of the men shook his head at her pushing the Padres ballcap he wore higher as he looked up the hill before settling his gaze on Savanah. "We've been here for days shooting. The caves we found were shallow, nothing more than hollows that went a few yards in. There's nowhere we can hide. We'd have known about it." The man looked back at the rest of his party. "I think we should try and make it back to town while there's a break in the storm."

He reminded Savanah of being in school when the kid next to you asks what the answer on a test is and then doesn't believe you when you tell him. She and Race had answered the group's call for help, and now someone wanted to argue against the rescue plan. Thankfully, Race stepped up as another of them made to get in the Civil Defense SUV and turn it around.

"This isn't a break, and this isn't just a storm. Above us is the eye of a Category 4 hurricane. It isn't going to last. There isn't enough time to make it into town."

Patience was usually something Savanah was good at, but she was running out and Garth wasn't going to wait for her to explain things. "I'm not taking you back to one of the caves you've been in. I'm taking us to a lava tube. And it isn't on any map. It's the only place that runs deep enough that the hurricane won't be able to reach."

She made eye contact with each of them. "We cannot stay here. I've lived here my entire life. And I'm telling you it's up there and it's the only place for us to go. Climb carefully. This is a'ā lava. It is jagged and it is sharp. It will slice your skin open so fast you won't even know you're bleeding."

Savanah turned away. They were going to follow her, or not. It was time for everyone to make their own choice. She began making her way up the hillside. Dying with them wouldn't do anyone any good. Her or them.

Race grabbed, barely catching the back of his bag on Savanah's back as she started climbing.

"We need to stick together." He waved at some of the film crew who were getting back into what little shelter the vehicles offered.

"You're right. We do." The frustration at the situation was beginning to take its toll. The knots in her stomach cinched tighter. There was no way to force any of them to do anything. Dragging them to safety against their will wasn't an option. She understood their fear, but they were going to have to work to survive. "We're running out of time."

"We can't leave them here alone, Savanah." Race barely caught her in time as a gust took her feet out from under her. "Let's get back in the vehicles and we'll come up with another plan."

"No. We can't stay here. It's time to make a choice. And they're making the wrong one. We need to go Race, and we need to go now." His face hardened and she clutched at his arm. Desperation filled her and she gave a cry. "I told you we weren't going to die. But if we stay here, there won't be any protection from the backside of the hurricane where it's going to pile up and stall over us. It's going to be worse than what we've seen already."

"They aren't trained for this..." His hands covered hers. "But I am."

Her tears mixed with the rain on her face. "Don't you do it, Race. I know what you're thinking. But you can't save them this way. You can't carry them to safety. This is one time the people you want to save have to help."

Her fingers went slack as Race pulled her hands from his jacket. She saw her plea bounce uselessly off the hardened shell of his resolve.

Savanah turned away and began scrambling over the rocks. The look in Race's eyes had been enough. The pain in her chest threatened to cripple her, but she forced herself to keep moving. She focused on searching for any crack or outcrop to cling to as her legs pushed her upward. A rock slid beneath her feet. Savanah used the momentum to bounce off the hillside and keep moving. The dull throb of the wound at her thigh bloomed as if it caught fire. The tape twisted, pulling the injured skin. She didn't stop. The pain helped to ground her and keep her moving.

She didn't waste what little time she had by looking back to see who was following. Not even when she heard the tormented sound of her name, from where Race stood watching her leave.

Race stood on the dirt road, his body shaking as if the wind still buffeted him. He roared Savanah's name after her as if somehow it would carry her to safety.

She didn't turn, didn't look back at him. Race could only watch and pray as Savanah picked her way cautiously up the steep hillside. The men and women who followed did their best to keep pace behind her. Seven scrambled over the rocks with Savanah. The four who'd chosen to stay behind huddled together, fearfully watching their disappearing comrades, from where they'd retreated inside one of the vans.

They hadn't been able to convince themselves to believe Savanah. Their minds could only grasp the safety of what they could see where the sun shone down on them. Race swept his eyes between the two vans, to the sky overhead. He weighed their options.

Going back to his SUV, he pulled it tight to the van once more, to build as much defense against the backside of the hurricane that would soon sweep over them. He had meant what he'd said. They needed to stay together. Their resources and their strengths were now divided. Race stared through the windshield, asking himself what advantage he could find that the storm couldn't take from them. His eyes searched the landscape. With a curse, he realized their only advantage was almost gone from his sight.

He went to the vehicle where the others remained and ripped the rear doors open.

"Get out. Now. Everyone. Take any food or water you have. Anything that we can use. Leave everything else," he barked.

His tone didn't leave room for any argument. He started opening the numerous boxes of gear they had stowed, looking for anything useful. He found a backpack and shoved a half-used roll of duct tape into it.

"I'm not . . ."

It was the man with the Padres cap who'd spoken against Savanah moments earlier. Race cut him off with a sharp look. "I said get out now. If you want to live. We're going after them."

Shouldering his large first aid kit, Race strode to the edge of the road and waited for the others to join him. He took the opportunity to use his satellite phone, to pin the current location and send the coordinates to Steve. It didn't go through. Whether it was the storm or the rock around him interfering with the signal, he couldn't tell. He put the phone away to conserve the battery. If it suddenly started pulling a signal, it would automatically send the message.

Race led the remaining film crew toward the spot where Savanah had begun her ascent. "Start climbing," he ordered.

He took up the position at the rear of their small group. Savanah was right. They shouldn't have separated, and he shouldn't have stood there arguing with her and wasting time. As he pushed the scared group of people in front of him to keep moving upward, he refused to consider anything but that the five of them would make it up the hill. And that Savanah would be at the top waiting for them with an *I told you so* look that would be the sweetest thing Race had ever seen.

CHAPTER THIRTY-FIVE

The opening to the lava tube was smaller than she remembered. Or maybe she was just bigger. Whichever it was, they needed to get inside. The sun was beginning to disappear, and Savanah could feel the eye buckling. The quiet calm forced to give way to the fury of the hurricane's body.

"Hurry. We need to get some of these rocks out of the way," Savanah shouted.

She lay on her back, Race's pack helping to cushion her against the jagged a'ā. Settling down, she put both feet against the largest boulder blocking the entrance to the lava tube. They didn't need to lift the VW bug sized boulder, they just needed to shift it. Several of the others realized what she was doing and crowded around her. They began pushing, but the large rock was wedged tight.

Come on. We're just asking for a little break here. "Again. Everybody. Push on the count of three."

Hands and feet covered everywhere they could reach on the rock. Arms and legs were intertwined, bodies lying half on top of one another as the group worked together. Savanah counted down and she could feel the collective strain of muscles. A small shout sounded as they heard the grate of rock against rock.

She counted again, ignoring her back as it began to protest. There was a cry as someone's hand slipped, blood instantly beginning to drip from where the jagged lava ripped the tender flesh open. But they didn't stop. Instead, everyone pushed again. Savanah's cheer of relief blended with the others' as the rock gave way.

Savanah knelt at the edge of the opening, holding her hand up. The others crowded behind her in silence. She bowed her head and placed both hands on the rock beside her.

To those who rest here, I humbly ask your permission that I may enter as may those who follow me. I ask that you grant us sanctuary from the storm. We come with respect in our hearts and love for all those who have passed before us.

Savanah gave time for the words to die out in her head. The darkness behind her eyes gave way to an image of what lay before her and she got to her feet. "Inside. Everyone, get inside."

She waited until the others were all through the opening before sliding into the darkness herself. Hands immediately reached out to help her to her feet. The light of several phones cast wild shadows on the walls as they looked around. Silence settled over the group one by one.

"What is this place?" one of the women asked in a hushed voice, indicating how much the surroundings affected them.

"It's a burial chamber." Savanah swung Race's bag from her shoulders and began going through it. She took out one of his shirts and a small bottle of sanitizing gel from within, then went to the woman who held her bleeding hand tight to her chest. "Let me see."

The cut was nasty. The woman would need antibiotics and stitches for sure. Lava rock was porous and full of bacteria. Savanah had known plenty of people who suffered excruciating infections because they hadn't bothered to clean a cut from the lava rock or coral well enough. But the woman would live, and that was the most important thing.

"Do any of you know first aid?" Savanah looked around at the faces watching her.

"I do." A young man stepped forward. "Jack," he offered his hand hesitantly.

"Nice to meet you, Jack." Savanah put the gel and clean shirt in his outstretched hand. There was a scruff of facial hair that made her think he wasn't one of the actors. She gave him instructions anyway. Talking loud enough so everyone heard.

"Use the whole bottle on it. Pull the edges open and make sure you get any pieces of rock or dirt out. Then wrap it tight with the shirt." Savanah chewed the inside of her lip. What she wouldn't give for one small roll of tape. She looked to the woman whose dark hair was coming loose from its ponytail. "What's your name?"

"Gloria."

"You're going to be fine, Gloria. But keep your hand above your heart until the bleeding stops. Okay?" Savanah waited for Gloria to respond before she turned away.

"Wait. Where are you going?" Gloria asked.

Savanah paused at the entrance, looking back at them. "I'm going back down for the others. You're protected from the storm here. Don't go inside any further, though. It isn't safe."

"We worried about a bear or something?" one of the men scoffed from where he stood at the back.

Savanah narrowed her eyes at the man who'd spoken. He looked to be in his early forties, but it was a fit forty. Below his shorts, she could see the muscular definition of his calves. She was betting a cyclist or runner. She marveled at the almost insolent tone of his voice. Obviously, the safety he now enjoyed had returned enough confidence that he was willing to mouth off already. Then again, maybe it was just nerves. There was plenty to be nervous about.

"No bears. But a wild boar would be just as bad."

It had been her decision to bring them to this sacred place. Anything they did here was her responsibility. In praying for permission, she knew what that meant.

"I brought you here because it was the only place I knew of that we could make it to and have any chance surviving the hurricane outside. This is a sacred place. There are children buried here. Families buried here. That's why it isn't on your maps. I'm asking you to respect where you're standing. Don't touch anything. Don't take any pictures." She let her words sink in, making eye contact with each of them.

"Don't make me regret saving you." She turned and started the short climb back up the loose rock of the entryway.

She rubbed her back where an ache was beginning. She didn't have the time or the luxury of giving in to her body's shortcomings. The sound of the wind outside told her the storm was returning while Race and the others were still out there.

Savanah stopped at the entrance and looked back where the group stood watching her. Their eyes following her every move.

"One more thing. Stay together. If you think you hear voices or noises deeper inside, don't go investigating. I won't tell you it's your imagination. You need to stay here, as close to the entrance as is safe. And for God's sake, whatever you do, don't go off following what you think is calling your name."

The uneven air pressure waiting outside saved her from the sudden rush of questions as it sucked the breath from her lungs.

The way down proved to be so much harder than the way up had been.

Savanah spent most of the descent on her backside, using her hands and feet as breakfalls as she slid from one crack to the next. She would have been cursing Race and the others if all her focus hadn't been on not making the wrong move and sliding to her death. Or worse, surviving the fall. The small cuts and bruises already covering her hands were nothing compared to what would happen if she lost her grip.

The clear sky of the storm's eye had almost disappeared, and rain was once again falling. Visibility was down to only a few feet. She was nowhere near the bottom where the vans were parked.

"Thank God," Savanah sighed, as she saw a head appear a few feet below her. Relief made her weak as she realized that the rest of the film crew had decided to climb up, after all.

Digging in so her own position was secure, she reached down and grabbed a handful of jacket to help pull up the woman who didn't even know she was there. Savanah smiled into the surprised face.

Leaning forward, Savanah yelled against the increasing volume of the wind and rain. "Keep going straight up. You're almost there. You can't miss the opening. The others are inside."

She helped the remaining three that followed make their way past her, until finally the only one left was Race. Savanah hadn't seen him look up. She didn't think he knew she was there waiting for him anymore than the others had.

Maybe they would decide later to be mad at one another when they'd survived and gotten everyone out safely. For now, it was enough they'd found the lava tube. Savanah couldn't help herself.

"Civil Defense Director Weston. How are you enjoying working with us here on the west side so far?"

Chapter Thirty-Six

The rain began to pour down again, the wind whipping above their heads. Race kept the group moving. If Savanah had turned off left or right, he'd never find her. He had to hope she'd kept a straight course and that they'd run into the entrance to wherever she'd taken the other part of the group. He grunted as a gust flattened him into the rock before trying to rip him backwards. Small chunks of lava skittered past as they all clawed for handholds that would keep them from being tossed down the hillside by the ferocious winds.

It was too loud to talk. The people above him couldn't hear but still he continued to encourage them to keep going. He refused to think what would happen if Savanah was wrong. Dying on the side of a mountain because a hurricane beat you to death didn't sound like a good way to die.

Race whipped his head up at the sound of Savanah's voice. Race couldn't believe she sat wedged into the rocks just above him. The others were already climbing past where she waited for him. He took her outstretched hand just as a gust rocked him, forcing his body to slam down against hers. Yelling was his only choice. "What are you doing?"

"Coming back to rescue you."

"You shouldn't have."

The rockface was treacherous. Rainwater ran so heavily, it pulled rocks along with it. They both turned in time to see a half-grown tree sliding toward them. Race ducked his head back against Savanah's and used his body to cover as much of her as possible.

"As exciting as this is, are you ready to get out of here?" Savanah asked as he held himself over her.

"I thought you'd never ask," Race answered. He waited a few more minutes before chancing a look over his shoulder for any more projectiles.

Race pulled her up. They began moving in unison, Race keeping tight to Savanah's backside to offer what protection he could as the sky let loose its wrath.

"There. You can see the entrance." Savanah pointed above her another twenty yards. They were almost home free.

There was a thunder beginning behind them that was different from the howl of the wind and pounding of the rain. Underneath the deafening roar came a constant tapping, like the sound of a wood chipper. Savanah started to turn, but Race's hand on her back stopped her.

"Don't look back. Keep going." Race pushed Savanah with enough strength she was forced to keep her eyes in front of her. Race knew what the sound was. He could see everything around them lifting from the ground as it was sucked into the vacuum at their backs. The seconds they would lose turning around to see death coming might be what got them killed.

Savanah slipped and Race was there, almost picking her up around the waist, half-dragging her as he refused to let them stop. If he hadn't been there, Race wasn't sure Savanah could have kept the wind from sweeping her away.

They scrambled furiously, clawing their way the last few feet to the ledge. Race threw them down flat as a blast of rock and tree branches exploded against the rock only feet from them. Savanah rolled onto her back and stared at the terrifying scene unfolding.

A funnel cloud snaked down from the sky. It was nothing like her offhand comparison to the shimmering waterspouts of its Hawaiian counterpart. What was coming down from the sky was unfathomable devastation. Even the darkness of its color spoke to the destruction it was bringing.

Race put his arm around Savanah and pulled her toward the safety of the lava tube entrance while she stared, transfixed by the tornado as it stretched earthward. He knew the almost graceful sway of all that power was captivating in a horrific way.

The tornado roared in victory as it overruled the laws of nature. The clouds that birthed such an inconceivable monster continued to feed it. Its base above them expanding steadily. Rather than diminishing as it reached for the earth, it sucked the strength from everything around it and grew.

Race flinched with her as the tornado touched the earth and began making its mark upon the indestructible lava face of the Big Island. An unbelievable sight even as they watched it with their own eyes. The power of the tornado was like a giant jackhammer dragging across the land. The funnel tore loose things that were rooted deep within the lava. It flung rocks the size of trucks as if it were flicking bugs from the face of the island.

Savanah grasped for Race blindly when one of the vans suddenly appeared in the whirling cloud moving steadily toward them.

"Get down," Race shouted, shoving Savanah ahead of him into the opening. The moment there were vehicles flying through the air, it was time to quit watching. The sight had been enough to snap Race out of the trance the tornado had put them under.

The earth now provided protection from the winds and rain outside, but the noise couldn't be held back. Even muted by the walls of solid rock around them, it was still terrifying. It was no wonder that everyone had moved deeper into the darkness to escape what was outside. They huddled together, staring at Race and Savanah as they rolled through the opening.

All eyes fixed on the opening, watching in fear as if some piece of what was happening outside might find its way in.

Race brushed himself off. He'd hit the loose gravel and rolled to the bottom of the slope into the cavern. He heard labored breathing behind him and turned to see Savanah still on her hands and knees. A sharp moan rent the air, and he didn't have to see her face to know what was happening.

"Tell me what to do." He slid to his knees beside her.

"Don't do anything. Don't touch me," Savanah hissed through clenched teeth.

"Savanah. I can help you. Tell me what to do." His wrapped his arms around her, making to pick her up, to be answered by vehement jerks of her head.

He'd thrown her through the entrance. She'd only been out there because she was coming back for him and the others. She was down on her knees now, enduring this pain, because of him. Race watched, knowing it was his fault.

CHAPTER THIRTY-SEVEN

Savanah could feel the land beneath her from where she was still on her hands and knees. The mountains of the Big Island stood almost 14,000 feet tall from the ocean's surface. Measured from the summits, it was more than 33,000 feet to where their base was rooted in the ocean floor.

She'd seen the pictures of Category 5 tornadoes. Giant things that looked as wide as a town. Not until now, as her island home shuddered and moaned, did she realize she'd never quite believed it.

The island trembled.

This wasn't the gentle tumbling like ice cubes tripping about in some giant glass. Savanah gasped as the island shuddered in shock. The concentrated power of the tornado landed like a boxer's punch, the fury reverberating through the bone and sinew of a body that had no choice but to absorb it. Savanah felt another terrible shudder, and knew the tornado had pulled back, only to touch down again.

She gasped as pain stabbed through her focus. Too late, Savanah realized her body had absorbed the energy of the tornado touching down upon her island home. A second explosive shockwave ripped through her, and her body buckled.

Her head snapped back and a cry slipped out before she could stop it. After everything she had been through in the last few hours, Savanah wasn't surprised. There wasn't enough warning to fight it, even if there'd have been something she could have done. Her last coherent thought was to be thankful it hadn't happened while they'd been climbing up the hillside.

Her muscles were locked in place. It wouldn't matter what position she was in. There was no way to stop it. Savanah's head snapped up and her teeth clamped together as the first full spasm hit. She bit down on her lip to stifle any further cries out as she prepared for another one. It wouldn't be long before they rolled into one another to become an unending fist to her spine. Savanah began to pray for it. The sooner it got to that point, the sooner it would come to an end.

Race had taken her at her word and moved away. She knew because she couldn't feel his heat beside her anymore. She pushed thoughts of him out of her mind as she focused all her energy on staying conscious as another spasm rocked her.

Savanah was past talking. She was afraid to try. There was the sound of his voice and the others in the background. But all her attention was focused inward as her body tried to turn inside out.

Race started emptying the bags he was carrying. "I need a battery. Wires. Anything you have."

"Stay with me Savanah. Don't you leave me," Race called as he worked frantically.

Several of the people they'd rescued stepped forward. "What are you looking for?"

Race looked up in surprise. He'd forgotten about them. "I need something that will deliver an electrical shock."

Suddenly everyone was pulling things out of the hastily grabbed bags they'd carried. The pile grew as Race continued reassuring Savanah he was with her. His desperation was growing as he heard the low sounds of her suffering increase.

"Let us help you."

A man from the film crew stepped forward. "We can put something together that will deliver a charge."

Race looked him over. He was one of those who'd gone up with Savanah. Above the Def Leopard shirt and beard were intelligent eyes.

"Filming on location means finding a way to get the job done even when things stop working. It isn't just about knowing how to work a camera. We know how to rig up anything to get the most out of all the equipment. I'm not saying we can make it work in the manner you want. But can we rig something? Sure," he told Race.

Race had expected to use the battery on his satellite phone. It was more powerful than the cellphone in his pocket. The man scoffed, handing it back to him. Race watched as they opened several of the backpacks they'd carried. The pile suddenly grew, but now with wires and electronics. A multipurpose tool appeared. Its attachments were worked so effectively Race knew it meant the tool was well used. Within minutes, they handed him what they'd made from the cameras' battery packs.

"You never know when someone's going to say, 'Film this.' Being a cameraman means you're always ready," one of them shrugged.

The minutes it took to assemble the makeshift taser felt like hours to Race. He couldn't imagine what it felt like for Savanah as he went back to her. Other than the gasps of air she took intermittently, she hadn't tried speaking. Now that he was next to her, he could hear soft moans of pain beneath her ragged breaths. He didn't know whether she'd heard them talking. Or even if she could hear him now.

"This won't be perfect. You'll have to find a way to tell me if it's too strong." Race pulled her clothes away from her skin, exposing her tanned flesh. Her clothes were soaked, and he watched as water droplets ran across her skin to pool in the valley of her spine.

He ignored the intake of breath he heard from behind him as someone saw the scars across Savanah's hip. He laid a hand to her back, searching for an indication where he should put the makeshift electrodes. He jerked his fingers away in surprise as he felt the ripple as the muscles seized again.

Savanah grunted and Race wasn't sure whether that meant she understood his words.

He looked around for something to dry her skin. A shirt was shoved into his hands and Race recognized one of his own. He wiped away as much moisture as he could before placing the small pads he'd made from duct tape to her skin. Holding his breath, he connected the wires that would deliver the first shock to where he could see the gnarled muscles clenching.

As the first surge of electricity flashed through her, Savanah's head shot up. She heaved and emptied her stomach. The sound that escaped her pushed everyone but Race away.

"Too much," she panted.

There was a sound of shock from behind him, but the look Race shot over his shoulder silenced anything further.

"We need to turn down the intensity." He looked at the men who'd helped him put the makeshift device together. Fear for Savanah overrode everything else as he pleaded with them. "Help me help her."

The man with the Padres cap stepped forward, taking the improvised machine from Race's outstretched hand. "Jack, find a radio." He instructed over his shoulder as he and the bearded technician talked and examined what they'd put together.

Race watched as a young man dug through the pile of equipment. The multipurpose tool reappeared in the hand of the bearded cameraman, who moved quickly disconnecting the wires. Then he added the channel dial from one of the two-way radios the teenaged-looking Jack had found. He held the makeshift device out for inspection and offered an apology. "Sorry Kel, I should have thought of that."

"If Tim says this will work, it will. Best onsite tech I've ever worked with." Kel placed the impromptu taser back in Race's hand.

He'd thank them later. Race knelt beside Savanah.

"Savanah?" Race asked. It was up to her. She was the one enduring the pain of what she was going through, and what Race was trying to do as he tried to help.

Her head sawed spastically. "Try again," she managed before clenching her jaw back together.

Race held his breath as he delivered another shock. This time she didn't cry out, but the shudder was unmistakable as the electrical impulse flashed through her body.

"Al . . . most," Savanah gasped, taking several gulps of air after the second attempt.

Race turned the dial down another notch and made the connection. At Savanah's nod of acceptance, he began delivering a steady stream of pulses. He could almost see her sigh in relief as the electrical current began interrupting the excruciating contractions. It was working.

Race watched her closely. When he saw her arms start to quiver, he looked to Tim, the technician who'd wired the device and was still standing close watching. Race handed him the device to take over the electro-pulses so he could keep her from falling.

With a final contraction, Savanah's entire body began to quiver and without warning, her arms gave out. His arms already waiting around her,

Race caught her easily. Just as she'd been unable to stop the seizures, he knew she would be helpless to combat the weakness that followed. Just as she was that day at the pier. He listened to her struggle to breath, as if even the effort to fill her lungs was too much.

Race held her carefully as he watched her body for signs the seizure might return. He wasn't willing to move her and take the chance of reigniting the pain she'd gone through.

"These batteries are done," said Tim as he waved the makeshift taser in the air.

Race carefully peeled the corners of the pads from her skin. Everyone retreated slightly, leaving them room now that it appeared the emergency was over. Gathering Savanah in his arms, he settled his back against the rock wall so he could rest her in his lap. He held her in silence, content to wait for her to give him a sign she was beginning to recover from the grip of what had happened. He wasn't quite sure whether the heart he could feel pounding was hers, or his.

With every twitch of her body, his arms tensed. Race would have done anything to erase the last few moments for her. His arms around her were the only comfort he had to offer. Now that he'd experienced up close and in person what she went through, he was horrified to think what it was like for her.

"Are the small tremors I can still feel going through you painful?" he finally asked.

The movement of Savanah's head against his chest was more a twitch than a nod. Race thought it was a no. He didn't ask anything else. He didn't want her to think she had to move or talk. Not until she was ready.

"Not really." Savanah's voice was a whisper. Spoken as if the muscles of her throat weren't used to working. "They're more like when a muscle has gone to sleep and is waking back up."

A thousand tiny pin pricks. Race remembered when Savanah had told him she was good at pain. "Your throat sounds raw."

"A little." Her eyes flashed to Race. The question in them clear. "Should it be?"

He smoothed a raven lock from her cheek as he reassured her. "No. That's why I mentioned it. It doesn't make sense."

Savanah gave an audible sigh of relief. "I think it's more a caution against accidentally biting my tongue. You know, because I'm not in control of anything yet."

"I'm sorry if I hurt you . . ." His hands flexed tighter where they held on to her. "The first shock . . . was too much."

Savanah shook her head again. This time it was less jerk and more controlled. "You're handy to have around. My doctor is going to want to hear all about what you did." She attempted to laugh. "Think how much money I could have saved if I'd just bought a taser."

"Are you sure you're okay?" He wasn't sure he was.

"Better than I was a few minutes ago. Lucky for me you were here."

Race touched his forehead to hers. "If it weren't for you coming back for me . . . If I hadn't thrown you to the ground. That wouldn't have happened. The way I see it, everything about what just happened is my fault . . ."

She put a hand to his cheek. "It wasn't your fault, Race. You already know that can happen at any time. You've seen it before."

"Not when I was the one holding you." Race couldn't imagine what it had been like for her parents. Torture to have watched their daughter go through that. To hold her as it happens. "All I knew was I had to find a way to help you."

"Give me a few minutes and I'll show you another way you can help me." Her voice was regaining some of its strength.

"Whatever you need." Race knew he'd do anything she asked of him.

"That's never happened before. Throwing up from my seizures."

"Sorry. We should have known the first one would be too much," the bearded Tim called sheepishly from where he was sitting several feet away. "To be fair, it was the first time we put something like that together. Well, to be used on a person, anyway."

"Hey. It's just lucky for me you all were here. Thanks." Savanah looked around at the group.

"Now what do we do?" Gloria, asked, her injured hand still tucked high against her shoulder.

"We wait." Savanah gave an easy swing of her shoulders.

"For what?"

"Until it's over," Race finished for Savanah. "And then we get out of here."

"How long will that be?" someone else asked from the shadows.

"When it quits sounding like a freight train outside, someone feel free to take a look," Savanah offered with a laugh. "I think I'll wait a while before I go sticking my head out."

CHAPTER THIRTY-EIGHT

Returning to consciousness of her surroundings happened faster than Savanah expected. As impossible as it seemed, whatever Race had done had helped. Somehow, he'd managed to interrupt the spasms of the seizure and her nerves were beginning to fire in a normal manner. The episode was ending.

She didn't trust her tongue to talk and was glad that Race seemed content to sit with her in silence. Savanah didn't protest that he still had his arms around her. It provided a sense of security while she slowly regained control of her body, one limb at a time.

"I haven't felt any contractions or tremors in a while now."

Race spoke quietly from where his head rested next to hers. Part of her didn't want to move. "No." She turned to look at him. "I'm sorry to put you through that."

"You're sorry . . ." Race laid his forehead to hers. Any other words drowned out by the anguished breath that passed from his lips.

A sense of calm went through Savanah as her breath mingled with Race's. She couldn't help the soft smile as they sat with their foreheads together. Savanah wondered whether Race knew what he was doing. The *honi*, the traditional Hawaiian greeting, meant so much more than hello. It was the sharing of one person's essence, their life's breath, with another. Two spirits taking the time to come together. Savanah couldn't help thinking maybe she and Race were meeting as equals for the first time as they sat in this sacred place. Surrounded by her ancestors and the land as they shared their life's breath.

She and Race may have been calm, but the others were not. What little light the opening allowed was gone. Evening had merged seamlessly with the thick layer of clouds that was Garth.

Now there was nothing but the terrible sound of the hurricane outside, and the blackness. She guessed few of them had ever experienced what it was like to be in an area utterly devoid of light. Though the thick walls of rock were what had saved them, the unknown in the blackness where the cavern wormed its way into the mountain side was unnerving.

Even if there had been cell service to this area, no signal would penetrate the rock that surrounded them. The group had used their phones for light, until Race instructed them to conserve, and only use one at the time. That meant the group crowded close together to share. Without that, it would be too dark to see anything even inches from their face.

One of the women looked up long enough to lock eyes. Her voice was surprisingly musical as she asked Savanah a hesitant question: "Why did you say that earlier? You know, about the voices?"

"Voices?" Race asked beside her. The lift to his eyebrows said he thought she was trying to scare the tourists. "What voices, Savanah?"

Savanah almost laughed. If the group wanted to talk to keep some of the eeriness of their surroundings at bay, she didn't think their choice of topic was going to help much. Asking her to detail her remarks would, without a doubt, result in the opposite.

She flashed Race a look through the side of her lashes before reaching for his flashlight. The intense beam shone bright as she swung the beam to highlight the petroglyphs carved at the entrance.

"When we arrived, I explained this is a burial chamber. It is an extremely sacred place that needs to be shown our respect."

"Is it *kapu*?" Jack, the one who'd assisted Savanah with Gloria's hand from earlier, asked.

Savanah nodded. "Very good, Jack. Yes, it is. *Kapu*, restricted or off limits. I only brought us here because I believed it was the only place we would survive what is happening outside." She shuddered at the memory of the tornado touching down. If she never saw another one of those in person, it would be too soon. "I'm positive we would not have survived what is out there."

Everyone gathered closer to hear. The bearded man who'd assisted Race switched on his phone, then placed a bottle of water over the beam. The prisms of light reflected through the water sent eerie shadows bouncing off the walls. Uneasy laughter sounded from the group, dying out in the draft that pulled the sound away deeper into the lava tube.

Everyone swallowed hard, trying to rid themselves of the lump that had suddenly formed in their throats. All except Savanah. It was a simple matter of respecting where she was. She knew that as long as you showed respect, there was nothing to fear.

The group noticed she wasn't laughing and quieted. "What does it being kapu have to do with hearing voices?" The question came from the man who'd been so quick with sarcasm once they were safe. Savanah noticed his arrogance seemed to have dimmed. "Devon. And sorry, about earlier."

The apology surprised Savanah. She thought better of him for it. Then again, with what they'd all been through, a bit of grace to overlook nervous behavior was in order. She made sure her smile reflected her acceptance of his words. She included everyone as she answered his question.

"You should respect sitting here as you would if you were sitting in any church or religious setting you recognize. I cautioned everyone to not go any deeper than necessary because there are things in the deeper recesses that shouldn't be disturbed." Savanah's eyes of iced blue held their collective gaze.

"Things?" Devon spoke up again.

"Again. This is a burial chamber containing the remains of entire families. That shouldn't be taken lightly." She had their undivided attention now.

"You said not to follow the voices. What voices?"

"Some of you are very fair." Savanah gave a slight nod toward the young woman sitting across from her who'd asked the question. Light blonde waves cascaded around the woman's shoulders. Savanah would have guessed she was in her early twenties.

"The *Menehune* are the little people of Hawaii," Savanah began.

"I've seen pictures. They look like a brown-skinned, happy dwarf with pointed ears," chimed in a woman whose dark hair lay in braids down her back.

Savanah blanched and shook her head quickly. "We would never describe them in such a manner. Yes, they are childlike themselves in spirit. They cannot help their mischievousness nor their love of children. But the Menehune were highly skilled craftsmen. They were known to be very shy of the much larger-in-stature Polynesians."

"Which is why they are depicted like what Rose said." Jack's observation seemed purposeful in Rose's direction.

"Yes," Savanah replied. "Depicting a happy dwarf sells more cookies."

There was an uncomfortable silence for several minutes. Interestingly enough, now that they were safe, the hurricane had become background noise to what was happening inside the lava tube.

"Your appearance . . ." Savanah finally went on, giving the blonde across from her a knowing smile, ". . . is not only striking, but vastly different than that of our little people. And your small stature disguises your age. You could be mistaken for a child."

She paused to consider her next words. "I was told from the time I could walk, to make sure I never followed an unseen voice into the forest. Parents know better than to leave their children unguarded in remote areas where the Menehune might still reside."

Savanah surveyed the passage where the darkness was like a living thing in the deeper region of the lava tube. "I didn't think it was fair *not* to warn you and risk that one of you might go missing."

"You're pulling our leg." The halfhearted accusation couldn't dispel the underlying fear that had blossomed to life. "Night marchers I've heard of. But you expect us to believe in fairies?"

Savanah shrugged. "These are stories I have heard since birth. It is not so much about what I believe as what you do." She felt the whispering touch of a hand to her shoulder and relaxed into it. The soft laughter, dropping like flower petals into the ocean, made her smile.

It was interesting to watch as most of the group sat unmoving. Unaware of what she felt. Deaf to what she could hear. Of all the people sitting around listening so intently to her, Savanah saw only two who shivered suddenly. She watched as they sat up straight, their heads moving to look around them for the source of the noise they thought they heard.

"There are those who believe the legend of the Menehune was born from the need to protect our children. When sailing ships began arriving at our shores, our children began to disappear, taken by slave traders who waited at the edge of the woods for the happy, trusting little ones to wander close enough."

The women gasped in horror as the men gave a collective grumble. Even though it had been centuries ago, the act of slavery felt even more despicable at the thought of it happening to a child. Savanah agreed. And if the legend of the Menehune helped save even one child, then or now, it was worth it.

"So, what else do we have to worry about?" The man who asked the question had been watching and listening intently. He was one of those that had gone with her up the hillside. Now that the group was back together, she could see the others deferring to him. She wondered if he might be the director for the film crew.

"The only thing we should be concerned with are the conditions outside." Savanah replied.

"What about inside?" Gloria asked.

Savanah hesitated. She loved sharing about her culture. But she wasn't willing to have it made fun of. There was no reason to trust these people. Race squeezed her hand, and she turned to meet his perceptive gaze. Searching his eyes, Savanah decided trust had to start with someone.

"Even among those of Hawaiian descent, it is recognized that each individual is sensitive to such things on a different level. While one might see a shadow in the corner of their peripheral vision, the person sitting next to them won't see anything. Another of you might hear something. Music, voices, even laughter..." The eyes of the two, who Savanah suspected had heard that very thing moments earlier, flew to gape at her wide-eyed. The slow sweep of her lashes affirmed she knew they'd heard, just as she had.

Savanah waved her hand. "The land, the island, is part of who we are. The ancestors of our people are not simply buried in the ground, their spirit lives on in every breath we take, every step . . ."

The group sat silent, waiting for her to go on. She took a breath. "So, if you see anyone walking around who doesn't look like our group or isn't dressed like we are, do not stare at them. Cast your eyes down and let them pass. Do not walk in front of them or cross their path."

"Night marchers."

"Some of them. Not all." Savanah was doing her best to tell them the truth.

"Now you are scaring me," Gloria said. Her dark ponytail swinging as she looked side to side nervously.

Savanah gave the woman a reassuring smile. "There isn't anything to be frightened of. But we would not want the unwarranted attention that would come from disrespecting anything here."

Savanah opened her hand to the still air of the cavern. "They are well aware we came here seeking shelter. And that we do not mean to disturb them. Before we entered, I asked permission of those who watch over this place and of those who are resting here. As long as your heart and mind harbor nothing other than that, we are welcome."

There was nervous laughter as everyone in the group tried to gauge the truth of what Savanah had said. In the end, it was the man Savanah suspected was the director who spoke up. "Thank you for sharing with us. And telling us honestly."

Race had been quiet beside her. That told her he wasn't bothered by where they were sitting. Maybe the tornado outside had been enough to override any fear for him, too. He must have felt her eyes on him, because he looked down with a smile as he pulled her closer.

"That's one way to keep everyone close so we can keep track of them."

"You don't seem overly concerned about it." Savanah dug her shoulder into his side.

"Would it surprise you if I told you there are more similarities between Australia and Hawaii than people might realize?" Race replied, suddenly solemn.

It didn't. Savanah had found similarities in the cultures of several countries. She shifted her weight trying to ease the throbbing in her leg.

"How's your leg?" Race asked, his hands instantly there to assist her. "I forgot all about that. It seems forever ago."

"I'll live." Savanah sighed. There was an exhaustion creeping over her, borne of more than just her back seizing up. She was having trouble keeping her eyes open and wondered if Race had noticed. She'd feel better if one of them stayed awake to keep an eye on everyone and everything. "I need to just rest a little."

"Go ahead. You look exhausted." He traced a finger across her cheek. "I'll keep watch."

Savanah couldn't help her eyes sliding back to the members of the group. Some talked in hushed tones, while others tried to find a comfortable place to close their eyes. No one had tucked off by themselves.

"Scout's honor. I won't let any of them walk off," Race assured Savanah, moving behind and leaning her back against him. He moved his head so he could whisper in her ear. "You weren't teasing them, were you?"

"I wouldn't do that. Not here." The solemn answer left no room for question.

"I'll watch them. Get some rest."

Savanah knew she needed to bolster her energy. "One more thing?"

"What do you need me to do?" Race kept his voice low to match hers.

"Nothing. Just sit with your arms around me. Like this." Savanah moved to face him. She situated herself between his knees, her legs to either side of his waist. His arms went around her immediately and she helped his hands find the lower portion of her spine where the ache was the strongest.

"This doesn't seem like a genuine request for help," Race chuckled. "Which doesn't mean I'm not totally down for it. Whatever *it* turns out to be. Though I should mention we are in full view of everyone," he teased softly.

"Don't move." Savanah shifted trying to get more comfortable where they sat on the ground. Looking up to his eyes she said again. "Don't move until I tell you. Promise?"

Race nodded, spreading his fingers so his large hands held her firmly. His fingers flexed as if to massage the muscles beneath, but Savanah gave a quick shake of her head. He stopped and did as she requested. Sat there unmoving with her in his lap, his hands holding steady to her lower back.

"I want to trace these and take the pain away," he told her as the palm of one hand settled over the ridges of the scars that decorated her hip.

"Those don't hurt anymore, Race." Savanah didn't want him wasting his thoughts for something in her past that no longer needed to be fixed.

"That doesn't make any difference." His arms pulled her closer.

"If you hold me and follow my instructions, you will be helping me to get rid of the pain."

"You're serious. How?" His voice showed doubt and eagerness.

"It's a Japanese technique called Reiki. My mother taught me. I'm not as good at it as she is. Because I'm tired, I don't really have enough energy by myself. That's where you come in. If we do it together, it should help. And it will be easier."

"I've got a lot to learn from you. How does it work?" He was focused solely on her.

Some of the others were quietly listening in as well, though they kept their distance. Savanah could feel the weight of their interest as they watched.

"I'm going to borrow your energy. Mine is low, and what I do have is tainted by the residual pain. By suffusing everything affected by the seizures with your inner strength that I'm going to borrow, the warmth that generates will help the muscles heal." Savanah gave Race a smile that she couldn't help. "I promise to give it back when I'm done."

CHAPTER THIRTY-NINE

"Can you do that?" Admiration for her filled Race's gaze.

"If I say not exactly, but yes, would you accept that?"

"I'd still like you to explain it to me." The bad boy smirk he gave said he wasn't going to let it go. His hands flexed tighter momentarily. "I like how intimate this feels already."

Savanah's nibbled on her lower lip. "The chakra system originated in India over three thousand years ago. There are seven chakra centers of energy in the body. These centers correspond to specific organs, and also to the emotional, physical, spiritual, and psychological health of the body. The chakras are filled with a pure healing energy. It's a matter of learning to release it or work with it. Chakras are a part of many healing practices: yoga, massage, mediation . . . and what we're about to do, Reiki."

"So, maybe a little slower. That's a lot to grasp," Race admitted.

Savanah answered with a hum of amused agreement. "The way we are sitting combines the Sacral Chakra and the Root Chakra. The combination of sensuality and survival are working in my favor. As is your interest in learning more."

Race suddenly found himself wishing the other inhabitants of the cave away. "Oh, I am definitely interested in more."

"Would it be easier if I said your energy likes mine? So, when I give it back, I'll feel better and so should you," Savanah laughed.

"I think a better question is, does *your* energy like mine?" Race asked.

Color rose in her cheeks at the heated look he stroked over her. Her voice was full of warmth as she answered, "You already know the answer to that."

Race felt an instant rush of desire at the reminder of how good their bodies had been together. Maybe their natural instincts had been far more intuitive than their intellects in dealing with each other by the colored influences of the world they lived in. Her soft words caressed his skin like the scent of plumeria or gardenias on the wind. Sweet and heavy, through even the darkest night, when it assails your senses, and draws you to it.

"Oh please . . ." Savanah rolled her eyes.

He liked her unexpected admission that she'd enjoyed his lovemaking. Enough to endure her playful front of exasperation. He didn't bother tempering his satisfied smile.

She cleared her throat as if trying to get his attention. "Are you ready?"

"Lead the way."

Her face grew focused. "Keep your hands right below my waist but keep your fingers together. That keeps the energy concentrated. Think of it like you're holding a ball made of light. If you spread your fingers, the light will leak out."

"Will I feel anything?"

"I can't answer that. I'm not sure."

"Will you?"

Savanah nodded as she gave a laugh filled with promise. "Definitely."

"What will you feel?" Race asked.

"There usually isn't this much talking, Director," Savanah teased, one eyebrow raised as her lips twitched up. "A warmth. A sense of calm. As if I'm bathing in sunlight."

"Can you guide it? Like a spotlight?" Race vowed it was his last question. He would save the rest for later.

"That's what the chakras are for. What you are trying to do or to heal determines which chakra you should concentrate on and the position of your hands. When you see me move my hands, move one of yours to the base of my neck and the other over the base of my spine. When you move them, try not to lose contact with my body if you can help it," Savanah instructed.

"Got it." Race wanted to try this with her naked. He was only human, and right now he was seriously turned on. And he was secure enough to admit his physical arousal was hitting new heights with the mental foreplay of Savanah's words, and something else he wasn't quite sure how to describe. It was a feeling of being connected he'd never experienced before. It seemed natural that doing this *sans* clothes would make it more effective.

"Okay. Here we go." Savanah closed her eyes.

"Wait. Do I need to close my eyes too?"

Savanah opened her eyes back up only to be captured by the intensity of Race's gaze. "No. You don't have to. You can if you want to."

"I don't want to. I want to watch you."

"You might change your mind on that. But okay."

Savanah closed her eyes once more and took a deep breath. Holding it, she placed her hands across her abdomen, mirroring Race's hands on her back. The noises around her began to fade as she focused on only the two of them.

Like she was opening a door between them, she went in search of the light of his essence. Not surprised that it was already calling her.

She pictured their hands as if they were energy magnets. Where Race was touching her, she envisioned a bright glow. Soon she could feel warmth generating from where her mind could see the pool of Race's strength. And then his energy began to pour into her. Like sunlight streaming through a sheer cloth, it passed through her skin and into her body where his hands contacted her skin. Savanah could feel her fingers tingling with the outpouring of his strength as if she held them above a live wire. Now that Race's energy was beginning to fill her, she opened herself and let her energy flow down through her other chakras and into her hands.

She'd called to Race's energy. Hers flowed of its own accord.

Savanah's mind envisioned what was happening in the spiritual sense. She watched as the energies began to mix, swirling slowly at first like two animals getting to know one another. A hesitant dip together only to pull back before rushing together again. Her head tipped back and her lips parted to drag in a breath with the flare of sensuous pleasure at their fusion.

As if she were holding the mass of healing light, Savanah directed it through the bone and muscle beneath Race's fingers. The aura of the injured area dark against the light of their combined energy.

Her breathing should have been calm, but there was so much power. The bright light of Race's energy consumed the uncharacteristic pallor of hers. His burned so bright, it was almost white. Savanah smiled as her energy flared with the influx of Race's, where they met inside her Sacral Chakra.

She moved her hands slowly from her abdomen. It wasn't necessary for her to open her eyes to know where to stop. She could feel the energy as it followed her legs. It didn't so much come from her hands as her hands acted as guide. She stopped when her left hand was directly over the gunshot wound. As she'd done for her back, she now did for her thigh. Letting her hands hover over the area so the energy had time to help it begin the healing process.

"Relax, Race," Savanah told him softly, without opening her eyes. "You're thinking too hard."

His energy was wavering slightly, and she could feel the subtle tensing of his body beneath hers. He'd done a masterful job of remaining focused up to this point. She just needed him to stay with her a few minutes longer.

"We're almost done. I just need to return what I borrowed."

Returning his energy took almost no effort. Savanah gave a prayer of gratitude as his light hovered with hers. It was as clear in her mind's eye as anything she'd ever experienced in the physical world. She didn't release it because she wasn't holding it. As if his energy knew it was no longer needed, it expanded a last time, pushing its brightness into every corner of her being. Then with a rush of wind, it was gone.

Her body bowed forward and she opened her eyes. She knew her face held the same glow as his. Despite what he'd said, his eyes were closed. Her hands went to his chest and she felt him drag in air, filling his lungs slowly.

"I felt that." His eyes were glowing as they looked at her with wonder.

Savanah nodded. "It would appear you did."

"I like this Reiki stuff."

"I figured you would." There was a lot to like about Reiki. Though Savanah wasn't sure she'd ever been as successful before as they had just been.

"I feel recharged, like I had the best sleep of my life or something. Am I supposed to feel like that? I didn't feel bad to begin with." Race's eyes swept over her, concern edging out the pleasure in his voice. "Did it help you?"

Reaching a hand to the smooth line of his jaw, Savanah drew his lips to hers. The kiss she gave him was meant as her answer. But instead of a simple press to the warmth of his mouth, Savanah was drawn to the expanse of his lower lip. The heat that blossomed flowed instantly into her. She was grateful that Race's response to her kiss trapped the soft moan of desire that had escaped.

"It would seem your body is still trying to help." She whispered against his cheek as she appreciated the feel of his skin to hers.

Savanah didn't protest when Race turned her in his arms. For all his questions earlier, he was suddenly quiet as he insisted she close her eyes and rest. There was an arrogant smile at the corner of his mouth as if he was proud of what had just happened. She couldn't believe how attractive his arrogance suddenly seemed when it was directed at taking care of her. Best she could attribute it to was she was possibly losing her mind.

The sounds from the horrific winds were beginning to die down outside. The rain, too, was slowing to a steady downpour. Before Savanah drifted off to sleep, she and Race agreed. It was far better to wait until daylight to attempt to leave. Walking in the dark when they couldn't see the damage around them would be dangerous. After seeing the tornado pick up the vehicle, they weren't counting on any of those still being drivable. Which meant they would be walking out.

Savanah gave an involuntary shudder. She didn't know if the sight of a vehicle flying through the air would ever leave her.

She snuggled deeper into Race's embrace. They had survived. The sun would rise tomorrow and they would face it together.

He studied Savanah as she slept in his arms. Rather than the lines of exhaustion and pain her face had shown earlier, she had a relaxed glow. Race thought back to what it had felt like as she'd performed the Reiki on herself.

He hadn't ever participated in something like what Savanah had done. There was no denying how incredible it had been.

Her instructions had been simple: maintain contact with her body and move only when she did. When her hands moved from her abdomen, he had slid one of his smoothly up her spine. Suddenly he had been filled with the image of a golden path sweeping behind his hand where it travelled over her.

Even now, there was no mistaking the heat he had clearly felt radiating between them. A combination of Savanah's body heat with his own had filled him in a way he hadn't experienced before. He'd watched, enthralled, at the glowing calm that filled her face. Race tried not to blink. He didn't want to miss a moment of what was happening. But as if blinded by light, his eyes had closed of their own accord.

"Thank you." He'd heard her soft whisper. Race wasn't sure to whom or for what.

He hadn't wanted the experience to end. Race thought about telling her she could take anything she wanted from him. All through the night, or for however long it would take. She'd said she was returning what she borrowed, but he wasn't prepared for the feeling that rushed into him. His body flexed unexpectedly, suddenly overflowing with energy.

Saying he liked whatever it was Savanah had done was an understatement.

Race looked down at Savanah sleeping in his arms. There was a slight smile on her lips, as if even in sleep she knew exactly what he was thinking. Race knew that shouldn't be possible, but something was telling him, when it came to the woman in his arms, there were different rules that applied.

He added the Reiki to the list of extraordinary things about Savanah Jordan he had begun compiling.

Race had another reason for insisting they wait out the night, other than it being the safest thing to do. He kept it to himself. Savanah had done enough for one day.

Chapter Forty

Savanah's eyes opened. Her eyes adjusted quickly to the low light, a benefit of coming from the blackness of sleep. The light that filtered from the opening of the lava tube was enough for her to see small groups of bodies scattered across the rock floor, leaning on one another in a futile attempt to get comfortable.

Bare ground was rarely comfortable. Sleeping on solid rock was miserable. No matter how flat the rock was.

The inside of the lava tube was incredibly smooth, thanks to its formation by the centuries-old pahoehoe lava flow. She laughed softly so she wouldn't wake anyone. Smooth should not be confused with soft. They were *so* not the same thing.

She'd had the good fortune of sleeping the night held entirely on top of Race. Savanah didn't see any sign of him now and had no recollection of him leaving.

She took her time, cautiously stretching her body before gingerly rising to her feet. Even with Race acting as a cushion, she would be glad to sleep in a real bed.

Looking around, Savanah still didn't see him. He surely hadn't gone walking further into the depths of the tube. Looking toward the opening,

Savanah could see the beginnings of daylight. He'd be out there assessing the damage. She was sure of it.

Without waking the others, Savanah made her way outside to find Race.

She didn't have to go far. Once outside the lava tube entrance, she spotted the orange safety vest with Civil Defense across the back. He turned at the sound of rocks sliding behind him

Race jumped the few feet to where Savanah stood.

"Did you check the vehicles?" She began twisting her hair to put it up out of her way. Race reached a hand and stopped her.

"Wait. I just want to look at you. Like this, with the sun rising over the mountain behind you like a golden halo around your head. The perfect harmony of you, here . . ." Race swept his arm to encompass the wild mountainside.

Savanah shook her head, her hair spilling around her.

"I don't mind if you leave it down. It's incredible just the way it is." He reached to wind the espresso silk through his fingers. "Your hair is beautiful. A wild mane framing the beauty of your face."

He gave an embarrassed laugh. "The same way your lashes do around the incredible glacial pattern of your eyes. I don't think I'll ever grow tired of staring into them. Or at you."

"It will be in my way when we climb down," Savanah answered without thinking.

Then his words penetrated her practicality. She stopped winding her hair, sending a shot of warmth from beneath her lashes as she looked up at him. "But duly noted, Director. Thank you. And I'll remember that for next time."

She waited until he dropped his hand to finish the job of winding it out of her way.

"The vehicles are trashed. We aren't driving them anywhere. I didn't find the one the tornado sent flying yesterday." Race pulled a protein bar and a bottle of water from his pocket and handed them to her.

Savanah broke the bar in half and gave part back to Race. She did the same with the water, drinking half the bottle before handing it back to him. The sky was clear above them. It was always that way. The bigger the storm, the clearer the day that follows it. Every bit of cloud and haze had been blown away.

Whatever damage it had done, Garth was gone now. Savanah felt a quickening of her heartbeat at the thought of what they'd find once they got back to recognizable civilization.

"We should get the others up. The walk might take us longer than we think. There's no way to know how much of the road washed out. It wasn't much of a road to start with," Race mused.

Savanah agreed. "We need to get you back. You're supposed to be giving orders. A lot of people will be waiting for you."

She was thinking that Race going missing was not going to look very good for him. Coming after her probably jeopardized his job. She needed to get Director Weston back to his office. Savanah headed back into the lava tube to wake the group.

It wasn't long before their little group was making its way back down the jagged slope. Even in the dry dawn of the new day, Savanah marveled at what they had climbed over to survive yesterday. They were indeed lucky none of them had fallen and broken a leg, or worse. They would have found themselves crushed beneath the huge storm surge that had swept over and far up the cliffs, evident by the changes to the landscape around them. Sand and coral, pulverized trees, all littered the cracks and crevices they slowly made their way down.

No one said anything as they took in the aftermath. Rocks and trees thrown impossibly far up the hillside by the churning water. Savanah didn't take any photos. It was too devastating. She wasn't surprised the film crew did—the few who still had battery life in their cellphones. The sound of a picture snapping close to her made her turn and look at Race. She frowned to realize he was taking pictures as well.

"People need to know the extent of the damage. Even somewhere as remote as here. It isn't about fame and fortune." He inclined his head at the others. "This is about first-hand knowledge and what we can learn that will help us the next time."

Savanah almost didn't want to admit he was right. But she knew he was. Still, this was her home. This wasn't some unknown place in a textbook.

"Bird poop signs and all that . . ." Race gave her a smile as he took her hand.

The sound of a motor broke the stillness of the morning. Savanah looked around the width of Race's shoulders and was surprised to see military all-terrain vehicles bouncing toward them. She turned a surprised look to Race only to be greeted by his satisfied smile.

"I'm the CDD, remember. I have people like the Army and the National Guard on speed dial." He leaned in to claim her lips as if sealing his words.

Savanah steadied herself with her hands on his chest. The feel of being in his embrace was something she was getting used to. She was sorry as he drew back, ending the kiss.

"Once things died down and there was enough light to see, I kept climbing until I managed to get a message out from my sat phone. My man in Hilo has been taking care of things while I was . . ." His hand was still beneath her chin. His lips only inches from hers. "While I've been busy finding out what the people on the ground live through."

A loud voice cut through the air. "*Hūi.*"

It was Savanah's turn to look pleased. Her face broke into a grin as she leaned around Race's shoulders again and waved to her cousin as he jumped from the lead vehicle. "Ikaika."

Savanah turned a beaming smile to Race. "It isn't exactly the National Guard. I just called my '*ohana.*"

She was surprised to see Duke hit the ground behind Ikaika. Savanah wasn't expecting him. "Duke. What are you doing here?"

"Leayne called me before cells went out and told me where you'd gone. I went to your dad's as soon as I could. Ikaika was there with everyone. They knew you'd find somewhere to wait things out until they could come get you. I told Uncle Kyle to stay with everyone while I went with 'Kaika to find you."

He jerked a thumb behind him at where the military vehicles had come to a stop. "We were halfway here when these guys showed up so we told them *shoots*, they could come with us if they wanted."

"Hey. If you guys are *pau* with the vacation, we get cleaning up to do," Ikaika called as he pulled Savanah into a hug. "Everyone's going to be relieved to know we found you, Savanah. And I didn't even know you don't need your wheelchair no more. It's a day of blessing."

Savanah began laughing as the wonderful sound of her cousin's voice. His optimism came as naturally as breathing. His voice and his words affirmed that everything would be okay. No matter what they found once they got out of there. The people of Hawaii, the people of the Big Island, would recover. Together.

CHAPTER FORTY-ONE

Hurricane Garth wasn't the biggest hurricane on record to hit Hawaii. But as Race had observed, even a small storm could be devastating. And Garth hadn't been small by any means. The path it had taken when it suddenly looped around was unprecedented for the Hawaiian Islands. But thanks to the gut feeling of the new Civil Defense Director, fueled by constant prodding from Savanah, the island hadn't been caught totally unaware.

Meteorologists would spend months reviewing the data from before, during, and after the storm. Gleaning every bit of knowledge from every satellite image, every pressure reading. Garth had taken almost the exact track the Japanese station had predicted. As Savanah had feared, once it made the turn, the hurricane had begun picking up speed like a locomotive going downhill. That speed is what had allowed it to be sucked into the pressure flow that ran through the valley bisecting the northern end of the island before the mountains had a chance to break it apart.

Thankfully, that same speed had contributed to damages being less than the catastrophe that could have resulted had the storm continued at its snail's pace over the island. They'd gotten off lucky. At its peak, Garth's speed had topped out at almost fifty miles per hour. Had it been only a mile wide, it would have passed over the island in a little more than an hour. But the behemoth had been two hundred miles across. The island had endured the Category 4 hurricane for over six hours.

That width meant the Big Island wasn't the only island that had been affected. Maui, too, had been caught within Garth's reach. Thankfully, when Race jumped the gun, the Maui director had followed suit, both islands acting on impulse and preparing for a Hurricane Warning hours before that warning had officially come from the national offices. That had made the difference. Countless lives on Maui had been saved, just as Race had saved them on the Big Island.

As in the past, the lay of the land had played a role. It was just an unprecedented one. Not just in how the valley had all but sucked the hurricane through the island, but also due to the storm's massive size, it had ping-ponged from the Kohala mountains on one side of the valley to Hualalai and Mauna Kea, on the other. The slight ricochet had been enough to bounce it out back out to sea faster than would have happened otherwise. The mountains had also served their purpose by disrupting the smooth upper-level rotation of the hurricane once it started crowding up against them. The moment that happened, it began falling apart. Everyone agreed. They'd been damn lucky.

Thankfully, the tornado that had touched down near the lava tube where Race, Savanah and the film crew had taken refuge, had been the worst. It had been a blessing that it had spawned over such a remote location. Too intent on survival, none of their group had taken pictures of the funnel itself. However, others who'd seen if from a much safer distance, had. Those photos combined with the devastation shown in the photos they'd taken as they were being rescued, showed the power that had been unleashed.

The media was having a field day. The hotels and restaurants were full of logo-wearing reporters from news stations across the globe. Between filming the scars left on the land and hoping to get an interview with Race or Savanah, it didn't appear the reporters would leave any time soon. Which meant despite the damages, money was coming into the Big Island.

As for Onimura resort, CEO Clark Dieter was going to jail. There wasn't any damage at the resort that couldn't be repaired, and they only had to close a few buildings as they reopened for business. The people who had sheltered down in the kitchens had been well protected. Savanah hadn't worried knowing Leayne was in charge.

Which couldn't be said the other way around. The sight of the CEO tied up hadn't bothered the head of HR. It had been the blood Leayne found in the lobby when they'd come out after the storm. She had been beside herself with worry, even knowing that Savanah wasn't alone.

"The press conference is starting." Leayne said, walking into Savanah's office and taking a seat. "What do you think this one's about?"

"I'm pretty sure they've decided to keep Race for a while, so I can't imagine. They're probably just going to report on how all the recovery efforts and repairs are coming along."

Savanah hadn't heard much from Race over the last two months. The island had been busy trying to recover. There was a lot to do for the director of Civil Defense. And just because Garth was gone didn't mean they were in the clear. There were still three months left of the Pacific hurricane season, not to mention the usual flooding, earthquakes, and constant threat of lava eruptions.

A knock on the door took Leayne's and Savanah's attention away from the screen they'd been watching.

"Nice to see you again, Race." Leayne jumped from her chair. She nodded to Race as he moved out of her way. "I'll catch up with you later, Savanah."

Savanah thought Leayne was being a bit of a chicken. It wasn't as though her friend hadn't heard all about what had happened with Race when they'd gone out to rescue the crew from End of the World.

"Do you have a moment, Safety Director Jordan?" Race worked hard to keep his face set in a serious line. He'd missed her over the last sixty days. Looking at her across the desk, he was reminded just how much.

"Of course. I always have time for you, Director Weston." Savanah came around her desk, watching with curiosity as Race closed the door. "It's good to see you, Race. What brings you over here?" She waved her hand at the monitor. "I was expecting you to be speaking at the press conference."

He closed the gap between them, immediately gathering her in his arms. "I was thinking about that thing we did back in the cave. You know, that thing you did that made me forget all about the hurricane trying to kill us."

"Don't forget the tornado. And it was a lava tube. Not a cave. There's a difference, Race."

"Right. Lava tube, not a cave. And then there was that damn scary tornado." He kissed her lightly on the lips. He loved the way her lips tasted of her smile. "I was wondering if you'd agree to help me out. Maybe share a little light with me."

He was teasing her lips with his and her body was already pressing against him in happy anticipation of more.

"I'm sure we could arrange that sometime when your busy schedule

275

allows it." Savanah gave a soft gasp of need as Race's hands touched her bare skin. He'd pulled her shirt up far enough to separate it from her skirt.

"I have a special request this time." Race knew the door was closed. He wondered if he could convince her to lock it.

"You know I cooperate fully with Civil Defense and . . ." She felt desire spike in her stomach, before radiating out through her. The warmth of strong fingers suddenly at her thighs was enough of a shock that Savanah fell forward into Race's chest. She grabbed his shirt as she felt his palms begin to slide up.

His hands took her skirt with them, slowly exposing her thighs. "I think we'd be much more successful if we didn't have these troublesome clothes between us while we let our chakras continue becoming familiar with one another."

Savanah knew Race could feel her heart pounding as he lifted her off her feet. "My energy does seem to like yours," she teased as his lips stole the breath she'd been trying to take.

"Indeed. Despite how much you'd like to deny it, it does," Race told her as he covered her lips once more.

"We'd like to announce the creation of a new position," the mayor's voice came over Savanah's TV. "At the suggestion of Civil Defense Director Weston, we will be appointing an additional liaison to the Civil Defense office. The position will report directly to the Director . . ."

Savanah knew the mayor was talking. But she was too interested in Race's kiss.

"The mayor's office congratulates Savanah Jordan as the first person to be appointed as the Hawaii Civil Defense Field Director . . ."

There was the sound of celebrating outside the closed door of Savanah's office.

"Wait a minute. Did the mayor just say my name?" Savanah was sure she heard it.

"We'll be required to work very closely from now on. I'll tell you all about it, Field Director Jordan. Later . . ." Race went back to the business of relearning Savanah's lips. His hands continued exploring her skin, as the love in his heart wrapped firmly around hers. If she thought he was letting her go, he would just have to spend the rest of his life explaining otherwise.

Savanah sank into Race, her body melding with his as easily as her energy did. She could see it now. Even when they were at odds, it was a graceful dance of sparks flying. But ever since they'd walked into the sunlight after the storm, Savanah had felt the presence of something around her. Standing in Race's arms, she knew what it was. Despite everything that had been between them. In the dark of night. A hurricane trying to kill them. Surrounded by the souls of her ancestors. Savanah had realized Race wasn't different from her. It didn't matter where he was from. What mattered to her was the beating of their two hearts. The storm outside nothing compared to their love and the storm of passion they'd found for one another.

Thank you so much for reading *Storm of Passion*. If you've enjoyed the book, we would be grateful if you would post a review on the bookseller's website. Just a few words is all it takes! ♥

Made in the USA
Monee, IL
11 June 2022

97869023R10166